Modern Black Stories

With Study Aids

edited by
Martin Mirer

BARRON'S

BARRON'S EDUCATIONAL SERIES, INC.
Woodbury, New York • London • Toronto • Sydney

All inquiries should be addressed to:

Barron's Educational Series, Inc.
113 Crossways Park Drive
Woodbury, New York 11797

Library of Congress Catalog Card No. 70-162824

International Standard Book No. 0-8120-0425-6

PRINTED IN THE UNITED STATES OF AMERICA

345   510   16 15 14 13 12 11

Acknowledgments

The editor and the publisher, *Barron's Educational Series, Inc.*, of *Modern Black Stories* wish to make grateful acknowledgment for permission granted by the following publishers and journals to use their selections in this book:

"The Bench." From *An African Treasury* edited by Langston Hughes. Copyright © 1960 by Langston Hughes. Used by permission of Crown Publishers, Inc.

"Bruzz." Reprinted by permission of *Freedomways* magazine published at 799 Broadway, New York City. From Vol. 2, No. 2, 1962.

"The Convert." Copyright © 1963 by *Negro Digest*. Reprinted by permission.

"The Death of Tommy Grimes." Reprinted by permission of *Freedomways* magazine published at 799 Broadway, New York City. From Vol. 2, No. 3, 1962.

"Go Tell It on the Mountain." Reprinted from *Go Tell It On The Mountain* by James Baldwin. Copyright © 1953, 1952 by James Baldwin and used by permission of the publisher, The Dial Press.

"The Homecoming." Reprinted by permission of William Morris Agency, Inc. Copyright © 1946 by Frank Yerby.

"Invisible Man." Copyright © 1947 by Ralph Ellison. Reprinted from *Invisible Man*, by Ralph Ellison, by permission of Random House, Inc.

"Miss Cynthie." Permission for use of "Miss Cynthie" granted by Mrs. Jane Ryder Fisher.

"Mista Courifer." From *An African Treasury* edited by Langston Hughes. Copyright © 1960 by Langston Hughes. Used by permission of Crown Publishers, Inc.

"Native Son." From pp. 1-16 in *Native Son* (Perennial Edition) by Richard Wright. Copyright © 1940, by Richard Wright.

"Professor." Reprinted by permission of Harold Ober Associates Incorporated. Copyright © 1952 by Langston Hughes. Slightly edited.

"Rat Joiner Routs the Klan." Ted Poston, feature writer on the New York Post.

"A Summer Tragedy." Reprinted by permission of Harold Ober Associates Incorporated. Copyright © 1933 by Arna Bontemps.

"We're the Only Colored People Here" from *Maud Martha* by Gwendolyn Brooks. Copyright © 1953, by Gwendolyn Brooks Blakely.

Photographs and Painting

Grateful acknowledgment is also made to the following photographers and agents for permission to reprint their materials.

Contents

Introduction

All the stories in this collection are by Negro authors. With the exception of two stories by African writers, they show some aspect of the black experience in America, ranging in scope from tapping feet behind the footlights in a Harlem theater to the menace and outrageous brutality of the deep South.

The African writers found here, Adelaide Casely-Hayford of Sierra Leone *(Mista Courifer)* and Richard Rive of The Union of South Africa *(The Bench)*, also present problems concerned with being black.

A disclaimer is entered here against any intention to label these talented people as "Negro" writers. Their work meets all the standards of literary excellence and stands out because of intrinsic merit. Many of the writers in this volume have achieved recognition in the form of prizes, awards, grants and writing fellowships. They are writers who happen to be black, as other writers happen to be French or German. They are uniquely qualified to write about what it means to be black and can do so with an insight and passion denied to others. The desire to be judged solely on merit has been expressed by James Baldwin, represented in his book by a selection from his novel, *Go Tell It On The Mountain*, who has said, "I wanted to prevent myself from becoming. . .merely a Negro writer. I want to be known as an honest man and a good writer."

The Short Story

WHAT MAKES some stories good stories and others mediocre? You have read stories that have given you the feeling that you have read something satisfying, something that made an impression on you. On the other hand, you may have read other stories, perhaps in a magazine, that have caused you to say afterwards, "There wasn't much to that story; it was hardly worth reading." Would you like to know what makes a good story good?

Here are the ingredients of a good short story; when skilfully combined they produce an enduring work of art.

1. THE THEME. The story has to have a reason for being. The author starts with a kernel which he envelops with people and happen-

ings. The main idea, which usually can be expressed in a sentence or two, is the *theme* or message of the story.

2. THE BACKGROUND.   The story must take place somewhere and exist in time. The author gives us a setting for the story which includes the geographical location or the physical circumstances and the time or period during which the action takes place.

3. THE CHARACTERS.   Who are the people in the story? Do they seem real? Can we see them in their strengths and weaknesses as human beings we have known or might meet at any time? What qualities do the characters possess? People in a story stand revealed by what they do, by what they say, and by what others say about them. By these means a character develops during the course of the story.

4. THE PLOT.   People in a story do things to make the story move. There are incidents which involve the characters in a problem. Steps are taken to work out of the difficulty. All these actions or incidents engaged in by the characters constitute the plot.

5. CONFLICT.   A clash between characters in the story provides a *conflict* that leads to the development of the plot. The central character of the story may face a dilemma and be pulled in two different directions, in effect, a conflict between two parts of the individual. Sometimes the conflict is between a character and the circumstances of his life, the forces that hem him in. This is the tragedy of Bigger Thomas in "Native Son."

6. THE MOOD.   In some stories, an emotion may be just as important as the characters or the plot. The pervading feeling, or mood of the story, brought out by the author's choice of words or by the emotions of the characters may be fear, anger, joy, horror, grief, yearnings, etc.

When these elements are lacking or sketchily conceived, the end product is second-rate. Analyze any short story in terms of these components to see for yourself how the author has succeeded with his story.

To The Student

EACH of the stories in this collection is followed by a related series of questions designed to help you reach a depth of understanding that might otherwise not be possible.

The discussion questions serve to bring to your attention meanings of the author that might otherwise have been missed. It might not be clear to the casual reader whether or not the narrator in "Invisible Man" was consciously trying to follow his grandfather's dying advice to be humble. Pointed questions direct the student to a re-reading of key parts of the story in order to formulate an answer.

The vocabulary section will serve to broaden the base of the student's word fund, especially if he maintains a private vocabulary list to which additions are constantly made and if the words are conscientiously re-studied and used in speech or writing. Included in this section are many words with interesting origins, like *galvanized*, derived from the name, Luigi Galvani, an Italian scientist. This word is analyzed in the vocabulary section appended to "Native Son."

The analytic questions related to some particular aspect of short story technique will point the way to an understanding of the author's art in the creation of his story. These questions deal with setting, plot structure, characterization, theme, suspense, mood, etc. For example, the story, "The Homecoming," is followed by questions that establish the kind of person the lead character in the story is; also there are questions that will help you identify the conflict that the author, Frank Yerby presents as the focus of his story.

Finally, each story has some composition questions deriving from the story to provide practice in thinking about a suggested topic, in organizing ideas and in improving written communication. As an example of this kind of pupil activity there is a composition question centered about Cecilia in "Rat Joiner Routs the Klan." Cecilia's aunt was against her affair with Tapper Johnson and wanted her to marry some one of her choice. The question asks students to write an essay concerning the role one's family should play in courtship.

If you would like to read more short stories like those in this volume, at the end there is a list of additional readings which should be available in your school or public library.

By Richard Rive

The Bench

Mrs. Rosa Parks, a tired seamstress living in Montgomery, Alabama, refused to give up her bus seat to a white man. When ordered by the driver to move back, she declined to do so and was arrested. That was the beginning of the famous non-violent bus boycott, led by Dr. Martin Luther King. After mass arrests, car pools, harassment, court cases, and a year of protests, segregation on city buses in Montgomery was brought to an end.

In "The Bench", a simple young Kaffir tries the same tactic as Mrs. Parks. He does what he can to challenge the racial policies of the South African government. His act of defiance is to sit on a bench marked "Europeans Only" in a Johannesburg railway station. Is he arrested like Mrs. Parks? Is there a Dr. King to lead a mass protest against separate benches for whites and blacks? Mr. Rive's story is one little example of "man's inhumanity to man."

"WE FORM an integral part of a complex society, a society in which a vast proportion of the population is denied the very basic right of existence, a society that condemns a man to an inferior position because he has the misfortune to be born black, a society that can only retain its precarious social and economic position at the expense of an enormous oppressed mass!"

The speaker paused for a moment and sipped some water from a glass. Karlie's eyes shone as he listened. Those were great words, he thought, great words and true. Karlie sweated. The hot November sun beat down on the gathering. The trees on the Grand Parade in Johannesburg afforded very little shelter and his handkerchief was already soaked where he had placed it between his neck and his shirt collar. Karlie stared around him at the sea of faces. Every shade of color was represented, from shiny ebony to the one or two whites in the crowd.

Karlie stared at the two detectives who were busily making shorthand notes of the speeches, then turned to stare back at the speaker.

"It is up to us to challenge the right of any group who willfully and deliberately condemn a fellow group to a servile position. We must challenge the right of any people who see fit to segregate human beings solely on grounds of pigmentation. Your children are denied the rights which are theirs by birth. They are segregated educationally, socially economically . . ."

Ah, thought Karlie, that man knows what he is speaking about. He says I am as good as any other man, even a white man. That needs much thinking. I wonder if he means I have the right to go to any bioscope,[1] or eat in any restaurant, or that my children can go to a white school. These are dangerous ideas and need much thinking. I wonder what Ou Klaas would say to this. Ou Klaas said that God made the white man and the black man separately, and the one must always be 'baas'[2] and the other 'jong.'[3] But this man says different things and somehow they ring true.

Karlie's brow was knitted as he thought. On the platform were many speakers, both white and black, and they were behaving as if there were no differences of color among them. There was a white woman in a blue dress offering Nixeli a cigarette. That never could have happened at Bietjiesvlei. Old Lategan at the store there would have fainted if his Annatjie had offered Witbooi a cigarette. And Annatjie wore no such pretty dress.

These were new things and he, Karlie, had to be careful before he accepted them. But why shouldn't he accept them? He was not a colored man any more, he was a human being. The last speaker had said so. He remembered seeing pictures in the newspapers of people who defied laws which relegated them to a particular class, and those people were smiling as they went to prison. This was a queer world.

The speaker continued and Karlie listened intently. He spoke slowly, and his speech was obviously carefully prepared. This is a great man, thought Karlie.

The last speaker was the white lady in the blue dress, who asked them to challenge any discriminatory laws or measures in their own way. Why should she speak like that? She could go to the best bioscopes and swim at the best beaches. Why she was even more beautiful than Annatjie Lategan. They had warned him in Bietjiesvlei about coming to the city. He

---

[1] bioscope: motion picture theater
[2] baas (bahs):   boss (Afrikaans language)
[3] jong (yahng):   young man (Afrikaans language)

had seen the skollies [1] in District Six and he knew what to expect there. Hanover Street held no terrors for him. But no one had told him about this. This was new, this set one's mind thinking, yet he felt it was true. She had said one should challenge. He, Karlie, would astound old Lategan and Van Wyk at the Dairy Farm. They could do what they liked to him after that. He would smile like those people in the newspapers.

The meeting was almost over when Karlie threaded his way through the crowd. The words of the speakers were still milling through his head. It could never happen in Bietjiesvlei. Or could it? The sudden screech of a car pulling to a stop whirled him back to his senses. A white head was thrust angrily through the window.

"Look where you're going, you black. . . !"

Karlie stared dazedly at him. Surely this white man never heard what the speakers had said. He could never have seen the white woman offering Nxeli a cigarette. He could never imagine the white lady shouting those words at him. It would be best to catch a train and think these words over.

He saw the station in a new light. Here was a mass of human beings, black, white and some brown like himself. Here they mixed with one another, yet each mistrusted the other with an unnatural fear, each treated the other with suspicion, moved in a narrow, haunted pattern of its own. One must challenge these things the speaker had said . . . in one's own way. Yet how in one's own way? How was one to challenge? Suddenly it dawned upon him. Here was his challenge! *The bench.* The railway bench with "Europeans Only" neatly painted on it in white. For one moment it symbolized all the misery of the plural South African society.

Here was his challenge to the rights of a man. Here it stood. A perfectly ordinary wooden railway bench, like thousands of others in South Africa. His challenge. That bench now had concentrated in it all the evils of a system he could not understand and he felt a victim of. It was the obstacle between himself and humanity. If he sat on it, he was a man. If he was afraid he denied himself membership as a human being in a human society. He almost had visions of righting this pernicious system, if he only sat down on that bench. Here was his chance. He, Karlie, would challenge.

He seemed perfectly calm when he sat down on the bench, but inside his heart was thumping wildly. Two conflicting ideas now throbbed through him. The one said, "I have no right to sit on this bench." The other was the voice of a new religion and said, "Why have I no right to sit on this bench?" The one voice spoke of

---

[1] skollies (skahl'leez): young hoodlums (Afrikaans)

the past, of the servile position he had occupied on the farm, of his father, and his father's father who were born black, lived like blacks, and died like mules. The other voice spoke of new horizons and said, "Karlie, you are a man. You have dared what your father and your father's father would not have dared. You will die like a man."

Karlie took out a cigarette and smoked. Nobody seemed to notice his sitting there. This was an anticlimax. The world still pursued its monotonous way. No voice had shouted, "Karlie has conquered!" He was a normal human being sitting on a bench in a busy station, smoking a cigarette. Or was this his victory: the fact that he was a normal human being? A well-dressed white woman walked down the platform. Would she sit on the bench? Karlie wondered. And then that gnawing voice, "You should stand and let the white woman sit!" Karlie narrowed his eyes and gripped tighter at his cigarette. She swept past him without the slightest twitch of an eyelid and continued walking down the platform. Was she afraid to challenge — to challenge his right to be a human being? Karlie now felt tired. A third conflicting idea was now creeping in, a compensatory idea which said, "You sit on this bench because you are tired; you are tired therefore you sit." He would not move because he was tired, or was it because he wanted to sit where he liked?

People were now pouring out of a train that had pulled into the station. There were so many people pushing and jostling one another that nobody noticed him. This was his train. It would be easy to step into the train and ride off home, but that would be giving in, suffering defeat, refusing the challenge, in fact admitting that he was not a human being. He sat on. Lazily he blew the cigarette smoke into the air, thinking . . . His mind was away from the meeting and the bench: he was thinking of Bietjiesvlei and Ou Klaas, how he had insisted that Karlie should come to Cape Town. Ou Klaas would suck on his pipe and look so quizzically at one. He was wise and knew much. He had said one must go to Cape Town and learn the ways of the world. He would spit and wink slyly when he spoke of District Six and the women he knew in Hanover Street. Ou Klaas knew everything. He said God made us white or black and we must therefore keep our places.

"Get off this seat!"

Karlie did not hear the gruff voice. Ou Klaas would be on the land now waiting for his tot of cheap wine.

"I said get off the bench, you swine!" Karlie suddenly whipped back to reality. For a moment he was going to jump up, then he remembered who he was and why he was sitting there. He suddenly felt very tired. He looked up slowly into a very red face that stared down at him.

"Get up!" it said. "There are benches down there for you."

Karlie looked up, and said nothing. He stared into a pair of sharp, gray, cold eyes.

"Can't you hear me speaking to you? You black swine!"

Slowly and deliberately Karlie puffed at the cigarette. This was his test. They both stared at each other, challenged with the eyes, like two boxers, each knowing that they must eventually trade blows yet each afraid to strike first.

"Must I dirty my hands on scum like you?"

Karlie said nothing. To speak would be to break the spell, the supremacy he felt was slowly gaining.

An uneasy silence, then: "I will call a policeman rather than soil my hands on a Hotnot like you. You can't even open up your black jaw when a white man speaks to you."

Karlie saw the weakness. The white man was afraid to take action himself. He, Karlie, had won the first round of the bench dispute.

A crowd had now collected.

"Afrika!" shouted a joker.

Karlie ignored the remark. People were now milling around him, staring at the unusual sight of a black man sitting on a white man's bench. Karlie merely puffed on.

"Look at the black ape. That's the worst of giving these Kaffirs enough rope."

"I can't understand it. They have their own benches!"

"Don't get up! You have every right to sit there!"

"He'll get up when a policeman comes!"

"After all why shouldn't they sit there?"

"I've said before, I've had a native servant once, and a more impertinent . . .".

Karlie sat and heard nothing. Irresolution had now turned to determination. Under no condition was he going to get up. They could do what they liked.

"So, this is the fellow, eh! Get up there! Can't you read?"

The policeman was towering over him. Karlie could see the crest on his buttons and the wrinkles in his neck.

"What is your name and address! Come on!"

Karlie still maintained his obstinate silence. It took the policeman rather unawares. The crowd was growing every minute.

"You have no right to speak to this man in such a manner!" It was the white lady in the blue dress.

"Mind your own business! I'll ask your help when I need it. It's people like you who make these Kaffirs [1] think they're as good as white men. Get up, you!" The latter remark was addressed to Karlie.

"I insist that you treat him with proper respect."

The policeman turned red.

---

[1] Kaffirs: members of a black race in South Africa

"This ... this ..." He was lost for words.

"Kick up the Hotnot if he won't get up!" shouted a spectator. Rudely a white man laid hands on Karlie.

"Get up, you bloody. . . !" Karlie turned to resist, to cling to the bench, his bench. There was more than one man pulling at him. He hit out wildly and then felt a dull pain as somebody rammed a fist into his face. He was bleeding now and wild-eyed. He would fight for it. The constable clapped a pair of handcuffs on him and tried to clear a way through the crowd. Karlie still struggled. A blow or two landed on him. Suddenly he relaxed and slowly struggled to his feet. It was useless to fight any longer. Now it was his turn to smile. He had challenged and won. Who cared the rest?

"Come on, you swine!" said the policeman forcing Karlie through the crowd.

"Certainly!" said Karlie for the first time. And he stared at the policeman with all the arrogance of one who dared sit on a "European bench."

Questions for Discussion

1. IDENTIFY the leading character in the story. What was his occupation? What level of African society did he represent?

2. WHAT IS the central situation that the author leads up to?

3. POINT OUT the conflicts in the story, not overlooking the inner conflict in Karlie's mind.

4. WHY ARE the detectives making notes of the speech making?

5. THE BENCH in the railway station said "Europeans Only." What would the equivalent wording be in the South? What kind of symbol did the bench represent to Karlie as he approached it?

6. KARLIE EXPERIENCED conflicting emotions after making the decision to sit on the forbidden bench. Which gained the ascendancy?

7. WHAT DO you think of Karlie's tactic of not speaking to those who ordered him to get off the bench? Would he have been more effective if he had spoken out against discrimination? Why?

8. EXPLAIN WHY Karlie felt that he had won a victory not by the act of sitting on the bench, but by the feeling it gave him.

9. How DID Karlie regard his boss, Ou Klaas, who had encouraged him to take the trip to Cape Town?

10. KARLIE PRACTICED self-restraint until the very end of the incident when they began to pull him from the bench. At that point he struck out wildly. Would it have been better for him to be non-violent all through the incident? Explain.

11. WHAT MADE Karlie smile after the struggle as the policeman led him away?

12. WHAT IS the climax of the story?

13. WHAT EFFECT does the author accomplish with this story? Will it help to crack open the policy of apartheid? Explain.

14. DESCRIBE the central figure in the story, Karlie. What is the significance of this repeated observation about Karlie: "That needs much thinking?"

15. WHAT IS the theme of the story?

Building Vocabulary

Getting the meaning from the context. In each of the following sentences taken from the story, select from the choices given the word or phrase that means the same as the word in heavy type. Check your answer by looking up the word in the dictionary. Write the ones you get wrong in your special vocabulary list.

---

1. "We form an **integral** (in′tuh-gruhl) part of a complex society." (p. 1)

   A. intelligent   B. essential   C. unimportant   D. interior

2. "... A society that can only retain its **precarious** (prih-kair′ee-yus) ... position at the expense of an enormous oppressed mass." (p. 1)

   A. uncertain   B. careful   C. valuable   D. false

3. "... Challenge the right of any group who ... condemn a fellow group to a **servile** (sur′vill) position." (p. 2)

   A. senior group   B. respectful   C. odd   D. like a slave

4. "He almost had visions of righting this **pernicious** (puh-nish′-us) system ..." (p. 3)

   A. official   B. personal   C. wicked   D. racial

5. "Nobody seemed to notice his sitting there. This was an **anticlimax** (an-tih-kly′maks)." (p. 4)

   A. act of defiance   B. building to a peak   C. cloth cover   D. after the highest point

6. "A third conflicting idea was now creeping in, a **compensatory** (kom-pen′suh-toh-ree) idea ..." (p. 4)

   A. making up for   B. feeling alert   C. complaining   D. great longing for

7. "**Irresolution** (ir-rez-uh-loo′shun) had now turned to determination." (p. 5)

   A. opposition   B. indecision   C. irony   D. conclusion

8. "... He stared at the policeman with all the **arrogance** (ar′uh-gance) of one who dared sit on a 'European bench.'" (p. 6)

   A. superiority   B. annoyance   C. gracefulness   D. humility

The Setting

1. THE INCIDENTS in *The Bench* could not have taken place in just any country picked at random. The setting or background (including place, time and circumstances) is essential for the validity of the story. If you read only the first paragraph of the story containing the words ". . . a society that condemns a man to an inferior position because he has the misfortune to be born black . . ." what countries might that description apply to?

2. WHAT IS the first clue in the second paragraph regarding the locale of the story? Why does that clue rule out the United States as the setting for the story?

3. WHAT SEASON of the year is it? What is the climate during this season?

4. How DO you know the approximate date of the story?

5. WHAT ARE the political and social circumstances that form the background of the story?

6. WHERE HAD Karlie traveled from to reach the arena where the speeches were being made?

7. DESCRIBE the shift in scene as Karlie takes his way home. What is the atmosphere in the railway station?

Thinking and Writing

1. YOU KNOW something of the racial policies of the government of South Africa, known as apartheid. These are official policies with a complete set of laws limiting the civil rights of blacks. Are there laws restricting the use of benches in Southern railway stations in the United States? Write a comparison of discrimination against blacks in the United States and in South Africa.

2. PRETEND that you have just gotten off a train in the Johannesburg station where the story takes place. You see a crowd of people milling about a black man on a bench. Describe the incident as an outside observer would see it.

3. KARLIE LAID DOWN a challenge to the separatist policies of his country by occupying a forbidden bench. In the face of

degrading name-calling he remained silent. Suppose that Karlie had chosen to reply to his tormenters. Write what he might have said to explain how apartheid robs black people of dignity and their essential humanity.

e√∂

About the Author

Richard Rive was born in South Africa in 1931. He won a municipal scholarship to a local high school, then attended the University of Cape Town where his extra-curricular activity was track athletics. Mr. Rive teaches English literature in a Cape Town segregated high school. He combines teaching with a writing career. His short stories have appeared in many African magazines in several languages. The stories have been collected under the title *African Songs*, published in 1963. On the basis of the promise shown in this book, he was awarded a fellowship for traveling and writing and toured Africa and Europe. His first novel, *Emergency*, appeared in 1964. In addition, he has compiled and edited two anthologies of black writings: *Modern African Prose* (1964) and *Quartet* (1965), a collection of South African literature.

"Bruzz"

"Bruzz"

If a stranger walked into your store and you caught a glimpse of a gun in a shoulder holster under his jacket how could you tell if

BY SAMUEL THOMPSON

he was a policeman or a gangster?
Little Bruzz, who was minding
the store for his father, trusted to
his instinct.

Bruzz waited motionless until the big fly stopped moving. When his mouth was full of saliva he maneuvered his wad of gum into one cheek in order not to lose it. Taking careful aim, he let go — Splat! — and missed. The startled fly zoomed off into the blazing afternoon sunlight and Bruzz looked around halfheartedly for another target. It was hot. Scorching, middle-of-July, Mississippi hot.

The jukebox in Jodie's Place across the road began booming out for the millionth time, "Thass all right, baby; Baby, thas all right fo' you—." Bruzz sighed and wished he was old enough to be allowed inside Jodie's.

. . . Bet nobody'd make me set around mindin a ole grocery sto while evvybody else went fishin. Get me a big ole cole bottle a beer and stan aroun talkin big es anybody else in Moun' Bayou. An chase lil ole small fry come peekin in de do . . .

Bruzz squinted up, then down Highway 61 which bisected the tiny subdivision and ran straight through the town toward Greensville. Nothing was stirring as far as he could see in either direction. Nothing but heat waves dancing crazily on the white concrete. Everyone with good sense had escaped into the comparative cool inside the handful of shacks scattered for half a mile on either side of the highway, or they were at ease in Jodie's. In the shade of the great live oak tree in Mister Rob's front yard, two or three fat barred rocks [1] scratched disinterestedly for worms that knew better.

The Jenkins family, with the exception of Bruzz, had left early that morning for Cooter's Pond and a day of fishing. It was Bruzz's regular turn to mind the store and he had been left with a stern warning that to leave the porch was "same as askin" for a licking. The little boy's backside twitched sympathetically at the memory of the purplish welts his brother Lin had suffered for disobeying his father's orders. Lin, at fourteen, was the oldest of the Jenkins brood and by far the orneriest. Leastways he was until that hiding took the meanness out of him. Their sister Baby was too young at seven to take care of the store alone.

Aside from a few customers before noon there had not been much business and time and the heat were making the boy restless. Papa had said they would return about sundown and the sun was still high in the sky. Thinking of the long afternoon ahead the boy squirmed impatiently. He soon tired of unravelling the threads at the cuff of his faded denims. He wriggled his toes and tried knitting them together. He experimented with holding his breath as long as he could. Maybe

---

[1] barred rocks: striped pigeons

he could make his eyes pop out of his head. Once out at the pond he and Lin had killed a toad by holding down on the back of its neck until the creature's eyes had nearly popped out of its head. The memory of the toad's slow death sent a delicious little shiver of pleasure up Bruzz's spine, and he released the pent-up air in his lungs with a loud whoosh just as a dusty coupe slid to a stop beside the porch.

The car's sole occupant alighted, stretched and walked quickly onto the porch and the welcoming shade. He was stocky and powerfully built and dressed like city folks in spite of the intense heat, in a loud sport jacket. His face and throat were burned red, Bruzz noticed, not tanned like the white folks he had seen hereabouts. Mound Bayou was seldom a stopping place for white people. Everyone of its inhabitants was colored, and aside from a few drummers[1] and truck drivers who did business in town, no *white* person ever got out of his car. Bruzz permitted himself a sidelong glance at the coupe's license plates. They were Mississippi tags, all right.

The stranger removed his hat and fanned himself. He was nearly bald and drops of perspiration glistened on his pate. "Got anything cold to drink, son?" he asked in the most unmusical voice Bruzz had heard in all his eleven years. He spoke in such a manner

that his lips scarcely moved, a feat which fascinated the boy into awed immobility. He quickly recovered, however, and opened the cooler.

"Take yo pick, mistuh," he invited.

The stranger picked a bottle of pop and opened it. He downed the cooling liquid in two swallows, paid the boy for two and opened the second bottle. When his thirst was partially satisfied he turned to peer down the road in the direction from which he had come. He grunted and busied himself once more with the soda pop.

Meanwhile, Bruzz was brimming over with curiosity. He stood first on one foot and then the other, waiting for the stranger to speak again. He even spat out his gum to attract attention. Finally, when he could contain himself no longer he spoke, "Hot, aint it?"

Without answering the stranger turned to look closely at this dark imp of a youngster whose brown eyes danced with inner excitement. They were the kind of eyes he hadn't seen in recent weeks —harmless, mildly curious and friendly. The stranger's guard came down, his manner relaxed and he opened his mouth to speak. Suddenly the sound of a motor not far off made him stiffen. He whirled about and peered down the road in the direction of the noise. An ancient dump truck had turned onto the highway from a

1 drummers: traveling salesmen (colloq.)

side road and was coughing and sputtering toward them. The bare-torsoed driver, sweaty black and shining in the sun's fire, grinned and shouted "Hey!" to Bruzz as the vehicle bounced and jerked past the store.

"Hey! Mistuh Bowman," yelled the youngster in return. He turned to the stranger and explained, "Thass Mistuh Dan Bowman. Got the bigges hawg farm in Mon Bayou." The stranger affected disinterest in Bowman's affluence but watched in strained silence as the truck lurched out of sight behind clouds of dust. Apparently satisfied that he was in no danger, the man threw back his head and drained the second soda pop. His movement threw open his jacket revealing the butt of an automatic resting in a shoulder holster. Bruzz stood transfixed, his eyes riveted on the weapon. Suddenly he blurted out, "You lookin for a crook, mistuh? Is you a police?"

The stranger's head jerked around as if pulled by a string. "Why'd yuh ask that?" he demanded roughly, his small grey eyes searching the boy's face.

"You got a gun, aint you? I seen it."

The stranger was so relieved to discover only simple curiosity in the boy's question he allowed himself the luxury of a thin smile. "Well, I hafta carry a gun in my business, sonny," he lied easily. I—uh, I travel a lot." The youngster seemed satisfied with the explanation. "Now, you tell me some-thin. Don't you people have no cops in this burg?"

"Cops? You mean police?" Bruzz asked. The man nodded. "We doan need no cops in Moun Bayou," the boy stated simply. "Doan nothin but colored people live here. No white folks a-tall. We got a jail, but we doan need no cops," he repeated, wondering why this strange white man was afraid. In spite of the stranger's effort to appear only casually interested in the state of law enforcement in Mound Bayou Bruzz was not deceived. His childish innocence made him oddly sensitive to the man's inner terror.

Speaking half to himself so that Bruzz scarcely heard him the stranger murmured. "A guy could live. No cops." But after a moment's reverie he dismissed the thought with a shrug of his shoulders and turned to the boy. "Well, I outta get goin, sonny. You're a nice kid. Maybe I'll be seein ya some more." He dropped off the porch, climbed into the coupe and drove off in a cloud of dust. Bruzz stood shading his eyes against the glare and watched the car disappear in the distance. By the time the dust had settled it was peaceful once more in Mound Bayou.

But the excitement of the stranger's brief stop lingered. Returning to his perch on the lard tub Bruzz speculated idly on the strange ways of white folks. Anybody was crazy to wear a coat in this heat. Peckerwoods had some crazy notions, anyway. But then this stranger had not acted crazier than the rest of them, just scared. He acted as if he was running away from something, or someone. Maybe he was running away from the police. That could be the reason he asked about cops. He must be a big crook or a gangster, Bruzz figured, to be carrying a gun and worrying about the law.

Carried away by the force of his own lively imagination Bruzz debated with himself for several moments and then, his mind racing against fear, he went inside to the telephone on the counter. He paused only for a brief instant during which he could hear his heart pounding wildly against his chest. His hand reached out almost involuntarily, picked up the receiver and placed it against his ear. He heard himself ask for the county sheriff. When an indolent drawl identified an officer on the other end of the wire a fit of near panic gripped the boy. But prodded by his own audacity he drew a determined breath and glibly spun the most stupendous lie ever told in the short history of Mound Bayou, Mississippi.

". . . gangstuh from up Nawth . . . a big ol pistol inside his coat . . . try to hol up my papa's sto . . . we aint had no money nohow . . . big ol green car, yessuh . . . went thu town goin straight to Greenville . . . my name, suh? . . . yes suh . . . my name Bruzz Jenkins, suh . . ." He hung up. Nearly faint with excitement and horror at what he had done Bruzz rested against the counter. Then, his head still spinning, he made his way slowly out to the porch, selected a piece of ice from the cooler and sat trying to calm his jumping nerves.

In his mind's eye Bruzz could picture the entire chain of events he could take credit for setting in motion. A chase, perhaps—lots of shooting and—Phewee! —a tire shot flat on the gangster's car. The car swerves off the road and they start shooting it out again until—Bang!—the cops plug the gangster between the eyes, just like the movies he had seen. And there'd be lots of blood. Pools of blood.

The mental picture of the stranger lying in oceans of blood was so gory it shocked Bruzz back to a less sanguine reality and a sharp awareness of the magnitude of what he had done. He sucked in his breath so quickly he almost swallowed the chunk of ice. What if the stranger was not a gangster? Suppose he was only a tourist or a drummer? Or, what was worse, a policeman? If he was the law they would surely come and take him away to jail where he wouldn't be able to see Lin and Baby and Papa and Mama. What if he got lynched like he heard Luke Roberts was? Doubt gave way to fear and fear was almost as soon replaced by genuine terror that clutched at his tight little belly and brought huge tears into his eyes. Bruzz began to sob softly.

He wished Papa would come on home, but a watery look skyward told him he'd have a long wait. The thought of running away tempted him briefly but he quickly discarded the idea, as much afraid of a licking from his father as he was of the law. He was miserable. He rolled over on his stomach and pillowed his head in his arms. He continued to cry and ignored a runny nose. The jukebox at Jodie's started up again—"Thass all right baby; Baby, thass all right fo you—."

Above the sounds of his own sobs Bruzz heard the distant screaming of a police siren. He knew the end had come and his sobs crescendoed into a wailing that rivaled the noise of the approaching siren. Flattening himself against the porch floor Bruzz braced himself for the swift and painful hand of punishment. In a matter of almost seconds the car, dusty with a coat of red clay, pulled up to the store, its siren still growling.

Heads poked out of doorways and a few people drifted out of houses to see. A giant of a police officer eased his lanky frame out of the sedan and in two strides was standing over the prostrate form of the boy. He slapped him none too gently on the backside. "Git up," boy," he commanded. Bruzz rose weakly to a sitting position, still crying. "You the nigger called the sheriff a while ago bout a holdup?"

"Yessuh," sobbed Bruzz, wiping his nose with the back of his hand. He looked among the faces of his neighbors for a sign that would tell him everything would be all right. Instead, he saw only the noncommittal stares they always assumed whenever the law came around. His heart sank. He had never felt so alone.

The deputy pushed back his stetson and scratched his head in puzzlement. "Hey, Jeff," he called to the driver. "Looka heah what we got."

"Aint big enough," drawled the one called Jeff. "Throw him back, Red."

"Sho will," grinned the deputy. Then he became stern and Bruzz cringed. "Boy, you tol a lie, a whopper. Theah warnt no holdup heah, was they?"

"Nossuh," Bruzz shook his head sadly.

The deputy pondered a moment, then asked, "Wheah you folks at, lil nigger?"

"Fishin."

"Wal-al, you tell em Ah say to give you a good hidin for lyin to the law, ya heah? An after that tell em Sheriff Abernathy say you help us catch Two Finger Rawlins, the biggest crook in the country. Least he was until he try tuh draw on mah pardnuh Jeff, theah." This last was said for the benefit of the spectators. "Now, whatcha say? You gonna tell em all that, lil nigger?"

"Yes, Suh!" Bruzz wanted to dance a jig.

The deputy rubbed his hand on

the boy's head. "That's a smaht lil nigger theah," he announced to the crowd as he climbed back into the patrol car. Bruzz's shiny, tear-stained face had broken into a thousand smiles. It was wonderful once more to be alive and he wanted the world to know it.

The driver shifted gears noisily and the sedan started to roll away. It had moved only a few feet when it stopped. The officer called Red leaned out and addressed the boy.

"Nigger, how in hell you figgered that crook didn come from aroun heah?"

Bruzz's brow furrowed in mute testimony to his earnest search for an answer. The silence grew noisier as the seconds passed. Finally, it came, sure and honest.

"Ah reckon, suh, it was cuz— well, cuz he didn call me 'nigger.'"

Questions for Discussion

1. BRUZZ was an unusually observant little boy. For one thing, he noticed that the stranger's skin was burned red instead of tanned. What other instances of the boy's alertness can you mention?

2. WAS BRUZZ justified in calling the sheriff or was he simply a youngster who let himself be carried away by his imagination? Explain your answer.

3. SHOW HOW the sheriff is a product of his environment by his actions and his manner of speaking to Bruzz.

4. WHAT MADE the stranger stand out in Mound Bayou; how was he different from other white men in that area?

5. A GOOD short story centers around a single situation. What is the incident that is the focal point of this story?

6. WHAT CAN you say about the atmosphere the story provides? How does the author make you feel the intense heat of mid-summer?

7. AFTER his call to the sheriff, Bruzz suffered second thoughts about his impulsive action. What was the nature of the mental anguish he experienced?

8. WHAT DOES the author primarily show in this story; (a) life in the South; (b) the capture of a gangster; (c) the contempt whites have for blacks; (d) how a boy's imagination works? Explain your choice. How would you state the theme (basic idea) of the story?

9. THERE ARE two white people who appear in the all-colored town of Mound Bayou: the crook and the sheriff. Compare the way each of these men looks upon the little black boy, Bruzz.

10. Do YOU feel sorry for the crook? What feeling does the author want you to have towards Two Finger Rawlins?

Building Vocabulary

Getting the meaning from the context. In each of the following sentences taken from the story, select from the choices given the word or phrase that means the same as the word in heavy type. Check your answer by looking up the word in a dictionary. Write the ones you get wrong in your private vocabulary list.

1. "... just as a dusty **coupe** (koop) slid to a stop ..." (p. 15)

   A. poultry pen   B. wagon   C. two-door auto   D. dump truck

2. "... a feat which fascinated the boy into awed **immobility** (im-oh-bil'ih-tee)." p. 15)

   A. fixedness   B. staring   C. astonishment   D. motion

3. "... The stranger affected disinterest in Bowman's **affluence** (af'loo-ins) ..." (p. 16)

   A. poverty   B. residence   C. friendliness   D. wealth

4. ". . . BRUZZ stood **transfixed** (trans-fikst')." (p. 16)

   A. trembling   B. astounded   C. perplexed   D. made motionless

5. "... His hand reached out almost **involuntarily** (in-vol-un-tair'ih-lee) ..." (p. 17)

   A. shakily   B. automatically   C. consciously   D. numbly

6. "... But **prodded** (prod'id) by his own audacity ..." (p. 17)

   A. urged   B. frightened   C. doomed   D. drew back

7. "... When an **indolent** (in'-dull-ent) drawl identified an officer on the other end of the wire ..." (p. 17)

   A. indulgent   B. forceful   C. high-pitched   D. lazy

8. "... The mental picture of the stranger lying in oceans of blood was so gory it shocked Bruzz back to a less **sanguine** (sang'gwin) reality ..." (p. 17)

   A. doubtful   B. sorrowful   C. bloodthirsty   D. sensible

9. "... he saw only the **noncommital** (non-kuh-mit'l) stares they always assumed ..." (p. 18)

   A. hateful   B. haughty   C. blank   D. neutral

10. "... Then he became stern and Bruzz **cringed** (krinjd)." (p. 18)

    A. shrank   B. cried out   C. smiled   D. jumped

Local Color

"BRUZZ" IS AN EXAMPLE of a story with local color. This term signifies a story that focuses on a certain locality and the circumstances and people that are peculiar to that area. Such a story portrays a distinctive way of life in a particular section of the country and emphasizes the geographical setting together with the speech, mannerisms, attitudes, and way of life of the people in that region.

1. How ACCURATE is the author in reproducing the speech that is characteristic of Mississippi? Let us take a sentence spoken by the sheriff as an example: "Theah warnt no holdup heah, was they?" Would you identify this manner of speaking as (a) dialect or (b) colloquial speech?

2. THE GEOGRAPHICAL background is especially important in a story of local color. Mention some of the details the author gives to convey the atmosphere of a Mississippi town drowsing under a hot summer sun.

3. IN WHAT WAY do each of the following attributes of Mound Bayou contribute to local color: (a) the jukebox (b) the old dump truck (c) a big hog farm?

4. PEOPLE ARE slow of movement in a hot climate. How does the author show that the inhabitants of Mound Bayou are sluggish in the pursuit of their day's activities?

5. WHAT PECULIAR attitude do the native whites in this part of the country show toward their fellow black citizens?

6. IN WHAT WAY do these two words contribute to local color: *orneriest* (p. 14) and *peckerwoods* (p. 16)? Consult a dictionary to find out the meanings of these words and whether they are dialect or colloquial.

⁂

Thinking and Writing

1. IN REPORTING to the sheriff's office that a gangster tried to hold up his father's store, Bruzz, of course, was greatly exaggerating. If the story were true, write an account of the robbery, including dialogue, and bearing in mind that the robber's manner of speaking was quite different from Bruzz's.

2. IMAGINE THAT you were driving through Mississippi and had lost your way. You found yourself in a little town called Mound Bayou and made a stop at the Jenkins' store to refresh yourself and to get directions. Write a description of the little black boy who would be serving you.

⁂

About the Author

Samuel Thompson has been a reporter and a labor union journalist. At one time he worked as a reporter for two black newspapers in New York City, *The New York Age* and *The Amsterdam News*. More recently he has been an editor of *The Pilot*, which is a publication of the National Maritime Union.

By Lerone Bennett, Jr.

The Convert

When the Supreme Court ruled that separate but equal facilities were no longer valid, Rev. Aaron Lott took it to mean that segregation might no longer be practiced in interstate transportation. He thought it meant there would be no more Jim Crow waiting rooms or coaches crossing state lines. In Melina, Mississippi, the white folks seemed to be unaware of this important step toward civil rights. Things went on just the same as before.

Rev. Lott was convinced that he was appointed by God to test the new law. He was determined to go through the white waiting room and into a first class coach in order to attend the Baptist convention in St. Louis.

The white folks in Melina weren't having any part of the Supreme Court. What happened to Rev. Lott is told by a close friend, Booker Brown, a colored undertaker. The story is related in the vernacular, that is, the language spoken in that particular community.

A MAN don't know what he'll do, a man don't know what he is till he gets his back pressed up against a wall. Now you take Aaron Lott: there ain't no other way to explain the crazy thing he did. He was going along fine, preaching the gospel, saving souls, and getting along with the white folks; and then, all of a sudden, he felt wood pressing against his back. The funny thing was that nobody knew he was hurting till he preached that Red Sea sermon where he got mixed up and seemed to think Mississippi was Egypt. As chairman of the deacons board, I felt it was my duty to reason with him. I appreciated his position and told him so, but I didn't think it was right for him to push us all in a hole. The old fool—he just laughed.

"Brother Booker," he said, "the Lord—He'll take care of me."

I knew then that the man was heading for trouble. And the very next thing he did confirmed it.

The white folks called the old fool downtown to bear witness that the colored folks were happy. And you know what he did: he got down there amongst all them big white folks and he said: "Things ain't gonna change here overnight, but they gonna change. It's inevitable. The Lord wants it."

Well sir, you could have bought them white folks for a penny. Aaron Lott, pastor of the Rock of Zion Baptist Church, a man white folks had said was wise and sound and sensible, had come close—too close—to saying that the Supreme Court was coming to Melina, Mississippi. The surprising thing was that the white folks didn't do nothing. There was a lot of mumbling and whispering but nothing bad happened till the terrible morning when Aaron came a-knocking at the door of my funeral home. Now things had been tightening up— you could feel it in the air—and I didn't want no part of no crazy scheme and I told him so right off. He walked on past me and sat down on the couch. He had on his preaching clothes, a shiny blue suit, a fresh starched white shirt, a black tie, and his Sunday black shoes. I remember thinking at the time that Aaron was too black to be wearing all them dark clothes. The thought tickled me and I started to smile but then I noticed something about him that didn't seem quite right. I ran my eyes over him closely. He was kinda middle–sized and he had a big clean–shaven head, a big nose, and

thin lips. I stood there looking at him for a long time but I couldn't figure out what it was till I looked at his eyes; they were burning bright, like light bulbs do just before they go out. And yet he looked contented, like his mind was resting somewheres else.

"I wanna talk with you, Booker," he said glancing sideways at my wife. "If you don't mind, Sister Brown—"

Sarah got up and went in the living quarters. Aaron didn't say nothing for a long time; he just sat there looking out the window. Then he spoke so soft I had to strain my ears to hear.

"I'm leaving for the Baptist convention," he said. He pulled out his gold watch and looked at it. "Train leaves in 'bout two hours."

"I know *that*, Aaron."

"Yeah, but what I wanted to tell you was that I ain't going Jim Crow. I'm going first class, Booker, right through the white waiting room. That's the law."

A cold shiver ran through me.

"Aaron," I said, "don't you go talking crazy now."

The old fool laughed, a great big body-shaking laugh. He started talking 'bout God and Jesus and all that stuff. Now, I'm a God-fearing man myself, but I holds that God helps those who help themselves. I told him so.

"You can't mix God up with these white folks," I said. "When you start to messing around with segregation, they'll burn you up and the Bible, too."

He looked at me like I was Satan.

"I sweated over this thing," he said. "I prayed. I got down on my knees and I asked God not to give me this cup. But He said I was the one. I heard Him, Booker, right here—he tapped his chest—in my heart."

The old fool's been having visions, I thought. I sat down and tried to figure out a way to hold him, but he got up, without saying a word, and started for the door.

"Wait!" I shouted. "I'll get my coat."

"I don't need you," he said. "I just came by to tell you so you could tell the board in case something happened."

"You wait," I shouted, and ran out of the room to get my coat.

We got in his beat-up old Ford and went by the parsonage to get his suitcase. Rachel—that was his wife—and Jonah were sitting in the living room, wringing their hands. Aaron got his bag, shook Jonah's hand, and said, "Take care of your Mamma, boy." Jonah nodded. Aaron hugged Rachel and pecked at her cheek. Rachel broke down. She throwed her arms around his neck and carried on something awful. Aaron shoved her away.

"Don't go making no fuss over it, woman. I ain't gonna be gone forever. Can't a man go to a church meeting 'thout women screaming and crying."

He tried to make light of it, but you could see he was touched by the way his lips trembled. He held his hand out to me, but I wouldn't take it. I told him off good, told him it was a sin and a shame for a man of God to be carrying on like he was, worrying his wife and everything.

"I'm coming with you," I said. "Somebody's gotta see that you don't make a fool of yourself."

He shrugged, picked up his suitcase, and started for the door. Then he stopped and turned around and looked at his wife and his boy and from the way he looked I knew that there was still a chance. He looked at the one and then at the other. For a moment there, I thought he was going to cry, but he turned, quicklike, and walked out of the door.

I ran after him and tried to talk some sense in his head. But he shook me off, turned the corner, and went on up Adams Street. I caught up with him and we walked in silence, crossing the street in front of the First Baptist Church for whites, going on around the Confederate monument.

"Put it off, Aaron," I begged. "Sleep on it."

He didn't say nothing.

"What you need is a vacation. I'll get the board to approve, full pay and everything."

He smiled and shifted the suitcase over to his left hand. Big drops of sweat were running down his face and spotting up his shirt.

His eyes were awful, all lit up and burning.

"Aaron, Aaron, can't you hear me?"

We passed the feed store, Bill Williams' grocery store, and the movie house.

"A man's gotta think about his family, Aaron. A man ain't free. Didn't you say that once, didn't you?"

He shaded his eyes with his hand and looked into the sun. He put the suitcase on the ground and checked his watch.

"Why dont' you think about Jonah?" I asked. "Answer that. Why don't you think about your own son?"

"I am," he said. "That's exactly what I'm doing, thinking about Jonah. Matter of fact, he started *me* to thinking. I ain't never mentioned it before, but the boy's been worrying me. One day he was downtown here and he asked me something that hurt. 'Daddy,' he said, 'how come you ain't a man?' I got mad, I did, and told him: 'I am a man.' He said that wasn't what he meant. 'I mean,' he said, 'how come you ain't a man where white folks concerned.' I couldn't answer him, Booker, I'll never forget it till the day I die. I couldn't answer my own son, and I been preaching forty years."

"He don't know nothing 'bout it," I said. "He's hot-headed, like my boy. He'll find out when he grows up."

"I hopes not," Aaron said, shaking his head. " I hopes not."

Some white folks passed and we shut up till they were out of hearing. Aaron, who was acting real strange, looked up in the sky and moved his lips. He came back to himself, after a little bit, and he said: "This thing of being a man, Booker, is a big thing. The Supreme Court can't make you a man. The NAACP can't do it. God Almighty can do a lot, but even He can't do it. Ain't nobody can do it but you."

He said that like he was preaching and when he got through he was all filled up with emotion and he seemed kind of ashamed—he was a man who didn't like emotion outside the church. He looked at his watch, picked up his bag and said, "Well, let's git it over with."

We turned into Elm and the first thing I saw at the end of the street was the train station. It was an old red building, flat like a slab. A group of white men were fooling around in front of the door. I couldn't make them out from that distance, but I could tell they weren't the kind of white folks to be fooling around with.

We walked on, passing the dry goods store, the barber shop, and the new building that was going up. Across the street from that was the sheriff's office. I looked in the window and saw Bull Sampson sitting at his desk, his feet propped up on a chair, a fat brown cigar sticking out of his mouth. A ball about the size of a sweet potato started burning in my stomach.

"Please Aaron," I said. "Please.

You can't get away with it. I know how you feel. Sometimes I feel the same way myself, but I wouldn't risk my neck for these niggers. They won't appreciate it; they'll laugh at you."

We were almost to the station and I could make out the faces of the men sitting on the benches. One of them must have been telling a joke. He finished and the group broke out laughing.

I whispered to Aaron: "I'm through with it. I wash my hands of the whole mess."

I don't know whether he heard me or not. He turned to the right without saying a word and went on in the front door. The string-beany man who told the joke was so shocked that his cigarette fell out of his mouth.

"Y'all see that," he said. "Why, I'll—"

"Shut up," another man said. "Go git Bull."

I kept walking fast, turned at the corner, and ran around to the colored waiting room. When I got there, I looked through the ticket window and saw Aaron standing in front of the clerk. Aaron stood there for a minute or more, but the clerk didn't see him. And that took some not seeing. In that room, Aaron Lott stood out like a pig in a chicken coop.

There were, I'd say, about ten or fifteen people in there, but didn't none of them move. They just sat there, with their eyes glued on Aaron's back. Aaron cleared his throat. The clerk didn't look up;

he got real busy with some papers. Aaron cleared his throat again and opened his mouth to speak. The screen door of the waiting room opened and clattered shut.

It got real quiet in that room, hospital quiet. It got so quiet I could hear my own heart beating. Now Aaron knew who opened that door, but he didn't bat an eyelid. He turned around real slow and faced High Sheriff Sampson, the baddest man in South Mississippi.

Mr. Sampson stood there with his legs wide open, like the men you see on television. His beefy face was blood-red and his gray eyes were rattlesnake hard. He was mad; no doubt about it. I had never seen him so mad.

"Preacher," he said, "you done gone crazy?" He was talking low-like and mean.

"Nosir," Aaron said. "Nosir, Mr. Sampson."

"What you think you doing?"

"Going to St. Louis, Mr. Sampson."

"You must done lost yo' mind, boy."

Mr. Sampson started walking towards Aaron with his hands on his gun. Twenty or thirty men pushed through the front door and fanned out over the room. Mr. Sampson stopped about two paces from Aaron and looked him up and down. That look had paralyzed hundreds of niggers, but it didn't faze Aaron none—he stood his ground.

"I'm gonna give you a chance,

preacher. Git on over to the nigger side and git quick."

"I ain't bothering nobody, Mr. Sampson."

Somebody in the crowd yelled: "Don't reason wit' the nigger, Bull. Hit em."

Mr. Sampson walked up to Aaron and grabbed him in the collar and throwed him up against the ticket counter. He pulled out his gun.

"Did you hear me, deacon. I said, 'Git.' "

"I'm going to St. Louis, Mr. Sampson. That's cross state lines. The court done said—"

Aaron didn't have a chance. The blow came from nowhere. Laying there on the floor with blood spurting from his mouth, Aaron looked up at Mr. Sampson and he did another crazy thing: he grinned. Bull Sampson jumped up in the air and came down on Aaron with all his two hundred pounds. It made a crunchy sound. He jumped again and the mob, maddened by the blood and heat, moved in to help him. They fell on Aaron like mad dogs. They beat him with chairs; they beat him with sticks; they beat him with guns.

Till this day, I don't know what come over me. The first thing I know I was running and then I was standing in the middle of the white waiting room. Mr. Sampson was the first to see me. He backed off, cocked his pistol, and said: "Booker, boy, you come one mo' step and I'll kill you. What's a

matter with you niggers today? All y'all gone crazy?"

"Please don't kill him," I begged. "You ain't got no call to treat him like that."

"So you saw it all, did you? Well, then, Booker you musta saw the nigger preacher reach for my gun?"

"He didn't do that, Mr. Sampson," I said. "He didn't—"

Mr. Sampson put a big hairy hand on my tie and pulled me to him.

"Booker," he said sweetly. "You saw the preacher reach for my gun, didn't you?"

I didn't open my mouth—I couldn't I was so scared—but I guess my eyes answered for me. Whatever Mr. Sampson saw there musta convinced him 'cause he throwed me on the floor besides Aaron.

"Git this nigger out of here," he said, "and be quick about it."

Dropping to my knees, I put my hand on Aaron's chest; I didn't feel nothing. I felt his wrist; I didn't feel nothing. I got up and looked at them white folks with tears in my eyes. I looked at the women, sitting crying on the benches. I looked at the men. I looked at Mr. Sampson. I said, "He was a good man."

Mr. Sampson said, "Move the nigger."

A big sigh came out of me and I wrung my hands.

He grabbed my tie and twisted it, but I didn't feel nothing. My eyes were glued to his hands;

there was blood under the finger-nails, and the fingers—they looked like fat little red sausages. I screamed and Mr. Sampson flung me down on the floor.

He said, "*Move the nigger.*"

I picked Aaron up and fixed his body over my shoulder and carried him outside. I sent for one of my boys and we dressed him up and put him away real nice-like and Rachel and the boy came and they cried and carried on and yet, somehow, they seemed prouder of Aaron than ever before. And the colored folks—they seemed proud, too. Crazy. Didn't they know? Couldn't they see? It hadn't done no good. In fact, things got worse. The Northern newspapers started kicking up a stink and Mr. Rivers, the solicitor, announced they were going to hold a hearing. All of a sudden, Booker Taliaferro Brown became the biggest man in that town. My phone rang day and night: I got threats, I got promises, and I was offered bribes. Everywhere I turned somebody was waiting to ask me: "Whatcha gonna do? Whatcha gonna say?" To tell the truth, I didn't know myself. One day I would decide one thing and the next day I would decide another.

It was Mr. Rivers and Mr. Sampson who called my attention to that. They came to my office one day and called me a shifty, no-good nigger. They said they expected me to stand by "my statement" in the train station that I saw Aaron reach for the gun.

I hadn't said no such thing, but Mr. Sampson said I said it and he said he had witnesses who heard me say it. "And if you say anything else," he said, "I can't be responsible for your health. Now you know"—he put that bloody hand on my shoulder and he smiled his sweet death smile—"you *know* I wouldn't threaten you, but the boys"—he shook his head—"the boys are real worked up over this one."

It was long about then that I began to hate Aaron Lott. I'm ashamed to admit it now, but it's true: I hated him. He had lived his life: he had made his choice. Why should he live my life, too, and make me choose? It wasn't fair; it wasn't right; it wasn't Christian. What made me so mad was the fact that nothing I said would help Aaron. He was dead and it wouldn't help one whit for me to say that he didn't reach for that gun. I tried to explain that to Rachel when she came to my office, moaning and crying, the night before the hearing.

"Listen to me, woman," I said. "Listen, Aaron was a good man. He lived a good life. He did a lot of good things, but he's *dead, dead, dead*! Nothing I say will bring him back. Bull Sampson's got ten niggers who are going to swear on a stack of Bibles that they saw Aaron reach for that gun. It won't do me or you or Aaron no good for me to swear otherwise."

What did I say that for? That woman like to had a fit. She got down on her knees and she begged me to go with Aaron.

"Go wit' him," she cried. "Booker. *Booker*! If you's a man, if you's a father, if you's a friend, go wit' Aaron."

That woman tore my heart up. I ain't never heard nobody beg like that.

"Tell the truth, Booker," she said. "That's all I'm asking. Tell the truth."

"Truth!" I said. "Hah! That's all you niggers talk about: truth. What do you know about truth? Truth is eating good, and sleeping good. Truth is living, Rachel. Be loyal to the living."

Rachel backed off from me. You would have thought that I had cursed her or something. She didn't say nothing; she just stood there pressed against the door. She stood there saying nothing for so long that my nerves snapped.

"Say something," I shouted. "Say something—anything!"

She shook her head, slowly at first, and then her head started moving like it wasn't attached to her body. It went back and forth, back and forth, back and forth. I started towards her, but she jerked open the door and ran out into the night, screaming.

That did it. I ran across the room to the filing cabinet, opened the bottom drawer, and took out a dusty bottle of Scotch. I started drinking, but the more I drank the soberer I got. I guess I fell asleep 'cause I dreamed I buried Rachel and that everything went along fine until she jumped out of the casket and started screaming. I came awake with a start and knocked over the bottle. I reached for a rag and my hand stopped in mid-air.

"Of course," I said out loud and slammed my fist down on the Scotch-soaked papers.

I didn't see nothing.

Why didn't I think of it before?

I didn't see nothing.

Jumping up, I walked to and fro in the office. Would it work? I rehearsed it in my mind. All I could see was Aaron's back. I don't know whether he reached for the gun or not. All I know is that *for some reason* the men beat him to death.

Rehearsing the thing in my mind, I felt a great weight slip off my shoulders. I did a little jig in the middle of the floor and went upstairs to my bed, whistling. Sarah turned over and looked me up and down.

"What you happy about?"

"Can't a man be happy?" I asked.

She sniffed the air, said, "Oh," turned over, and mumbled something in her pillow. It came to me then for the first time that she was 'bout the only person in town who hadn't asked me what I was going to do. I thought about it for a little while, shrugged, and fell into bed with all my clothes on.

When I woke up the next morning, I had a terrible headache and my tongue was a piece of sandpaper. For a long while, I couldn't figure out what I was doing laying there with all my clothes on. Then it came to me: this was the big day. I put on my black silk suit, the one I wore for big funerals, and went downstairs to breakfast. I walked into the dining room without looking and bumped into Russell, the last person in the world I wanted to see. He was my only child, but he didn't act like it. He was always finding fault. He didn't like the way I talked to Negroes; he didn't like the way I talked to white folks. He didn't like this; he didn't like that. And to top it off, the young whipper-snapper wanted to be an artist. Undertaking wasn't good enough for him. He wanted to paint pictures.

I sat down and grunted.

"Good morning, Papa." He said it like he meant it. He wants something, I thought, looking him over closely, noticing that his right eye was swollen.

"You been fighting again, boy?"

"Yes, Papa."

"You younguns. Education— that's what it is. Education! It's ruining you."

He didn't say nothing. He just sat there, looking down when I looked up and looking up when I looked down. This went on through the grits and the eggs and the second cup of coffee.

"Whatcha looking at?" I asked.

"Nothing, Papa."

"Whatcha thinking?"

"Nothing, Papa."

"You lying, boy. It's written all over your face."

He didn't say nothing.

I dismissed him with a wave of my hand, picked up the paper, and turned to the sports page.

"What are you going to do, Papa?"

The question caught me unawares. I know now that I was expecting it, that I wanted him to ask it; but he put it so bluntly that I was flabbergasted. I pretended I didn't understand.

"Do 'bout what, boy? Speak up!"

"About the trial, Papa."

I didn't say nothing for a long time. There wasn't much, in fact, I could say; so I got mad.

"Questions, questions, questions," I shouted. "That's all I get in this house—questions. You never have a civil word for your pa. I go out of here and work my tail off and you keep yourself shut up in that room of yours looking at them fool books and now soon as your old man gets his back against the wall you join the pack. I expected better than that of you, boy. A son ought to back his pa."

That hurt him. He picked up the coffee pot and poured himself another cup of coffee and his hand trembled. He took a sip and watched me over the rim.

"They say you are going to chicken out, Papa."

"Chicken out? What that mean?"

"They're betting you'll 'Tom.' "

I leaned back in the chair and took a sip of coffee.

"So they're betting, huh?" The idea appealed to me. "Crazy—they'd bet on a funeral."

I saw pain on his face. He sighed and said: "I bet, too, Papa."

The cup fell out of my hand and broke, spilling black water over the tablecloth.

"You did what?"

"I bet you wouldn't 'Tom.'"

"You little fool." I fell out laughing and then I stopped suddenly and looked at him closely. "How much you bet?"

"One hundred dollars."

I stood up.

"You're lying," I said. "Where'd you get that kind of money?"

"From Mamma."

"Sarah!" I shouted. "Sarah! You get in here. What kind of house you running, sneaking behind my back, giving this boy money to gamble with?"

Sarah leaned against the door jamb. She was in her hot iron mood. There was no expression on her face. And her eyes were hard.

"I gave it to him, Booker," she said. "They called you an Uncle Tom. He got in a fight about it. He wanted to bet on you, Booker. *He* believes in you."

Suddenly I felt old and used up. I pulled a chair to me and sat down.

"Please," I said, waving my hand. "Please. Go away. Leave me alone. Please."

I sat there for maybe ten or fifteen minutes, thinking, praying.

The phone rang. It was Mr. Withers, the president of the bank. I had put in for a loan and it had been turned down, but Mr. Withers said there'd been a mistake. "New fellow, you know," he said, clucking his tongue. He said he knew that it was my lifelong dream to build a modern funeral home and to buy a Cadillac hearse. He said he sympathized with that dream, supported it, thought the town needed it, and thought I deserved it. "The loan will go through," he said. "Drop by and see me this morning after the hearing."

When I put that phone down, it was wet with sweat. I couldn't turn that new funeral home down and Mr. Withers knew it. My father had raised me on that dream and before he died he made me swear on a Bible I would make it good. And here it was on a platter, just for a word, a word that wouldn't hurt nobody.

I put on my hat and hurried to the courthouse. When they called my name, I walked in with my head held high. The courtroom was packed. The white folks had all the seats and the colored folks were standing in the rear. Whoever arranged the seating had set aside the first two rows for white men. They were sitting almost on top of each other, looking mean and uncomfortable in their best white shirts.

I walked up to the bench and swore on the Bible and took a seat. Mr. Rivers gave me a little smile and waited for me to get myself set.

"State your name," he said.

"Booker Taliaferro Brown." I took a quick look at the first two rows and recognized at least ten of the men who killed Aaron.

"And your age?"

"Fifty-seven."

"You're an undertaker?"

"Yessir."

"You been living in this town all your life?"

"Yessir."

"You like it here, don't you, Booker?"

Was this a threat? I looked Mr. Rivers in the face for the first time. He smiled.

I told the truth. I said, "Yessir."

"Now, calling your attention to the day of May 17th, did anything unusual happen on that day?"

The question threw me. I shook my head. Then it dawned on me. He was talking about—

"Yessir," I said. "That's the day Aaron got—" Something in Mr. Rivers' face warned me and I pulled up—"that's the day of the trouble at the train station."

Mr. Rivers smiled. He looked like a trainer who'd just put a monkey through a new trick. You could feel the confidence and the contempt oozing out of him. I looked at his prissy little mustache and his smiling lips and I got mad. Lifting my head a little bit, I looked him full in the eyes: I held the eyes for a moment and I tried to tell the man behind the eyes that I was a man like him and that

he didn't have no right to be using me and laughing about it. But he didn't get the message. He chuckled softly, turned his back on me, and faced the audience.

"I believe you were with the preacher that day."

The water was getting deep. I scrooched down in my seat, closed the lids of my eyes, and looked dense.

"Yessir, Mr. Rivers," I drawled. "Ah was, Ah was."

"Now, Booker—" he turned around— "I believe you tried to keep the nigger preacher from getting out of line."

I hesitated. It wasn't a fair question. Finally, I said: "Yessir."

"You begged him not to go to the white side?"

"Yessir."

"And when that failed, you went over to *your* side—the *colored* side—and looked through the window?"

"Yessir."

He put his hand in his coat pocket and studied my face.

"You saw *everything*, didn't you?"

"Just about." A muscle on the inside of my thigh started tingling.

Mr. Rivers shuffled some papers he had in his hand. He seemed to be thinking real hard. I pushed myself against the back of the chair. Mr. Rivers moved close, quick, and stabbed his finger into my chest.

"Booker, did you see the nigger

preacher reach for Mr. Sampson's gun?"

He backed away, smiling. I looked away from him and I felt my heart trying to tear out of my skin. I looked out over the courtroom. It was still: wasn't even a fly moving. I looked at the white folks in front and the colored folks in back and I turned the question over in my mind. While I was doing that, waiting, taking my time, I noticed, out of the corner of my eye, that the smile on Mr. Rivers' face was dying away. Suddenly, I had a terrible itch to know what that smile would turn into.

I said, "Nosir."

Mr. Rivers stumbled backwards like he had been shot. Old Judge Sloan took off his glasses and pushed his head out over the bench. The whole courtroom seemed to be leaning in to me and I saw Aaron's widow leaning back with her eyes closed and it seemed to me at that distance that her lips were moving in prayer.

Mr. Rivers was the first to recover. He put his smile back on and he acted like my answer was in the script.

"You mean," he said, "that you didn't see it. It happened so quickly that you missed it?"

I looked at the bait and I ain't gonna lie: I was tempted. He knew as well as I did what I meant, but he was gambling on my weakness. I had thrown away my funeral home, my hearse, everything I owned, and he was standing there like a magician, pulling them out of a hat, one at a time, dangling them, saying: "Looka here, looka here, don't they look pretty?" I was on top of a house and he was betting that if he gave me a ladder I would come down. He was wrong, but you can't fault him for trying. I looked him in the eye and went the last mile.

"Aaron didn't reach for that gun," I said. "Them people, they just fell on—"

"Hold it," he shouted. "I want to remind you that there are laws in this state against perjury. You can go to jail for five years for what you just said. Now I know you've been conferring with those NAACP fellows, but I want to remind you of the statements you made to Sheriff Sampson and me. Judge—" he dismissed me with a wave of his hand—"Judge, this *man*—"he caught himself and it was my turn to smile—"this *boy* is lying. Ten niggers have testified that they saw the preacher reach for the gun. Twenty white people saw it. You've heard their testimony. I want to withdraw this witness and I want to reserve the right to file perjury charges against him."

Judge Sloan nodded. He pushed his bottom lip over his top one.

"You can step down," he said. "I want to warn you that perjury is a very grave offense. You—"

"Judge, I didn't—"

"Nigger!" He banged his gavel.

"Don't you interrupt me. Now git out of here."

Two guards pushed me outside and waved away the reporters. Billy Giles, Mr. Sampson's assistant, came out and told me Mr. Sampson wanted me out of town before sundown. "And he says you'd better get out before the Northern reporters leave. He won't be responsible for your safety after that."

I nodded and went on down the stairs and started out the door.

"Booker!"

Rachel and a whole line of Negroes were running down the stairs. I stepped outside and waited for them. Rachel ran up and throwed her arms around me. "It don't take but one, Booker," she said. "It don't take but one." Somebody else said: "They whitewashed it, they whitewashed it, but you spoiled it for 'em."

Russell came out then and stood over to the side while the others crowded around to shake my hands. Then the others sensed that he was waiting and they made a little aisle. He walked up to me kind of slow-like and he said, "Thank you, sir." That was the first time in his whole seventeen years that that boy had said "sir" to me. I cleared my throat and when I opened my eyes Sarah was standing beside me. She didn't say nothing; she just put her hand in mine and stood there. It was long about then, I guess, when I realized that I wasn't seeing so good. They say I cried, but I don't believe a word of it. It was such a hot day and the sun was shining so bright that the sweat rolling down my face blinded me. I wiped the sweat out of my eyes and some more people came up and said a lot of foolish things about me showing the white folks and following in Aaron's footsteps. I wasn't doing no such fool thing. Ol' Man Rivers just put the thing to me in a way it hadn't been put before—man to man. It was simple, really. Any man would have done it.

Questions for Discussion

1. THIS STORY is told in the first person from the point of view of one who took a personal part in the events. The language is colloquial, that which would be used in talking to a friend. How effective is the use of the vernacular in telling this story of Southern violence? Would the story have been just as interesting if told by some one else, by Sheriff Sampson, perhaps?

2. How IMPORTANT is the setting for this story? Could the story have been placed in a different setting without losing its impact?

3. THE FIRST three paragraphs set the mood and prepare the reader for a somber story. Does the story fulfill the expectations of the first part? Are we prepared for the death to follow? In what way is this first section similar to the topic sentence in a paragraph?

4. Is THE BRUTALITY of Sheriff Sampson too incredible or is it convincing? Can you cite similar incidents that have taken place in the South?

5. WHAT TRAITS of character did Rev. Lott possess? If he had known that defiance of Jim Crow in Melina, Mississippi, would lead to his death, would he have hesitated to put the Supreme Court decision to the test? Explain your answer.

6. COMPLAINTS have been made that older people do not listen to their children and alienation is the result. Show how two fathers in this story *did* listen to their children and respected their good will so much that they were ready to sacrifice even their lives.

7. BOOKER WAS LIKE the 38 people who heard Kitty Genovese scream for help in a New York City street but did nothing to stop her murder because they didn't want to get involved. Booker did not want to get involved because he had too much to lose by telling the truth. What did he have to *gain* by telling the truth at the hearing?

8. WHAT PRESSURES were put on Booker before the hearing?

9. TRUTHFULNESS has always been regarded as a guiding principle of conduct. Booker kept saying it wouldn't make any difference if he told the truth because Aaron could not be brought back to life and he decided to conceal the facts of the vicious murder. Does this indicate a defect in Booker's character?

10. BOOKER CAME to the hearing undecided how to testify. When

the crucial question was put to him he told the truth, knowing it would bring his world crashing down and possibly mean his death. What motivated Booker's decision?

11. THE PREACHER'S WIDOW said in gratitude to Booker after the hearing, "It don't take but one." What did she mean by that?

12. THE LAST WORDS of the story are: "Any man would have done it." *Would* any man have done what Booker did?

13. COMPARE the qualities of character of Booker and Rev. Aaron Lott and show how their characters played a large part in the story.

14. How DOES the element of suspense enter into the story?

15. How DOES the author make you feel the atmosphere of menace in the story?

16. WHAT IS the meaning of the title?

The Plot

1. THE PLAN of the story is made clear in the beginning paragraphs. The narrator tells us that Aaron Lott was heading for trouble. The series of events leading to his death and the complications following his murder taken together constitute the plot. What event in Washington, D. C. started the chain of happenings in Melina, Mississippi?

2. THE PROBLEM faced by Aaron Lott was how to break through the practice of segregation in Southern states. What course of action did he take to meet this problem?

3. AARON'S COURSE led to a major catastrophe. What happened? This might be identified as a crisis in the story.

4. POLYBIUS, a Greek historian, wrote in the second century B.C.: "There is . . . no accuser so terrible as the conscience that dwells in the heart of every man." Apply this quotation to Booker and show what conflict was going on in his mind.

5. WHAT HINTS does the narrator give as to the resolution of the extremely difficult quandary in which he finds himself, as Aaron tries to control his life from beyond the grave?

6. AT WHAT POINT did the plot reach its climax (the peak of action)?

7. THE OPENING of the story is: "A man don't know what he'll do, a man don't know what he is till he gets his back pressed up against a wall." Although these words are meant to apply to Aaron, they also have meaning for Booker. How significant is this sentence in explaining the action the narrator took to end the war with his own conscience?

8. WHAT WAS the solution arrived at in the story? Did you feel satisfied with it? Did you think it was contrived or grew naturally out of the circumstances of the story?

Thinking and Writing

1. THE REV. LOTT first showed his resentment of segregation by a Red Sea sermon wherein he compared ancient Egypt with Mississippi. Write out that sermon showing how the tyranny and bondage of antique times find their parallel in sections of the United States.

2. SUPPOSE you were in the courtroom at the hearing into the death of Rev. Aaron Lott. Tell what was the purpose of the hearing, what was at stake and then describe the effect on the spectators when star witness Booker Brown denied Aaron reached for the sheriff's gun.

3. ASSUME that you are seventeen-year-old Russell, the undertaker's son. Write an explanation of your fight with another student who called your father an Uncle Tom and why you bet that your father would tell the truth about Rev. Lott's death at the hearing.

4. WHAT POSITION do you take on Aaron Lott's death? Did he die a martyr's death to no purpose, or do you think his death served as an inspiration that would produce far-reaching results in undermining segregation? Write a paper on your interpretation of the death of the deacon.

5. IF SUPREME COURT decisions do not have much effect on changing the pattern of segregation in the South nor in reducing violent racial incidents, what would you suggest can be done to achieve racial harmony? Write an essay setting forth your ideas in an organized fashion.

Word Study

Since the story is told on a colloquial level by a member of the black community of a town in Mississippi, we find the vocabulary to be composed of everyday words in common usage, sprinkled with a number of localisms or slang expressions. Most of these words or phrases will not be found in a dictionary, but it is possible to pinpoint their meaning from their use in the context. For example, on page 25, the expression occurs "he felt wood pressing against his back." By reference to the ideas preceding and following we become aware that Aaron Lott felt he had taken all he could endure and that it was time to strike back. In other words, he felt that he was being pushed against the wall, or "feeling wood."

In the same way, see if you can reason out the meaning of the following terms according to the ideas surrounding the unfamiliar words.

---

1. ". . . You could have bought them white folks for a penny." (page 26)

2. ". . . string-beany man." (page 29)

3. ". . . it wouldn't help one whit." (page 31)

4. ". . . young whippersnapper." (this one is in the dictionary) (page 33)

5. ". . . I was flabbergasted." (this, too, is in the dictionary) (page 33)

6. ". . . to chicken out" (page 33)

7. ". . . to 'Tom'" (page 34)

8. ". . . hot iron mood." (page 34)

9. ". . . prissy little mustache." (page 35)

10. ". . . scroonched down in my seat." (page 35)

About the Author

ℒerone Bennett, Jr. was born in 1928 in Mississippi. After grad-uating from college in Atlanta, Georgia, he carved out a highly successful career in journalism, first in the newspaper and then in the magazine field. Before becoming an editor of *Ebony* maga-zine in 1960, he held an editorial post with an Atlanta newspaper. He has written several books, in addition to short stories and poems. Mr. Bennett's writings are largely about the historical con-tributions of Negroes to the building of America. His works are: *Before the Mayflower*: a history of the Negro in America 1619-1962 (1962); *The Negro Mood,* about race relations in the U. S. (1964); *What Manner of Man;* a biography of Martin Luther King, Jr. (1964); *Confrontation, Black and White,* about the struggle of the American Negro for social and economic equality (1965); *Black Power U.S.A.,* about the Reconstruction period in the South following the Civil War (1967); *Pioneers in Protest,* stories of twenty outstanding personalities who were leaders in the struggle against racial bias, from Crispus Attucks, Revolu-tionary War hero to W. E. B. Du Bois, Afro-American scholar (1968).

In 1969 Mr. Bennett took a leave of absence from *Ebony* to serve as a professor of black history at Northwestern University in Chicago.

The
Death
of
Tommy
Grimes

The Death of Tommy Grimes

By R. J. Meaddough III

Tommy had become part of the ground. At least he felt that way as he watched the dew and the daylight make giant shiny cobwebs of the treetops. The sun had not yet risen and a mist lay over the ground, which made the forest seem rather spooky to him.

His nose itched and he longed to scratch it, maybe just nudge it a little, but Pa said don't move, don't twitch, don't even breathe hard. Not one arm, one hand, even one finger, he said. "He knows the woods," Pa told him; "you'll never know he's there; suddenly he'll just *be* there looking at you, just looking."

It started so long ago, Tommy remembered, almost a year, when he was just eleven. That night, in the henyard, with the weasel's eyes glistening in the flashlight. He never even fired a shot, just stood there with his mouth open, foolish, while the weasel dashed into the woods.

And Pa knocking the rifle from his hands and asking, "Why didn't

44

Dawn was just breaking in the forest. The stillness gave way only to the rustling of small creatures and the chirping of crickets. There was a tranquility and beauty that had spanned the centuries. But death was lurking in the forest. There was a hunter. The hunter was very young, not even twelve years old, yet he was a skilled marksman. The quarry he brought down forms the basis for a surprise ending to this story of racial hate in the deep South.

you shoot? What you waiting on? What's wrong with you, boy?"

"Pa, I . . . I couldn't, Pa. I just couldn't."

Pa hunkered down and pulled on a blade of grass. He didn't say anything for a minute, just knelt there chewing on that grass.

"You never did like to kill nothing did you, boy? Even when you was small."

Tommy looked at the ground without saying anything and his father sighed, "Tommy, dammit, a man *always* dies a little when he kills something, but it just plain has to be done. Some animals just ain't no damn good and got to be *killed.* Understand?"

He nodded without answering, still looking at the ground, and Pa stood up with a groan and they walked into the henhouse without speaking. They counted forty-three dead pullets, lying in red and white patches of feathers, blood and confusion.

So he began to practice with the rifle, shooting at moving targets, and the rifle became part of his arm. It seemed so long that Pa practiced with him, so long. Again and again he would take a deep breath, let some out, then squeeze the trigger. So long, so very long.

Tommy felt beads of sweat form on his forehead despite the chill that remained in the forest air. Soon the beads would form into droplets and run down his face and burn his eyes. There was a handkerchief in his coat pocket just a few inches away but he could not, dare not reach for it. But soon it would be over. Soon.

It got so that he could hit anything he aimed at, even things a good bit out. And sometimes, when he turned real quick, he would see pride in Pa's eyes. But then Pa would always make his face blank and say, "We-e-ell, Tommy," real grim-like, "you're getting better but you need more practice."

Pa taught him how to track animals and how to lead quail, and how to lean into the rifle to take up the recoil. And Pa showed him how to lie quiet so the forest forgot he was there and Nature went on about her business.

And the time came last night when Pa came home and mentioned that some of the men were going into the forest to get a buck; and how it might be some good shooting because bucks were fast, real fast.

He bent his head to eat his beans, yet he knew without looking that his father was watching him, way out of the corner of his eye. He knew too, that Pa wouldn't have said a word if Ma was there —she was always saying he was too young for something or other —but she was visiting overnight up in Colliersville. And he thought how it must be for Pa when the other men bragged about their boys, and him so scared to kill a weasel, and he knew what he had to do.

"Pa," he murmured, "think maybe I could go a time at that old buck?"

"Boy, this ain't no old buck, it's a young one," Pa said, making like he was surprised. "Boy, you might get hurt."

"Some time, I think I'd like to take my turn," he answered, face even closer to the beans.

"Well I'll think about it, boy," Pa mumbled, but he couldn't hide a gleam in his eye.

Tommy slowly, ever so slowly, rubbed his forehead along his sleeve and watched the gloom in front of him. Somewhere out there Pa had circled around and was trampling through the woods, scaring everything away, away toward the clearing where he lay waiting.

He laughed in his mind when he thought of the last time when Pa had gone down to the Hut for a drink with the "boys," as he called them. And when he came out his eyes were gleaming like the mischief and he wobbled into the yard like he didn't know how to walk. He had gone downstairs in his pajamas and they sat on the back porch and listened to the crickets and looked at the stars. Maybe afterwards Pa would let him go into the Hut and talk with the men and drink liquor. But right then he had to be satisfied with listening to Pa tell stories that he had heard at the Hut and then squeeze his arm at the end and laugh, oh my, how he would laugh. Then he filled his pipe and stared out across the backyard toward the north pasture.

"Dawn in the forest is a beautiful thing, boy, beautiful. All the colors and wild flowers, fresh streams, cool breeze, you feel like, boy, feel it! Even though there ain't a sound you feel it. You see a flash of white and you know some rabbit's going home. Or you might see a chuck burrowing in. And the trees," he whispered, "They just stand there watching you. Been there before you came, be there after you gone."

"Gee Pa," he murmured, "you make it sound so nice I don't know's I want to *hunt* tomorrow."

Pa smiled. "It *is* nice, boy, real nice, but things got to be done to keep it that way. Fox eats a rabbit, he keeps the rabbit population down, else they'd overrun the land. Same here. You hunt 'cause you hungry and got to eat, that's one reason. Then you might hunt for the sport—pit your mind against animal cunning—'course I don't hold much with that, but

some do. Some do. But there's some varmints that do damage and just plain got to be killed. Understand?"

"I . . . think so. But what about what you said about a man dying when he kills something?"

"Man kills once and he starts to get callous. Next time it ain't so hard. Then you get so's you make a decision that something's got to die and you kill it, just like that. Then you. dead, boy. You got no feeling no more so you just as good as dead. You just ain't had time to lay down."

Tommy wiggled his toes and got no response. They felt like sticks of wood, stilts that somebody had glued on his legs. An ant left the ground and started climbing his arm until he blew, softly, blew the ant into some brave new world. The mist was thinning and the sun began to shine dully through the trees. Pa was right, he thought. Seems as if everything had a place in the scheme of things. Birds ate worms they found on the ground. Then they got eaten by bigger birds. Rabbits got eaten by foxes and foxes by bobcats, and bobcats by bears or something all the way up to elephants. And elephants were killed by man. Pa said that man preyed on himself, whatever that meant, but everything had a place, and when they got out of place they upset the balance. Like too many rabbits or squirrels or anything.

A twig snapped like dynamite

and he froze on the ground and swiveled the gun to the left and waited. Slowly, clumsily, with three blades of grass waving like pennants ahead of him, a porcupine strolled into view, made his way through the sunlight, and vanished into the grass. Tommy laughed, out loud almost, he could hardly keep from blowing up he was so relieved, so happy. Instead he settled down again to wait.

But things had changed somehow. The sunlight was duller, almost disappearing and he felt a chill again as he had before the sun came up. And the silence somehow nettled him . . . *the silence!* Not a sound! No crickets, no chirping, no rustling, nothing. There was something out there! The happy-scared feeling ran up and down Tommy's back and his breath came in painful gasps. His chest hammered, almost pushing his lungs into his mouth with its rhythm which seemed to be saying: *Soon! Soon! Soon they would be calling him Tom Grimes like his father. Soon he would be able to go into the Hut and drink liquor with the rest of the men. Soon the waiting would be over. Soon he would be grown. Soon. Soon. Soon. Soon! Soon! Soon!*

There! In the bushes! A little pinch of color behind the bramble bush moving light and easy, so very easy, behind the bushes. He slid down still further behind the gun and spread his feet wide, toes digging into the soft earth. Put the whole side of your body be-

hind the gun to take the recoil," Pa had said. "Spread your legs wide to brace yourself. Make the gun, your arm, your hip, your leg into one long line." Tommy drew his breath in and nearly gagged trying to hold it, sighting along the clean black ridges of the rifle. The outline was clear behind the bush, creeping, sniffling, gliding along.

"You won't see it, or hear it, or smell it, or anything," Pa had told him. "You'll just feel it, and it'll be there."

Tommy breathed out and in, let some of the air out and chokingly began to squeeze the trigger. Would it never go off, his mind asked, reeling and stumbling and clinging desperately to reality, and the earth stuttered. The light blinked. His ears rang. His nose reacted to the smell of smoke and the taste of ink crept into his mouth. There was a rustling sound in the bushes and a thrashing, a terrible thrashing and rattling, but it stopped. Suddenly it stopped. Tommy blinked. It was over; just like that, it was over.

He got to his feet and the stiffness forced him to lean against a tree trunk. Before there had been nothing, then suddenly there was something, a small patch of color the same as Pa's jacket. Tommy blinked and listened for the crashing sound of someone coming through the forest—but there was nothing. Nothing. He strained his ears and heard new-sprung crickets and birdcalls, but no crashing, no rustling, no voice, and he started for the bush and then stopped, trembling.

"Pa?" he whispered, "Pa-a-a?" There was no sound except his own voice, twisted and shapeless and mocking, twirling through the trees like vapors in the dull, chilly air. "Pa! Pa! Pa!"

Then came the rushing and the crashing to the left and the tall husky figure coming out of the gloom saying, "Boy? What's wrong, boy?" And Tommy ran over and slammed his head against his father's chest. "Pa! I thought I killed you, Pa, I thought I killed you, Pa. I thought I killed a man!"

"Now, Tommy, it's all right, everything's all right," Pa said, walking behind the bush and kneeling and then rising and coming back.

"See?" he said. "What did I tell you? Right through the heart. Now that's good shooting. Come on over here and look; come on, now."

So he looked, and then it wasn't so bad.

Later, much later, they walked the mile from town to the Hut and walked inside together. There were some men sitting at tables and they looked up as Pa hoisted him onto the bar, running his fingers through his dark, blond hair.

"Boys, I wanna tell you my boy became a man today. Yessir, killed his first nigger."

"No!" a man said. "Who?"

"Swamp-buck got away from the chain gang yes-tidy."

"Git out!" the man said.

"Yessir, got him right through the heart."

The man grabbed Tommy and hugged him around the knees. "You a man now, boy!" he yelled, "you a real live honest-to-goodness 'fore God man!"

And Pa, his blue eyes agleam, yelled out, "Bartender! Don't just stand there! Give this man a drink!"

The man sat Tommy down on the bar and the liquor made him cough a bit as it coursed down his throat and it made his ears ring like the tolling of bells. But he smiled happily as the feeling of warmth like Mississippi sunshine spread through his insides. For now he belonged.

Questions for Discussion

1. How DOES the author use flashback (the technique of going back in time) in the story?

2. WHAT IS the setting for the story, that is, where it takes place and when? Show how important the setting is for the plot development.

3. WHAT EVIDENCE do you find that the author is familiar with the outdoor background of the story?

4. SOME FATHER-SON relationships show a great lack of understanding between the two generations, like John Grimes and his father in "Go Tell It on the Mountain," by John Baldwin. What kind of feeling is there between Tommy and his father?

5. IT IS Pa's observation that a man dies a little when he kills any creature. How does this piece of psychology apply to Pa himself?

6. DESCRIBE Tommy's emotions after the shot when his eye caught a scrap of color that looked like his father's jacket.

7. TOMMY'S SHOT had brought down a man. Why did his father think this called for a celebration?

8. WHAT IS your opinion of Pa's behavior? What kind of people are these in the story who think it is a feather in one's cap to kill a Negro?

9. DID YOU like Tommy at the beginning of the story? Did your attitude toward him change by the end of the story? Explain your answer.

10. THE LAST words of the story are "For now he belonged." To what did Tommy belong?

11. ACCORDING to Pa's philosophy Tommy died a little every time he killed in the course of hunting. The author implies more than this in the title. How do you interpret the title of the story?

12. With what feeling are you left at the end of the story? Has the author succeeded in arousing your emotions?

13. WHAT IS the author's purpose in writing this story?

Building Vocabulary

Getting the meaning from the context. For each of the following sentences taken from the story, select from the choices given the word or phrase that means the same as the word in heavy type. Check your answer by looking up the word in a dictionary. Write the ones you get wrong in your special vocabulary list.

---

1. "They counted forty-three dead **pullets** (puhl'itz), lying in red and white patches of feathers, blood and confusion." (p. 45)

   A. weasels   B. geese   C. young hens   D. turkeys

2. "Pa taught him how . . . to lead **quail** (kwale) . . ." (p. 46)

   A. ducks   B. birds   C. children   D. colts

3. "Pa taught him how . . . to lean into the rifle and take up the **recoil** (ree-koyl')." (p. 46)

   A. sighting   B. barrel   C. ammunition   D. rebound

4. ". . . Some of the men were going into the forest to get a **buck** . . ." (p. 46)

   A. money   B. cowboy   C. deer   D. horse

5. "But there's some **varmints** (vahr'mintz) that do damage and just plain got to be killed." (p. 47)

   A. monkeys   B. mischief makers   C. rascals   D. harmful animals

6. "Man kills once and he starts to get **callous** (kal'is)." (p. 47)

   A. hardened   B. sentimental   C. fearful   D. valiant

7. "Pa said that man **preyed** (praid) on himself . . ." (p. 47)

   A. sacrificed   B. seized   C. fasted   D. depended

8. ". . . He froze on the ground and **swiveled** (swiv'ld) the gun to the left . . ." (p. 48)

   A. turned   B. aimed   C. lifted   D. knocked

9. ". . . With three blades of grass waving like **pennants** (pen'intz) ahead of him, a porcupine strolled into view . . ." (p. 48)

   A. leaves   B. feathers   C. flags   D. tufts

10. "And the silence somehow **nettled** (net'ld) him . . ." (p. 48)

    A. irritated   B. stimulated   C. soothed   D. awed

❦

Suspense

1. THE ART the writer uses in maintaining the interest of the reader to the end is known as *suspense*. The story opens with Tommy lying in wait in the forest. The author doesn't tell why he is there. Our curiosity is aroused; we press on to learn what he is after. He is waiting very quietly for something. What words does the author use to show us how immobile he is?

2. WHEN DO we find out what Tommy is waiting for in the forest?

3. How DO the boy's thoughts add to the suspense of the story?

4. WHAT DEVICE does the author use to break the tension of silent waiting?

5. How DOES Tommy sense that there is something in front of him? How does the author give emphasis to this moment of crisis?

6. WHAT EFFECT does the description of Tommy's emotions have on the story's suspense when the boy realizes that at last he is going to draw a bead on his game?

7. How DOES the author surprise us when we feel that Tommy has accidentally shot his own father?

8. AT WHAT point does the story reach its climax, that is, the turning point after which everything falls into place?

9. AS PART of the author's technique of withholding information we are kept in the dark about the identity of the young hunter and his Pa until nearly the end of the story. How does the author reveal the race of these two?

10. THE AUTHOR builds up a number of tense scenes charged with emotion. At what point in the story did you find the suspense greatest?

❦

Thinking and Writing

1. YOU ARE familiar with the expression "as the twig is bent, so the tree will grow." Pa was training little Tommy to grow up in his own image, a fearful thing to contemplate. Write a description of the kind of man Tommy will become as the result of his father's instruction.

2. TOMMY WASN'T sure what Pa meant when he said that "man preyed on himself." Write an explanation of this statement, giving examples. Also, show how Pa and others like him preyed on other people.

3. THE ENDING of the story is very bitter, revealing a picture of brutal and debased people. Write another ending for this story if you think the author was too harsh in his characterization of southern attitudes.

ℰℊℴ

About the Author

R. J. Meaddough III is one of the new, young, talented, black writers of the sixties. He was born in New York City in 1935. He joined the Marine Corps when he was nineteen and after three years of service was discharged with the rank of sergeant. Deciding to complete his education, he attended New York University and received a degree in 1960. Subsequently, he became connected in a supervisory capacity with the arts and culture division of HARYOU-ACT, of the Anti-Poverty Program. As a member of the Harlem Writers Guild, his writings are concerned directly with the racial problem in the North as well as in the South.

His short stories have appeared in *Freedomways* magazine and have been collected in a volume entitled, *A White Negro With a Button Down Mind.*

From

Go Tell It
on The Mountain

By James Baldwin

The following selection is taken from the novel by James Baldwin,
GO TELL IT ON THE MOUNTAIN. *The book is about the inter-
relationships of three generations of the Grimes family, with their loves
and hatreds set against a background of deep religious devotion. The
central figure is John Grimes, a troubled boy, who faces his fourteenth
birthday with a feeling of doom.*

*His family had always taken it for granted that John would become
a preacher like his father. The relationship between John and his father
was not an amicable one and the boy could not see himself being
humble before his father as a minister of the Lord. John's superior in-
tellect led him to believe he could make anything of himself that he
wished. He had a private world in which he cut a very handsome figure
and was a very important person.*

*So, John was faced with a dilemma. Should he make his mother
whom he loved, happy, with a vow to become a preacher, or should
he follow the longings of his heart and take a path away from the
church?*

EVERYONE had always said that John would be a preacher when he grew up, just like his father. It had been said so often that John, without ever thinking about it, had come to believe it himself. Not until the morning of his fourteenth birth- day did he really begin to think about it, and by then it was al- ready too late.

His earliest memories—which were in a way, his only memories —were of the hurry and bright- ness of Sunday mornings. They all rose together on that day; his father, who did not have to go to work, and led them in prayer be- fore breakfast; his mother, who dressed up on that day, and looked almost young, with her hair straightened, and on her head the close-fitting white cap that was the uniform of holy women; his young brother, Roy, who was silent that day because his father was home. Sarah, who wore a red ribbon in her hair that day, and was fondled by her father. And the baby, Ruth, who was dressed in pink and white, and rode in her mother's arms to church.

The church was not very far away, four blocks up Lenox Avenue, on a corner not far from the hospital. It was to this hospital that his mother had gone when Roy, and Sarah, and Ruth were born. John did not remember very clearly the first time she had gone, to have Roy; folks said that he had cried and carried on the whole time his mother was away; he remembered only enough to be afraid every time her belly began to swell, knowing that each time the swelling began it would not end until she was taken from him, to come back with a stranger. Each time this happened, she became a little more of a stranger herself. She would soon be going away again, Roy said—he knew much more about such things than John. John had observed his mother closely, seeing no swelling yet, but his father had prayed one morning for the "little voyager soon to be among them," and so John knew that Roy spoke the truth.

Their church was called the Temple of the Fire Baptized. It was not the biggest church in Harlem, nor yet the smallest, but

John had been brought up to believe it was the holiest and best. His father was head deacon in this church—there were only two, the other a round, black man named Deacon Braithwaite—and he took up the collection, and sometimes he preached. The pastor, Father James, was a genial, well-fed man with a face like a darker moon. It was he who preached on Pentecost Sundays, and led revivals in the summertime, and anointed and healed the sick.

On Sunday mornings and Sunday nights the church was always full; on special Sundays it was full all day. The Grimes family arrived in a body, always a little late, usually in the middle of Sunday school, which began at nine o'clock. This lateness was always their mother's fault—at least in the eyes of their father; she could not seem to get herself and the children ready on time, ever, and sometimes she actually remained behind, not to appear until the morning service. When they all arrived together, they separated upon entering the doors, father and mother going to sit in the Adult Class, which was taught by Sister McCandless, Sarah going to the Infant's Class, John and Roy sitting in the Intermediate, which was taught by Brother Elisha.

When he was young, John had paid no attention in Sunday school, and always forgot the golden text, which earned him the wrath of his father. Around the time of his fourteenth birthday, with all the pressures of church and home uniting to drive him to the altar, he strove to appear more serious and therefore less conspicuous. But he was distracted by his new teacher, Elisha, who was the pastor's nephew and who had but lately arrived from Georgia. He was not much older than John, only seventeen, and he was already saved and was a preacher. John stared at Elisha all during the lesson, admiring the timbre of Elisha's voice, much deeper and manlier than his own, admiring the leanness, and grace, and strength, and darkness of Elisha in his Sunday suit, wondering if he would ever be holy as Elisha was holy. But he did not follow the lesson, and when, sometimes, Elisha paused to ask John a question, John was ashamed and confused, feeling the palms of his hands become wet and his heart pound like a hammer. Elisha would smile and reprimand him gently, and the lesson would go on.

Roy never knew his Sunday leslon either, but it was different with Roy—no one really expected of Roy what was expected of John. Everyone was always praying that the Lord would change Roy's heart, but it was John who was expected to be good, to be a good example.

John's birthday fell on a Saturday in March, in 1935. He awoke on his birthday morning with the feeling that there was menace in the air around him—that something irrevocable had occurred in him. He stared at a yellow stain on the ceiling just above his head. Roy was still smothered in the bedclothes, and his breath came and went with a small, whistling sound. There was no other sound anywhere; no one in the house was up. The neighbors' radios were all silent, and his mother hadn't yet risen to fix his father's breakfast. John wondered at his panic, then wondered about the time; and then (while the yellow stain on the ceiling slowly transformed itself into a woman's nakedness) he remembered that it was his fourteenth birthday and that he had sinned.

His first thought, nevertheless, was: "Will anyone remember?" For it had happened, once or twice, that his birthday had passed entirely unnoticed, and no one had said "Happy Birthday, Johnny," or given him anything—not even his mother.

Roy stirred again and John pushed him away, listening to the silence. On other mornings he awoke hearing his mother singing in the kitchen, hearing his father in the bedroom behind him grunting and muttering prayers to himself as he put on his clothes; hearing, perhaps the chatter of Sarah and the squalling of Ruth, and the radios, the clatter of pots and pans, and the voices of all the folk near-by. This morning not even the cry of a bed-spring disturbed the silence, and John seemed, therefore, to be listening to his own unspeaking doom. He could believe, almost, that he had awakened late on that great getting-up morning; that all the saved had been transformed in the twinkling of an eye, and had risen to meet Jesus in the clouds, and that he was left with his sinful body, to be bound in hell a thousand years.

. . . The darkness of his sin was in the hardheartedness with which he resisted God's power; in the scorn that was often his while he listened to the crying, breaking voices, and watched the black skin glisten while they lifted up their arms and fell on their faces before the Lord. For he had made his decision. He would not be like his father, or his father's fathers. He would have another life.

For John excelled in school, though not, like Elisha, in mathematics or basketball, and it was said that he had a Great Future. He might become a Great Leader of His People. John was not much interested in his people and still less in leading them anywhere, but the phrase so often repeated rose in his mind like a great brass gate, opening outward for him on a world where people did not live in the darkness of his father's house, did not pray to Jesus in the darkness of his father's church, where he would eat good food, and wear fine clothes, and go to the movies as often as he wished. In this world John, who was, his father said, ugly, who was always

the smallest boy in his class, and who had no friends, became immediately beautiful, tall, and popular. People fell all over themselves to meet John Grimes. He was a poet, or a college president, or a movie star; he drank expensive whisky, and he smoked Lucky Strike cigarettes in the green package.

It was not only colored people who praised John, since they could not, John felt, in any case really know; but white people also said it, in fact had said it first and said it still. It was when John was five years old and in the first grade that he was first noticed; and since he was noticed by an eye altogether alien and impersonal, he began to perceive, in wild uneasiness, his individual existence.

They were learning the alphabet that day, and six children at a time were sent to the blackboard to write the letters they had memorized. Six had finished and were waiting for the teacher's judgment when the back door opened and the school principal, of whom everyone was terrified, entered the room. No one spoke or moved. In the silence the principal's voice said:

"Which child is that?"

She was pointing at the blackboard, at John's letters. The possibility of being distinguished by her notice did not enter John's mind, and so he simply stared at her. Then he realized, by the immobility of the other children and by the way they avoided looking at him, that it was he who was selected for punishment.

"Speak up, John," said the teacher, gently.

On the edge of tears, he mumbled his name and waited. The principal, a woman with white hair and an iron face, looked down at him.

"You're a very bright boy, John Grimes," she said. "Keep up the good work."

Then she walked out of the room.

That moment gave him, from that time on, if not a weapon at least a shield; he apprehended totally, without belief or understanding, that he had in himself a power that other people lacked; that he could use this to save himself, to raise himself; and that, perhaps, with this power he might one day win that love which he so longed for. This was not, in John, a faith subject to death or alteration, nor yet a hope subject to destruction; it was his identity, and part, therefore, of that wickedness for which his father beat him and to which he clung in order to withstand his father. His father's arm, rising and falling, might make him cry, and that voice might cause him to tremble; yet his father could never be entirely the victor, for John cherished something that his father could not reach. It was his hatred and his intelligence that he cherished, the one feeding the other. He lived for the day when his father would be dying and he,

John, would curse him on his deathbed. And this was why, though he had been born in the faith and had been surrounded all his life by the saints and by their prayers and their rejoicing, and though the tabernacle in which they worshipped was more completely real to him than the several precarious homes in which he and his family had lived, John's heart was hardened against the Lord. His father was God's minister, the ambassador of the King of Heaven, and John could not bow before the throne of grace without first kneeling to his father. On his refusal to do this had his life depended, and John's secret heart had flourished in its wickedness until the day his sin first overtook him.

In the midst of all his wonderings he fell asleep again, and when he woke up this time and got out of his bed his father had gone to the factory, where he would work for half a day. Roy was sitting in the kitchen, quarreling with their mother. The baby, Ruth, sat in her high chair banging on the tray with an oatmeal-covered spoon. This meant that she was in a good mood; she would not spend the day howling, for reasons known only to herself, allowing no one but her mother to touch her. Sarah was quiet, not chattering today, or at any rate not yet, and stood near the stove, arms folded, staring at Roy with the flat black eyes, her father's eyes, that made her look so old.

Their mother, her head tied up in an old rag, sipped black coffee and watched Roy. The pale end-of-winter sunlight filled the room and yellowed all their faces; and John, drugged and morbid and wondering how it was that he had slept again and had been allowed to sleep so long, saw them for a moment like figures on a screen, an effect that the yellow light intensified. The room was narrow and dirty; nothing could alter its dimensions, no labor could ever make it clean. Dirt was in the walls and the floorboards, and triumphed beneath the sink where roaches spawned; was in the fine ridges of the pots and pans, scoured daily, burnt black on the bottom, hanging above the stove; was in the wall against which they hung, and revealed itself where the paint had cracked and leaned outward in stiff squares and fragments, the paper-thin underside webbed with black. Dirt was in every corner, angle, crevice of the monstrous stove, and lived behind it in delirious communion with the corrupted wall. Dirt was in the baseboard that John scrubbed every Saturday, and roughened the cupboard shelves that held the cracked and gleaming dishes. Under this dark weight the walls leaned, under it the ceiling, with a great crack like lightning in its center, sagged. The windows gleamed like beaten gold or silver, but now John saw, in the yellow light, how fine dust veiled their doubtful glory. Dirt crawled in the gray mop hung out of the windows to dry. John thought with shame and horror, yet in angry hardness of heart: *He who is filthy, let him be filthy still.* Then he looked at his mother, seeing, as though she were someone else, the dark, hard lines running downward from her eyes, and the deep, perpetual scowl in her forehead, and the downturned, tightened mouth, and the strong, thin, brown, and bony hands; and the phrase turned against him like a two-edged sword, for was it not he, in his false pride and his evil imagination, who was filthy? Through a storm of tears that did not reach his eyes, he stared at the yellow room; and the room shifted, the light of the sun darkened, and his mother's face changed. Her face became the face that he gave her in his dreams, the face that had been hers in a photograph he had seen once, long ago, a photograph taken before he was born. This face was young and proud, uplifted, with a smile that made the wide mouth beautiful and glowed in the enormous eyes. It was the face of a girl who knew that no evil could undo her, and who could laugh, surely, as his mother did not laugh now. Between the two faces there stretched a darkness and a mystery that John feared, and that sometimes caused him to hate her.

Now she saw him and she asked, breaking off her conversation with Roy: "You hungry, little sleepyhead?"

"Well! About time you was getting up," said Sarah.

He moved to the table and sat down, feeling the most bewildering panic of his life, a need to touch things, the table and chairs and the walls of the room, to make certain that the room existed and that he was in the room. He did not look at his mother, who stood up and went to the stove to heat his breakfast. But he asked, in order to say something to her, and to hear his own voice:

"What we got for breakfast?"

He realized with some shame, that he was hoping she had prepared a special breakfast for him on his birthday.

"What you *think* we got for breakfast?" Roy asked scornfully. "You got a special craving for something?"

John looked at him. Roy was not in a good mood.

"I ain't said nothing to you," he said.

"Oh, I *beg* your pardon," said Roy, in the shrill, little-girl tone he knew John hated.

"What's the *matter* with you today?" John asked, angry, and trying at the same time to lend his voice as husky a pitch as possible.

"Don't you let Roy bother you," said their mother. "He cross as two sticks this morning."

"Yeah," said John, "I reckon." He and Roy watched each other. Then his plate was put before

him: hominy grits and a scrap of bacon. He wanted to cry, like a child: "But, Mama, it's my birthday!" He kept his eyes on his plate and began to eat.

"You can *talk* about your Daddy all you want to," said his mother, picking up her battle with Roy, "but *one* thing you can't say—you can't say he ain't always done his best to be a father to you and to see to it that you ain't never gone hungry."

"I been hungry plenty of times," Roy said, proud to be able to score this point against his mother.

"Wasn't *his* fault, then. Wasn't because he wasn't *trying* to feed you. That man shoveled snow in zero weather when he ought've been in bed just to put food in your belly."

"Wasn't just *my* belly," said Roy indignantly. "He got a belly, too, I *know* it's a *shame* the way that man eats. I sure ain't asked him to shovel no snow for me." But he dropped his eyes, suspecting a flaw in his argument. "I just don't want him beating on me all the time," he said at last. "I ain't no dog."

She sighed, and turned slightly away, looking out of the window. "Your Daddy beats you," she said, "because he loves you."

Roy laughed. "That ain't the kind of love I understand, old lady. What you reckon he'd do if he didn't love me?"

"He'd let you go right on," she flashed, "right on down to hell where it looks like you is just determined to go anyhow! Right on, Mister Man, till somebody puts a knife in you, or takes you off to jail!"

"Mama," John asked suddenly, "is Daddy a good man?"

He had not known that he was going to ask the question, and he watched in astonishment as her mouth tightened and her eyes grew dark.

"That ain't no kind of question," she said mildly. "You don't know no better men, do you?"

"Looks to me like he's a mighty good man," said Sarah. "He sure is praying all the time."

"You children is young," their mother said, ignoring Sarah and sitting down again at the table, "and you don't know how lucky you is to have a father what worries about you and tries to see to it that you come up right."

"Yeah," said Roy, "we don't know how lucky we *is* to have a father what don't want you to go to movies, and don't want you to play in the streets, and don't want you to have no friends, and he don't want this and he don't want that, and he don't want you to do *nothing*. We so *lucky* to have a father who just wants us to go to church and read the Bible and beller like a fool in front of the altar and stay home all nice and quiet, like a little mouse. Boy, we sure is lucky, all right. Don't know what I done to be so lucky."

She laughed. "You going to find out one day," she said, "you mark my words."

"Yeah," said Roy.

"But it'll be too late, then," she said. "It'll be too late when you come to be . . . sorry." Her voice had changed. For a moment her eyes met John's eyes, and John was frightened. He felt that her words, after the strange fashion God sometimes chose to speak to men, were dictated by Heaven and were meant for him. He was fourteen—was it too late? And this uneasiness was reinforced by the impression, which at that moment he realized had been his all along, that his mother was not saying everything she meant. What, he wondered, did she say to Aunt Florence when they talked together? Or to his father? What were her thoughts? Her face would never tell. And yet, looking down at him in a moment that was like a secret, passing sign, her face did tell him. Her thoughts were bitter.

"I don't care," Roy said, rising. "When *I* have children I ain't going to treat them like this." John watched his mother; she watched Roy. "I'm *sure* this ain't no way to be. Ain't got no right to have a houseful of children if you don't know how to treat them."

"You mighty grown up this morning," his mother said. "You be careful."

"And tell me something else," Roy said, suddenly leaning over his mother, "tell me how come he don't never let me talk to him like I talk to you? He's my father, ain't he? But he don't never listen to me—no, I all the time got to listen to him."

"Your father," she said, watching him, "knows best. You listen to your father, I guarantee you you won't end up in no jail."

Roy sucked his teeth in fury. "I ain't looking to go to no *jail*. You think that's all that's in the world is jails and churches? You ought to know better than that, Ma."

"I know," she said, "there ain't no safety except you walk humble before the Lord. You going to find it out, too, one day. You go on, hardhead. You going to come to grief."

And suddenly Roy grinned. "But you be there, won't you. Ma—when I'm in trouble?"

"You don't know," she said, trying not to smile, "how long the Lord's going to let me stay with you."

Roy turned and did a dance step. "That's all right," he said. "I know the Lord ain't as hard as Daddy. Is he, boy?" he demanded of John, and struck him lightly on the forehead.

"Boy, let me eat my breakfast," John muttered—though his plate had long been empty, and he was pleased that Roy had turned to him.

"That sure is a crazy boy," ventured Sarah, soberly.

"Just listen," cried Roy, "to the little saint! Daddy ain't never going to have no trouble with her —*that* one, she was born holy. I bet the first words she ever said was: 'Thank you, Jesus.' Ain't that so, Ma?"

"You stop this foolishness," she said, laughing, "and go on about your work. Can't nobody play the fool with you all morning."

"Oh, is you got work for me to do this morning? Well, I declare," said Roy, "what you got for me to do?"

"I got the woodwork in the dining-room for you to do. And you going to do it, too, before you set foot out of *this* house."

"Now, why you want to talk like that, Ma? Is I said I wouldn't do it? You know I'm a right good worker when I got a mind. After I do it, can I go?"

"You go ahead and do it, and we'll see. You better do it right."

"I *always* do it right," said Roy. "You won't know your old woodwork when *I* get through."

"John," said his mother, "you sweep the front room for me like a good boy, and dust the furniture. I'm going to clean up in here."

"Yes'm," he said, and rose. She *had* forgotten about his birthday. He swore he would not mention it. He would not think about it anymore.

When he had finished and the room was ready for Sunday, John felt dusty and weary and sat down beside the window in his father's easy chair. A glacial sun filled the streets, and a high wind filled the air with scraps of paper and frosty dust, and banged the hanging signs of stores and storefront churches. It was the end of winter, and the garbage-filled snow that had been banked along the edges of sidewalks was melting now and filling the gutters. Boys were playing stickball in the damp, cold streets; dressed in heavy woolen sweaters and heavy pants, they danced and shouted, and the ball went *crack!* as the stick struck it and sent it speeding through the air. One of them wore a bright-red stocking cap with a great ball of wool hanging down behind that bounced as he jumped, like a bright omen above his head. The cold sun made their faces like copper and brass, and through the closed window John heard their coarse, irreverent voices. And he wanted to be one of them, playing in the street, unfrightened, moving with such grace and power, but he knew this could not be. Yet, if he could not play their games, he could do something they could not do; he was able, as one of his teachers said, to think. But this brought him little in the way of consolation, for today he was terrified of his thoughts. He wanted to be with these boys in the street, heedless and thoughtless, wearing out his treacherous and bewildering body.

But now it was eleven o'clock, and in two hours his father would be home. And then they might eat, and then his father would lead them in prayer, and then he would give them a Bible lesson. By and by it would be evening and he would go to clean the church, and remain for tarry service. Suddenly, sitting at the window, and with a violence unprecedented, there arose in John a flood of fury and tears, and he bowed his head, fists clenched against the windowpane, crying, with teeth on edge: "What shall I do? What shall I do?"

Then his mother called him; and he remembered that she was in the kitchen washing clothes and probably had something for him to do. He rose sullenly and walked into the kitchen. She stood over the washtub, her arms wet and soapy to the elbows and sweat standing on her brow. Her apron, improvised from an old sheet, was wet where she had been leaning over the scrubbing-board. As he came in, she straightened, drying her hands on the edge of the apron.

"You finish your work, John?" she asked.

He said: "Yes'm," and thought how oddly she looked at him; as though she were looking at someone else's child.

"That's a good boy," she said. She smiled a shy, strained smile. "You know you your mother's right-hand man?"

He said nothing, and he did not smile, but watched her, wondering to what task this preamble led.

She turned away, passing one damp hand across her forehead, and went to the cupboard. Her back was to him, and he watched her while she took down a bright, figured vase, filled with flowers only on the most special occasions, and emptied the contents into her palm. He heard the chink of money, which meant that she was going to send him to the store. She put the vase back and turned to face him, her palm loosely folded before her.

"I didn't never ask you," she said, "what you wanted for your birthday. But you take this, son, and go out and get yourself something you think you want."

And she opened his palm and put the money into it, warm and wet from her hand. In the moment that he felt the warm, smooth coins and her hand on his, John stared blindly at her face, so far above him. His heart broke and he wanted to put his head on her belly where the wet spot was, and cry. But he dropped his eyes and looked at his palm, at the small pile of coins.

"It ain't much there," she said.

"That's all right." Then he looked up, and she bent down and kissed him on the forehead.

"You getting to be," she said, putting her hand beneath his chin and holding his face away from her, "a right big boy. You going to be a mighty fine man, you know that? Your mamma's counting on you."

And he knew again that she was not saying everything she meant; in a kind of secret language she was telling him today something

that he must remember and understand tomorrow. He watched her face, his heart swollen with love for her and with an anguish, not yet his own, that he did not understand and that frightened him.

"Yes, Ma," he said, hoping that she would realize, despite his stammering tongue, the depth of his passion to please her.

"I know," she said, with a smile, releasing him and rising, "there's a whole lot of things you don't understand. But don't you fret. The Lord'll reveal to you in His own good time everything He wants you to know. You put your faith in the Lord, Johnny, and He'll surely bring you out. Everything works together for good for them that love the Lord."

He had heard her say this before—it was her text, as *Set thine house in order* was his father's—but he knew that today she was saying it to him especially; she was trying to help him because she knew he was in trouble. And this trouble was also her own, which she would never tell to John. And even though he was certain that they could not be speaking of the same things— for then, surely, she would be angry and no longer proud of him —this perception on her part, and this avowal of her love for him lent to John's bewilderment a reality that terrified and a dignity that consoled him. Dimly, he felt that he ought to console her, and he listened, astounded, at the words that now fell from his lips:

"Yes, Mama. I'm going to try to love the Lord."

At this there sprang into his mother's face something startling, beautiful, unspeakably sad—as though she were looking far beyond him at a long, dark road, and seeing on that road a traveler in perpetual danger. Was it he, the traveler? or herself? or was she thinking of the cross of Jesus? She turned back to the washtub, still with this strange sadness on her face.

"You better go on now," she said, "before your daddy gets home."

Questions for Discussion

1. How IS this story largely a study of attitudes? What is the attitude of each character toward each other?

2. WHAT QUALITIES distinguish John from the other members of his family?

3. WHAT SORT of power did his self-recognition of intellectual superiority give John?

4. WHAT FANTASIES did John have after deciding he would not be a preacher like his father, but have a completely different kind of life?

5. WHAT WAS John's greatest emotional problem at this stage of his life?

6. VERY OFTEN children in the same family may be quite different from each other. How is that true in the case of the Grimes children?

7. How DOES Roy feel about his father? Explain how this is an example of the generation gap. Who was responsible for the gap, Roy or his father?

8. THE SETTING of a story often plays a role in the kind of action that may take place. Show how the Grimes' dirt-encrusted apartment governed some of the events in the story.

9. How DO the boys participate in the work of the household? Are household chores unmanly? Do you think that boys should be excused from household chores? Why?

10. John felt sure that everybody had forgotten his birthday. Somehow, mothers remember these occasions. In what way did John's mother observe his birthday?

11. AN AUTHOR calls upon the reader to draw conclusions from hints he gives. When John's mother told him she was counting on him, he felt there was a hidden meaning in her words. What would you infer from that statement of faith, knowing the problem that John was facing?

Building Vocabulary

€ach of the following words occurs in the story on the page in paren-
thesis. Pick out the correct meaning from the group below. If you
are in doubt about a word, go back to the page on which it is found
and try to guess the meaning from the context, that is, from the way it
is used in the sentence. Look in the dictionary for the meaning of those
words you don't know; add them to your private vocabulary list.

1. **anointed** (p. 56)
   (uh-noint'id)
   A. found difficult   B. called
   the doctor   C. rubbed with
   oil   D. came on time

2. **irrevocable** (p. 57)
   (ih-rev'uh-kuh-bl)
   A. unalterable   B. foolish
   C. amiable   D. friendly

3. **squalling** (p. 57)
   (skwawl'ing)
   A. blowing   B. singing
   C. waving   D. crying

4. **immobility** (p. 58)
   (im-uh-bil'ih-tee)
   A. barrier   B. motionless-
   ness   C. speeding   D. crowd

5. **apprehended** (p. 59)
   (ap-ree-hend'id)
   A. deprived   B. menaced
   C. understood   D. praised

6. **tabernacle** (p. 59)
   (tab'uh-nakl)
   A. awe   B. place of worship
   D. roof   D. box

7. **precarious** (p. 59)
   (prih-kair'ih-yus)
   A. uncertain   B. high
   C. cheap   D. expensive

8. **morbid** (p. 60)
   (maw'bid)
   A. unhealthy   B. petty
   C. old   D. frightened

9. **reinforced** (p. 62)
   (ree-in-fawst')
   A. weakened   B. adjusted
   C. injured   D. strengthened

10. **improvised** (p. 64)
    (im-pruh-vizd')
    A. destroyed   B. made do
    C. broken   D. acted strangely

Use of Dialogue

AN AUTHOR uses dialogue (that is, conversation between characters) to lend variety to his narration and to reveal things indirec-
tly about his people. In effect, dialogue provides a change of pace.
Notice the balance that Baldwin employs between direct telling

(narration) and dialogue in this selection from *Go Tell It on the Mountain*. By so doing he keeps up the reader's interest and moves the story.

In dialogue a great deal is revealed about character. By what they say people reveal their personality, whether they are weak or strong, whether they are to be admired or despised, whether they are to be pitied or condemned. As they disclose what they are thinking, the characters in a story reveal their background, their educational and social level. Consider the conversation of the Grimes family around the breakfast table and see what it tells us about the writer's art and about the various members of the family.

1. THE DIALOGUE on pages 61-63, largely between rebellious Roy and his patient mother, might be compressed in narrative form to a few lines like these:

When John went into the kitchen for breakfast his brother, Roy, was complaining about his father's strictness. His mother countered Roy's arguments by saying that father knew best and all he was trying to do was to keep his children out of jail.

Compare this statement with the dialogue in the story. Which is the more interesting way to learn about Roy's feelings regarding his father?

2. Is THE DIALOGUE in this selection realistic? How?

3. Do THE CHARACTERS speak in different ways? Show how the speech of each is distinctive or similar.

4. WHAT DOES the dialogue tell you about the educational and social background of the characters in the story?

5. WHAT IS the level of English usage in the dialogue called?

6. How DOES the dialogue show the conflicts among the members of the family?

7. WHAT TRAITS of character does Roy reveal in his vehement criticism of his father's actions?

8. IN THIS DIALOGUE do you feel that John's mother has put up a good defense against the charges that Roy has brought? What does the conversation indicate about the personality of Mrs. Grimes?

9. DIALOGUE is an indirect way of finding out about people's thoughts and characters. The attitude of Roy toward his father is implied from what he says; the author does not tell us directly

in so many words. Which method requires more active reader participation in a story? Which method do you prefer?

10. WHAT PERSONALITY differences among the members of the Grimes family are brought out in this conversation?

11. RE-WRITE the dialogue on page 62 in Standard English.

⟡

Thinking and Writing

1. IF YOU were John and given some money for your birthday by your mother, how would you spend the money to bring the greatest enjoyment? Write a composition describing the possible ways you might spend the money and the one thing you would *finally* spend it on.

2. THE ROOMS in which John's family live were pictured as being begrimed and impossible to clean no matter how hard they tried. Write a description of the apartment in which you live.

3. WRITE an account of a typical breakfast scene in your house, possibly including the preparations for breakfast, where the members of the family sit, the room where the meal is eaten, or the conversation around the table.

4. THE GRIMES FAMILY spent almost all day on Sunday praying in church. Write an account of how you spend Sundays.

⟡

About the Author

James Baldwin was born in Harlem in 1924, one of nine children. His father, a preacher, was a bitter, proud, and harsh man who directed his son toward a career in the Holy Roller Church. As a boy preacher, from the ages of fourteen to seventeen, James Baldwin fired his congregation with the word of the Lord. After graduation from DeWitt Clinton High School, in New York, he moved to Greenwich Village to write, while earning his living with such jobs as factory worker, dishwasher and waiter. With a writing fellowship, he went to Paris to develop his literary talent and produced *Go Tell It on the Mountain* in 1953 and *Notes of a Native Son*, an analysis of Negro-white relationships in 1955. He produced *Giovanni's Room*, a novel with a European background, in 1956. As an intellectual leader of the Negro protest movement, Baldwin has written many essays about racial discrimination, including such collections as *Nobody Knows My Name*, in 1961 and *The Fire Next Time*, in 1963.

The
Homecoming

The Homecoming

By Frank Yerby

Sergeant Willie Jackson was returning to his hometown. He had fought with valor in the Pacific and suffered a serious war injury. There was no cheering crowd and no brass band waiting to greet the hero as he got off the train. There were only the heat and the dust of a small southern town.

Willie came back a different person from the youth who had gone off to the war. He had done a lot of thinking while in the army and was unwilling to go back to being any one's "boy". His personal declaration of independence got him into trouble with the townspeople. The situation became grimly threatening for Willie Jackson.

The train stretched itself out long and low against the tracks and ran very fast and smooth. The drive rods flashed out of the big pistons like blades of light, and the huge counter-weighted wheels were blurred solid with the speed. Out of the throat of the stack, the white smoke blasted up in stiff, hard pants, straight up for a yard; then the backward rushing mass of air caught it, trailing it out over the cars like a veil.

In the Jim Crow coach, just back of the mail car, Sergeant Willie Jackson pushed the window up a notch higher. The heat came blasting in the window in solid waves, bringing the dust with it, and the cinders. Willie mopped his face with his handkerchief. It came away stained with the dust and sweat.

"Damn," he said without heat, and looked out at the parched

72

fields that were spinning backward past his window. Up on the edge of the skyline, a man stopped his plowing to wave at the passing train.

"How come we always do that?" Willie speculated idly. "Don't know a soul on this train —not a soul—but he got to wave. Oh, well . . ."

The train was bending itself around a curve, and the soft, long, lost, lonesome wail of the whistle cried out twice. Willie stirred in his seat, watching the cabins with the whitewash peeling off spinning backward past the train, lost in the immensity of sun-blasted fields under a pale, yellowish white sky, the blue washed out by the sun swath, and no cloud showing.

Up ahead, the water tower was rushing toward the train. Willie grinned. He had played under that tower as a boy. Water was always leaking out of it, enough water to cool a hard, skinny, little black body even in the heat of summer. The creek was off somewhere to the south, green and clear under the willows, making a little laughing sound over the rocks. He could see the trees that hid it now, the lone clump standing up abruptly in the brown and naked expanse of the fields.

Now the houses began to thicken, separated by only a few hundred yards instead of by miles. The train slowed, snorting tiredly into another curve. Across the diagonal of the bend, Willie could see the town, all of it—a few dozen buildings clustered around the Confederate Monument, bisected by a single paved street. The heat was pushing down on it like a gigantic hand, flattening it against the rust-brown earth.

Now the train was grinding to a stop. Willie swung down from the car, carefully keeping his left leg off the ground, taking the weight on his right. Nobody else got off the train.

The heat struck him in the face like a physical blow. The sunlight brought great drops of sweat out on his forehead, making his black face glisten. He stood there in the full glare, the light pointing up the little strips of colored ribbon on his tunic. One of them was purple, with two white ends. Then there was a yellow one with thin red, white, and blue stripes in the middle and red and white stripes near the two ends. Another was red with three white stripes near the ends. Willie wore his collar loose, and his uniform was faded, but he still stood erect, with his chest out and his belly sucked in.

He started across the street toward the Monument, throwing one leg a little stiffly. The white men who always sat around it on the little iron benches looked at him curiously. He came on until he stood in the shadow of the shaft. He looked up at the statue of the Confederate soldier, complete with knapsack and holding

73

the musket with the little needle-type bayonet ready for the charge. At the foot of the shaft there was an inscription carved in stone. Willie spelled out the words:

"No nation rose so white and pure; none fell so free of stain."

He stood there, letting the words sink into his brain.

One of the tall loungers took a sliver of wood out of his mouth and grinned. He nudged his companion.

"What do it say, boy?" he asked.

Willie looked past him at the dusty, unpaved streets straggling out from the Monument.

"I ask you a question, boy." The white man's voice was very quiet.

"You talking to me?" Willie said softly.

"You know Goddamn well I'm talking to you. You got ears, ain't you?"

"You said boy," Willie said. "I didn't know you was talking to me."

"Who the hell else could I been talking to, nigger?" the white man demanded.

"I don't know," Willie said. "I didn't see no boys around."

The two white men got up.

"Ain't you forgetting something, nigger?" one of them asked, walking toward Willie.

"Not that I knows of," Willie declared.

"Ain't nobody ever told you to say sir to a white man?"

"Yes," Willie said. "They told me that."

"Yes what?" the white man prompted.

"Yes nothing," Willie said quietly. "Jus plain yes. And I don't think you better come any closer, white man."

"Nigger, do you know where you're at?"

"Yes," Willie said. "Yes, I knows. And I knows you can have me killed. But I don't care about that. Long time now I don't care. So please don't come no closer white man. I'm asking you kindly."

The two men hesitated. Willie started toward them, walking very slowly. They stood very still, watching him come. Then at the last moment, they stood aside and let him pass. He limped across the street and went into the town's lone Five and Ten Cent Store.

"How come I come in here?" he muttered. "Ain't got nobody to buy nothing for." He stood still a moment, frowning. "Reckon I'll get some post cards to send the boys," he decided. He walked over to the rack and made his selections carefully: the new Post Office Building, the Memorial Bridge, the Confederate Monument. "Make this look like a real town," he said. "Keep that one hoss outa sight." Then he was limping over to the counter, the cards and the quarter in his hand. The salesgirl started toward him, her hand outstretched to take the money. But just before she reached him, a white woman came toward the counter, so the girl went on past Willie, smiling sweetly, saying, "Can I help you?"

"Look a here, girl," Willie said sharply. "I was here first."

The salesgirl and the woman both turned toward him, their mouths dropping open.

"My money the same color as hers," Willie said. He stuffed the cards in his pocket. Then deliberately he tossed the quarter on the counter and walked out the door.

"Well, I never!" the white woman gasped.

When Willie came out on the sidewalk, a little knot of men had gathered around the Monument. Willie could see the two men in the center talking to the others. Then they all stopped talking at once and looked at him. He limped on down the block and turned the corner.

At the next corner he turned again, and again at the next. Then he slowed. Nobody was following him.

The houses thinned out again. There were no trees shading the dirt road, powder-dry under the hammer blows of the sun. Willie limped on, the sweat pouring down his black face, soaking his collar. Then at last he was turning into a flagstone driveway curving toward a large, very old house, set well back from the road in a clump of pine trees. He went up on the broad, sweeping veranda, and rang the bell.

A very old black man opened the door. He looked at Willie with a puzzled expression, squinting his red, mottled old eyes against the light.

"Don't you remember me, Uncle Ben?" Willie said.

"Willie!" the old man said. "The Colonel sure be glad to see you! I go call him—right now!" Then he was off, trotting down the hall. Willie stood still, waiting.

The Colonel came out of the study, his hand outstretched.

"Willie," he said. "You little black scoundrel! Damn! You aren't little any more, are you?"

"No," Willie said. "I done growed."

"So I see! So I see! Come on back in the kitchen, boy. I want to talk to you."

Willie followed the lean, bent figure of the old white man through the house. In the kitchen, Martha, the cook, gave a squeal of pleasure.

"Willie! My, my, how fine you's looking! Sit down! Where you find him, Colonel Bob?"

"I just dropped by," Willie said.

"Fix him something to eat, Martha," the Colonel said, "while I pry some military information out of him."

Martha scurried off, her white teeth gleaming in a pleased smile.

"You've got a mighty heap of ribbons, Willie," the Colonel said. "What are they for?"

"This here purple one is the Purple Heart," Willie explained. "That was for my leg."

"Bad?" the Colonel demanded.

"Hand grenade. They had to

take it off. This here leg's a fake."

"Well, I'll be damned! I never would have known it."

"They make them good now. And they teaches you before you leaves the hospital."

"What are the others for?"

"The yellow one means Pacific Theater of War," Willie said. "And the red one is the Good Conduct Medal."

"I knew you'd get that one," the Colonel declared. "You always were a good boy, Willie."

"Thank you," Willie said.

Martha was back now with coffee and cake. "Dinner be ready in a little," she said.

"You're out for good, aren't you, Willie?"

"Yes."

"Good. I'll give you your old job back. I need an extra man on the place."

"Begging your pardon, Colonel Bob," Willie said, "I ain't staying here. I'm going North."

"What! What the clinking ding dang ever gave you such an idea?"

"I can't stay here, Colonel Bob. I ain't suited for here no more."

"The North is no place for niggers, Willie. Why, those dang-blasted Yankees would let you starve to death. Down here a good boy like you always got a white man to look after him. Any time you get hungry you can always come up to most anybody's back door and they'll feed you."

"Yes," Willie said. "They feed me all right. They say that's Colonel Bob's boy, Willie, and they give me a swell meal. That's how come I got to go."

"Now you're talking riddles, Willie."

"No, Colonel Bob, I ain't talking riddles. I seen men killed. My friends. I done growed inside, too, Colonel Bob."

"What's that got to do with your staying here?"

Martha came over to the table, bearing the steaming food on the tray. She stood there holding the tray, looking at Willie. He looked past her out the doorway where the big pines were shredding the sunlight.

"I done forgot too many things," he said slowly. "I done forgot how to scratch my head and shuffle my feet and grin when I don't feel like grinning."

"Willie!" Martha said. "Don't talk like that! Don't you know you can't talk like that?"

Colonel Bob silenced her with a lifted hand.

"Somebody's been talking to you," he declared, "teaching you the wrong things."

"No. Just had a lot of time for thinking. Thought it up all by myself. I done fought and been most killed and now I'm a man. Can't be a boy no more. Nobody's boy. Not even yours, Colonel Bob."

"Willie!" Martha moaned.

"Got to be a man. My own man. Can't let my kids cut a buck and wing on the sidewalk for pennies. Can't ask for handouts round the back door. Got to come in the front door. Got to git it myself. Can't git it, then I starves proud, Colonel Bob."

Martha's mouth was working, forming the words, but no sound came out of it, no sound at all.

"Do you think it's right," Colonel Bob asked evenly, "for you to talk to a white man like this—any white man—even me?"

"I don't know. All I know is I got to go. I can't even say yessir no more. Ever time I do, it choke up in my throat like black vomit. Ain't coming to no more back doors. And when I gits old, folks going to say Mister Jackson—not no Uncle Willie."

"You're right, Willie," Colonel Bob said, "You better go. In fact, you'd better go right now."

Willie stood up and adjusted his overseas cap.

"Thank you, Colonel Bob," he said. "You been awful good to me. I reckon I be going."

Colonel Bob did not answer. Instead he got up and held the screen door open. Willie went past him out the door. On the steps he stopped.

"Good-by, Colonel Bob," he said softly.

The old white man looked at Willie as though he were going to say something, but then he thought better of it and closed his jaw down tight.

Willie turned away to go, but Uncle Ben was scurrying through the kitchen like an ancient rabbit.

"Colonel Bob," he croaked. "There's trouble up in town. Man want you on the phone right now! Say they's after some colored soldier. Lawdy!"

"Yes," Willie said. "Maybe they after me."

"You stay right there," Colonel Bob growled, "and don't move a muscle! I'll be back in a minute." He turned and walked rapidly toward the front of the house.

Willie stood very still, looking up through a break in the trees at the pale, whitish blue sky. It was very high and empty. And in the trees, no bird sang. But Colonel Bob was coming back now, his face very red, and knotted into hard lines.

"Willie," he said, "did you tell two white men you'd kill them if they came nigh you?"

"Yes. I didn't say that, but that's what I meant."

"And did you have some kind of an argument with a white *woman?*"

"Yes, Colonel Bob."

"My God!"

"He crazy, Colonel Bob," Martha wailed. "He done gone plum outa his mind!"

"You better not go back to town," the Colonel said. "You better stay here until I can get you out after dark."

Willie smiled a little.

"I'm gonna ketch me a train," he said. "Two o'clock today. I'm gonna ketch it."

"You be kilt!" Martha declared. "They kill you sure!"

"We done run too much, Martha," Willie said slowly. "We done run and hid and anyhow we done got caught. And then we goes down on our knees and begs. I ain't running. Done forgot how. Don't know how to run. Don't know how to beg. Just knows how to fight, that's all, Martha."

"Oh, Jesus, he crazy! Told you he crazy, Colonel Bob!"

Colonel Bob was looking at Willie, a slow, thoughtful look.

"Can't sneak off in the dark, Colonel Bob. Can't steal away to Jesus. Got to go marching. And don't a man better touch me." He turned and went down the steps.

"Crazy," Martha wept. "Out of his mind!"

"Stop your blubbering!" Colonel Bob snapped. "Willie's no more crazy than I am. Maybe it's the world that's crazy. I don't know. I thought I did, but I don't." His blue eyes looked after the retreating figure. "Three hundred years of wounded pride," he mused. "Three centuries of hurt dignity. Going down the road marching. What would happen if we let them—no, it's God-damned impossible . . ."

"Looney!" Martha sobbed. "Plum tetched!"

"They'll kill him," Colonel Bob said. "And they'll do it in the meanest damned way they can think of. His leg won't make any difference. Not all the dang blasted ribbons in the world. Crazy thing. Willie, a soldier of the republic—wounded, and this thing to happen. Crazy." He stopped suddenly, his blue eyes

widening in his pale, old face. "Crazy!" he roared. "That's it! If I can make them think—That's it, that's it, by God!"

Then he was racing through the house toward the telephone.

Willie had gone on around the house toward the dirt road, where the heat was a visible thing, and turned his face in the direction of town.

When he neared the one paved street, the heat was lessening. He walked very slowly, turning off the old country road into Lee Avenue, the main street of the town. Then he was moving toward the station. There were many people in the street, he noticed, far more than usual. The sidewalk was almost blocked with men with eyes of blue ice, and a long, slow slouch to their walk. He went on quietly, paying no attention to them. He walked in an absolutely straight line, turning neither to the right nor the left, and each time they opened up their ranks to let him pass through. But afterwards came the sound of their footsteps falling in behind him, each man that he passed swelling the number until the sound of them walking was loud in the silent street.

He did not look back. He limped on his artificial leg making a scraping rustle on the sidewalk, and behind him, steadily, beat upon beat, not in perfect time, a little ragged, moving slowly, steadily, no faster nor slower than he was going, the white men came. They went down the street until they had almost reached the station. Then, moving his lips in prayer that had no words, Willie turned and faced them. They swung out into a broad semicircle, without hastening their steps, moving in toward him in the thick hot silence.

Willie opened his mouth to shriek at them, curse them, goad them into haste, but before his voice could rush past his dried and thickened tongue, the stillness was split from top to bottom by the wail of a siren. They all turned then, looking down the road, to where the khaki-colored truck was pounding up a billowing wall of dust, hurling straight toward them.

Then it was upon them, screeching to a stop, the great red crosses gleaming on its sides. The two soldiers were out of it almost before it was still, grabbing Willie by the arms, dragging him toward the ambulance. Then the young

officer with the single silver bar on his cap was climbing down, and with him an old man with white hair.

"This the man, Colonel?" the young officer demanded.

Colonel Bob nodded.

"All right," the officer said. "We'll take over now. This man is a combat fatigue case—not responsible for his actions."

"But I got to go!" Willie said. "Got to ketch that train. Got to go North where I can be free, where I can be a man. You hear me, lieutenant, I got to go!"

The young officer jerked his head in the direction of the ambulance.

"Let me go!" Willie wept. "Let me go!"

But the soldiers were moving forward now, dragging the slim form with them, with one leg sticking out very stiffly, the heavy heel drawing a line through the heat-softened asphalt as they went.

Questions for Discussion

1. ENUMERATE the hints the author gives as to the setting of the story.

2. A GOOD short story is centered around a single situation. What is the situation that gives rise to the tension in the story?

3. WHY DID the salesgirl in the Five and Ten Cent Store ignore Willie when a white woman came forward for service?

4. WHAT WERE the men of the town going to do to Willie when they moved in on him?

5. WILLIE SAYS, "I can't stay here, Colonel Bob. I ain't suited for here no more." In what way has Willie changed to make him unsuitable for the town he grew up in? How would this apply to a great number of Negroes in the South? What has caused Negroes in recent years to appear restive?

6. WHAT STRATAGEM did Colonel Bob use to save Willie?

7. WHAT KIND of man is Colonel Bob?

8. IN WHAT RESPECTS is Colonel Bob like the men of the town? In what respects is he different from them?

9. WHAT SOUTHERN characteristics did you detect in the people in this story?

10. THE CHARACTERS in this story might be taken as symbols. How is Willie a symbol for all the blacks of the South when he says "We done run too much?" In what way are Martha, Uncle Ben, and Colonel Bob also symbols?

11. How DOES the author create suspense in this story?

12. IN WHAT WAY is the title of the story ironic?

13. Do YOU think the people in the story speak naturally? How would you describe their manner of speaking?

14. Do YOU THINK this story is typical of the Negro experience in the South or is it an exaggeration? Explain your answer.

15. WHAT IS the theme of the story?

Characterization

CHARACTERIZATION is a process by which an author describes a character in such a way that he seems life-like if the characterization is well done. In "The Homecoming" Willie is real enough to us. We can see him dropping off the train favoring one leg and then limping off down the street. From that point on Willie says and does things that make him a personality, that endow him with certain character traits. This is the act of characterization.

1. THE AUTHOR does not describe nor analyze Willie as a person. He uses largely the methods of dialogue and incidents in the story to reveal the kind of person Willie is. In the dialogue with the bigoted ruffians at the Monument and his actions immediately afterward what qualities does Willie exhibit?

2. How DID Willie acquit himself as a soldier? What does this indicate about his character?

3. WILLIE EXPLAINS to Colonel Bob that he can't stay because he is unable to humble himself anymore, that he wants to stand up straight like a man. What adjectives would you apply to Willie for the position he takes in this scene?

4. How WOULD you characterize Willie for declining Colonel Bob's offer to get him out of town after dark and instead marching defiantly to the station?

5. WHAT CAN we guess about the kind of schooling that Willie received in the South?

6. WHAT PHRASES does the author use to present a picture of Willie's physical appearance?

7. How DID the author succeed in identifying the reader with his leading character? Did you feel sympathy for Willie Jackson? Why or why not?

Conflict

A STRUGGLE of some kind is inevitably an important part of any short story. That struggle may be a conflict between two people in the story or it may be a clash between an individual and his environment.

1. THERE ARE several incidents in "The Homecoming" that are sources of tension. Identify the first clash that occurs in this story? Was this conflict avoidable?
With which side did you sympathize in this conflict? Why?
What was the outcome of this clash?

2. WHAT WAS the nature of the second incident that gave rise to another clash involving Willie Jackson?

3. WILLIE HAS DECIDED on a course of action which brings him into conflict with his former employer, Colonel Bob, who wants to give him back his old job. Describe this particular problem.

4. AT THE END of the story there is a confrontation between Willie and the men of the town. Tell about the incident. How is a great catastrophe averted?
Trace the background of this kind of racial crisis.

5. THROUGHOUT the story we find Willie in conflict with a number of people in this small, hate-ridden town. Willie was also in conflict with everything the town stood for. Describe the conflict between Willie and his environment.

6. How DO Willie's conflicts in this story take on a larger meaning?

Word Study

*M*any of our words are made up of Latin or Greek prefixes and roots. If we know the meaning of the prefix it can be a great help in figuring out the sense of an unfamiliar word from the context. Here are ten common prefixes; five of them are from the Latin language and five from the Greek language.

Latin Prefixes

1. ab — meaning **from** or **away**, as in **abduct** (to take away)

2. bi — meaning **two**, as in **bi-annual** (twice a year)

3. de — meaning **down**, as in **de-mote** (to put down to a lower grade)

4. im — meaning **not**, as in **im-mature** (not mature)

5. semi — meaning **half**, as in **semi-annual** (half of a year)

Greek Prefixes

1. anti — meaning **against**, as in **anti-biotic** (against life-threatening organisms)

2. auto — meaning **self**, as in **au-tomobile** (a self-propelled vehicle)

3. dia — meaning **through**, as in **diagnosis** (literally, seeing through a symptom to recognize a disease)

4. micro — meaning **small**, as in **microscope** (an instrument to see small objects)

5. poly — meaning **many**, as in **polyandry** (having many husbands at the same time)

In the following sentences from the story are five words in heavy type containing Latin or Greek prefixes found in the group you have just studied. Taking particular note of the prefix in each case, tell what each word in heavy type means and how the prefix affects the meaning of the word. If you are in doubt about any word, consult the dictionary and list the word in your private vocabulary list.

1. "Willie stirred in his seat, watching the cabins . . . spinning backward past the train, lost in the **immensity** of sun-blasted fields . . ." (p. 73)

2. "Across the **diagonal** of the bend, Willie could see the town . . ." (p. 73)

3. "... A few dozen buildings ... **bisected** by a single paved street." (p. 73)

4. "He walked in an **absolutely** straight line ..." (p. 78)

5. "They swung out into a broad **semicircle**, ... moving in toward him in the thick hot silence." (p. 79)

Thinking and Writing

1. COLONEL BOB made a telephone call to save Willie from the mob. Write an account of what he probably said to the military authorities to cause them to send out an ambulance to pick up Willie.

2. AT THE FOOT of the Confederate Monument the inscription read "No nation rose so white and pure; none fell so free of stain." Do you think this is a valid epitaph of the Confederacy? Write a statement of your feelings regarding the absurdity or truthfulness of these words.

3. SUPPOSE you were in the Five and Ten Cent Store and witnessed the scene that was later described as Willie's having "some kind of an argument with a white woman." Write an account of what you saw and heard at the time. Also include your interpretation of the event.

4. LIKE ANY good short story, "The Homecoming" is made up of such constituent elements as plot, characters and setting. Which one of these do you think is emphasized in this story? Explain your answer at some length, making references to the story itself.

About the Author

Frank Yerby was born in Georgia in 1916. He received his M. A. from Fisk University in Nashville, Tennessee in 1938 and for the next three years taught English in several southern colleges. During World War II he worked on war production in the Ford factory in Detroit and at Fairchild Aircraft in Long Island.

His first published short story in 1944 won an O. Henry Award. At this period his writings were about Negro life in the South. Beginning in 1946 with the publication of *Foxes of Harrow,* Yerby has devoted himself to the writing of popular historical novels which have been tremendously successful from the point of view of sales and which have made him a wealthy man. *Foxes of Harrow,* a romantic story of the South after the Civil War, has sold more than two million copies and has been translated into twelve languages. Yerby has produced more than twenty novels, several of which have been made into motion pictures. Some of the more notable titles include *The Vixens* (1947), *The Golden Hawk* (1948) and *The Saracen Blade* (1952). In 1967 he published *Goat Song.* Altogether, his books have sold over twenty million copies.

Yerby has written all his novels while living abroad in France and Spain to escape the racial climate of the United States. He has said, "I love my country, but unfortunately, my country doesn't love me enough to let me live in it."

From

Invisible Man

BY RALPH ELLISON

Have you ever felt that nobody took notice of you, that people looked right at you and didn't know you were there because you were below their notice? Ralph Ellison wrote a remarkable novel, called INVISIBLE MAN complaining that white people look right through blacks as if they didn't exist.

The story is told in the first person and opens with the narrator as a high school student being invited to give his graduation speech as part of the program of entertainment at a gathering of the leading white men in the town. He wins a scholarship to a state Negro college from which he is later expelled. He goes to New York, finds a job in a paint factory, is injured in an explosion and nursed back to health by his landlady in a Harlem rooming house.

He joins a street political party and finds himself in conflict with a group of Black Nationalists who pursue him through the streets of Harlem during a riot. To escape them he drops through a manhole and takes up his abode in an underground room where he ponders the problem of making himself visible to the world.

Following is the first chapter of INVISIBLE MAN in which the narrator relates a degrading incident participated in by a group of black boys, of whom he is one.

It goes a long way back, some twenty years. All my life I had been looking for something, and everywhere I turned someone tried to tell me what it was. I accepted their answers too, though they were often in contradiction and even self-contradictory. I was naive. I was looking for myself and asking everyone except myself questions which I, and only I, could answer. It took me a long time and much painful boomeranging of my expectations to achieve a realization everyone else appears to have been born with: That I am nobody but myself. But first I had to discover that I am an invisible man!

And yet I am no freak of nature, nor of history. I was in the cards, other things having been equal (or unequal) eighty-five years ago. I am not ashamed of my

87

grandparents for having been slaves. I am only ashamed of myself for having at one time been ashamed. About eighty-five years ago they were told that they were free, united with others of our country in everything pertaining to the common good, and, in everything social, separate like the fingers of the hand. And they believed it. They exulted in it. They stayed in their place, worked hard, and brought up my father to do the same. But my grandfather is the one. He was an odd old guy, my grandfather, and I am told I take after him. It was he who caused the trouble. On his deathbed he called my father to him and said, "Son, after I'm gone I want you to keep up the good fight. I never told you, but our life is a war and I have been a traitor all my born days, a spy in the enemy's country ever since I gave up my gun back in the Reconstruction. Live with your head in the lion's mouth. I want you to overcome 'em with yeses, undermine 'em with grins, agree 'em to death and destruction, let 'em swoller you till they vomit or bust wide open." They thought the old man had gone out of his mind. He had been the meekest of men. The younger children were rushed from the room, the shades drawn and the flame of the lamp turned so low that it sputtered on the wick like the old man's breathing. "Learn it to the younguns," he whispered fiercely; then he died. But my folks were more alarmed over his last words than over his dying. It was as though he had not died at all, his words caused so much anxiety. I was warned emphatically to forget what he had said and, indeed, this is the first time it has been mentioned outside the family circle. It had a tremendous effect upon me, however. I could never be sure of what he meant. Grandfather had been a quiet old man who never made any trouble, yet on his deathbed he had called himself a traitor and a spy, and he had spoken of his meekness as a dangerous activity. It became a constant puzzle which lay unanswered in the back of my mind. And whenever things went well for me I remembered my grandfather and felt guilty and uncomfortable. It was as though I was carrying out his advice in spite of myself. And to make it worse, everyone loved me for it. I was praised by the most lily-white men of the town. I was considered an example of desirable conduct— just as my grandfather had been. And what puzzled me was that the old man had defined it as *treachery*. When I was praised for my conduct I felt a guilt that in some way I was doing something that was really against the wishes of the white folks, that if they had understood they would have desired me to act just the opposite, that I should have been sulky and mean, and that that really would have been what they wanted, even though they were fooled and thought they wanted me to act as I did. It made me afraid that some day they would look upon me as a traitor and I would be lost. Still I was more afraid to act any other way because they didn't like that at all. The old man's words were like a curse. On my graduation day I delivered an oration in which I showed that humility was the secret, indeed, the very essence of progress. (Not that I believed this—how could I, remembering my grand father?—I only believed that it worked.) It was a great success. Everyone praised me and I was invited to give the speech at a gathering of the town's leading white citizens. It was a triumph for our whole community.

It was in the main ballroom of the leading hotel. When I got there I discovered that it was on the occasion of a smoker, and I was told that since I was to be there anyway I might as well take part in the battle royal to be fought by some of my schoolmates as part of the entertainment. The battle royal came first.

All of the town's big shots were there in their tuxedoes, wolfing down the buffet foods, drinking beer and whiskey and smoking black cigars. It was a large room with a high ceiling. Chairs were arranged in neat rows around three sides of a portable boxing ring. The fourth side was clear, revealing a gleaming space of polished floor. I had some misgivings over the battle royal, by the way. Not from a distaste for fighting, but because I didn't care too much for the other fellows who were to take part. They were tough guys who seemed to have no grandfather's curse worrying their minds. No one could mistake their toughness. And besides, I suspected that fighting a battle royal might detract from the dignity of my speech. In those pre-invisible days I visualized myself as a potential Booker T. Washington. But the other fellows didn't care too much for me either, and there were nine of them. I felt superior to them in my way, and I didn't like the manner in which we were all crowded together into the servant's elevator. Nor did they like my being there. In fact, as the warmly lighted floors flashed past the elevator we had words over the fact that I, by taking part in the fight, had knocked one of their friends out of a night's work.

We were led out of the elevator through a rococo hall into an anteroom and told to get into our fighting togs. Each of us was issued a pair of boxing gloves and ushered out into a big mirrored hall, which we entered looking cautiously about us and whispering, lest we might accidentally be heard above the noise of the room. It was foggy with cigar smoke. And already the whiskey was taking effect. I was shocked to see some of the most important men of the town quite tipsy. They were all there—bankers, lawyers, judges, doctors, fire chiefs, teachers, merchants. Even one of the fashionable pastors.

.   .   .

A glove smacked against my head. I pivoted, striking out stiffly as someone went past, and felt the jar ripple along the length of my arm to my shoulder. Then it seemed as though all nine of the boys had turned upon me at once. Blows pounded me from all sides while I struck out as best I could. So many blows landed upon me that I wondered if I were not the only blindfolded fighter in the ring.

Blindfolded, I could no longer control my motions. I had no dignity. I stumbled about like a baby or a drunken man. The smoke had become thicker and with each new blow it seemed to sear and further restrict my lungs. My saliva became like hot bitter glue. A glove connected with my head, filling my mouth with warm blood. It was everywhere. I could not tell if the moisture I felt upon my body was sweat or blood. A blow landed hard against the nape of my neck. I felt myself going over, my head hitting the floor. Streaks of blue light filled the black world behind the blindfold. I lay prone, pretending that I was knocked out, but felt myself seized by hands and yanked to my feet. "Get going, black boy! Mix it up!" My arms were like lead, my head smarting from blows. I managed to feel my way to the ropes and

held on, trying to catch my breath. A glove landed in my mid-section and I went over again, feeling as though the smoke had become a knife jabbed into my guts. Pushed this way and that by the legs milling around me, I finally pulled erect and discovered that I could see the black, sweat-washed forms weaving in the smoky-blue atmosphere like drunken dancers weaving to the rapid drum-like thuds of blows.

Everyone fought hysterically. It was complete anarchy. Everybody fought everybody else. No group fought together for long. Two, three, four, fought one, then turned to fight each other, were themselves attacked. Blows landed below the belt and in the kidney, with the gloves open as well as closed, and with my eye partly opened now there was not so much terror. I moved carefully, avoiding blows, although not too many to attract attention, fighting from group to group. The boys groped about like blind, cautious crabs crouching to protect their mid-sections, their heads pulled in short against their shoulders, their arms stretched nervously before them, with their fists testing the smoke-filled air like the knobbed feelers of hypersensitive snails. In one corner I glimpsed a boy violently punching the air and heard him scream in pain as he smashed his hand against a ring post. For a second I saw him bent over holding his hand, then going down as a blow caught his unprotected head. I played one group against the other, slipping in and throwing a punch then stepping out of range while pushing the others into the melee to take the blows blindly aimed at me. The smoke was agonizing and there were no rounds, no bells at three minute intervals to relieve our exhaustion. The room spun round me, a swirl of lights, smoke, sweating bodies surrounded by tense white faces. I bled from both nose and mouth, the blood spattering upon my chest.

The men kept yelling, "Slug him, black boy! Knock his guts out!"

"Uppercut him! Kill him! Kill that big boy!"

Taking a fake fall, I saw a boy going down heavily beside me as though we were felled by a single blow, saw a sneaker-clad foot shoot into his groin as the two who had knocked him down stumbled upon him. I rolled out of range, feeling a twinge of nausea.

The harder we fought the more threatening the men became. And yet, I had begun to worry about my speech again. How would it go? Would they recognize my ability? What would they give me?

I was fighting automatically when suddenly I noticed that one after another of the boys was leaving the ring. I was surprised, filled with panic, as though I had been left alone with an unknown danger. Then I understood. The boys had arranged it among themselves. It was the custom for the two men left in the ring to slug it out for the winner's prize. I discovered this too late. When the bell sounded two men in tuxedoes leaped into the ring and removed the blindfold. I found myself facing Tatlock, the biggest of the gang. I felt sick at my stomach. Hardly had the bell stopped ringing in my ears than it clanged again and I saw him moving swiftly toward me. Thinking of nothing else to do I hit him smash on the nose. He kept coming, bringing the rank sharp violence of stale sweat. His face was a black blank of a face, only his eyes alive—with hate of me and aglow with a feverish terror from what had happened to us all. I became anxious. I wanted to deliver my speech and he came at me as though he meant to beat it out of me. I smashed him again and again, taking his blows as they came. Then on a sudden impulse I struck him lightly and as we clinched, I whispered, "Fake like I knocked you out, you can have the prize."

"I'll break your behind," he whispered hoarsely.

"For *them?*"

"For *me*, sonofabitch!"

They were yelling for us to break it up and Tatlock spun me half around with a blow, and as a joggled camera sweeps in a reeling scene, I saw the howling red faces crouching tense beneath the cloud of blue-gray smoke. For a moment the world wavered, unraveled, flowed, then my head cleared and Tatlock bounced before me. That fluttering shadow before my eyes was his jabbing left hand. Then falling forward, my head against his damp shoulder, I whispered,

"I'll make it five dollars more."

"Go to hell!"

But his muscles relaxed a trifle beneath my pressure and I breathed, "Seven?"

"Give it to your ma," he said, ripping me beneath the heart.

And while I still held him I butted him and moved away. I felt myself bombarded with punches. I fought back with hopeless desperation. I wanted to deliver my speech more than anything else in the world, because I felt that only these men could judge truly my ability, and now this stupid clown was ruining my chances. I began fighting carefully now, moving in to punch him and out again with my greater speed. A lucky blow to his chin and I had him going too—until I heard a loud voice yell, "I got my money on the big boy."

Hearing this, I almost dropped my guard. I was confused. Should I try to win against the voice out there? Would not this go against my speech, and was not this a moment for humility, for nonresistance? A blow to my head as I danced about sent my right eye popping like a jack-in-the box and settled my dilemma. The room went red as I fell. It was a dream fall, my body languid and fastidious as to where to land, until the floor became impatient and smashed up to meet me. A moment later I came to. An hypnotic voice said FIVE emphatically. And I lay there, hazily watching a dark red spot of my own blood shaping itself into a butterfly, glistening and soaking into the soiled gray world of the canvas.

When the voice drawled TEN I was lifted up and dragged to a chair. I sat dazed. My eye pained and swelled with each throb of my pounding heart and I wondered if now I would be allowed to speak. I was wringing wet, my mouth still bleeding. We were grouped along the wall now. The other boys ignored me as they congratulated Tatlock and speculated as to how much they would be paid. One boy whimpered over his smashed hand. Looking up front, I saw attendants in white jackets rolling the portable ring away and placing a small square rug in the vacant space surrounded by chairs. Perhaps, I thought, I will stand on the rug to deliver my speech.

Then the M.C. called to us, "Come on up here boys and get your money."

We ran forward to where the men laughed and talked in their chairs, waiting. Everyone seemed friendly now.

"There it is on the rug," the man said. I saw the rug covered with coins of all dimensions and a few crumpled bills. But what excited me, scattered here and there, were the gold pieces.

"Boys, it's all yours," the man said. "You get all you grab."

"That's right, Sambo," a blond man said, winking at me confidentially.

I trembled with excitement, forgetting my pain. I would get the gold and the bills, I thought. I would use both hands. I would throw my body against the boys nearest me to block them from the gold.

"Get down around the rug now," the man commanded, "and don't anyone touch it until I give the signal."

"This ought to be good," I heard.

As told, we got around the square rug on our knees. Slowly the man raised his freckled hand as we followed it upward with our eyes.

I heard, "These niggers look like they're about to pray!"

Then, "Ready," the man said. "Go!"

I lunged for a yellow coin lying on the blue design of the carpet, touching it and sending a surprised shriek to join those rising around me. I tried frantically to remove my hand but could not let go. A hot, violent force tore through my body, shaking me like a wet rat. The rug was electrified. The hair bristled up on my head as I shook myself free. My muscles jumped, my nerves jangled, writhed. But I saw that this was not stopping the other boys. Laughing in fear and embarrass-

ment, some were holding back and scooping up the coins knocked off by the painful contortions of the others. The men roared above us as we struggled.

"Pick it up, goddamnit, pick it up!" someone called like a bass-voiced parrot. "Go on, get it!"

I crawled rapidly around the floor, picking up the coins, trying to avoid the coppers and to get greenbacks and the gold. Ignoring the shock by laughing, as I brushed coins off quickly, I discovered that I could contain the electricity—a contradiction, but it works. Then the men began to push us onto the rug. Laughing embarrassedly, we struggled out of their hands and kept after the coins. We were all wet and slippery and hard to hold. Suddenly I saw a boy lifted into the air, glistening with sweat like a circus seal, and dropped, his wet back landing flush upon the charged rug, heard him yell and saw him literally dance upon his back, his elbows beating a frenzied tattoo upon the floor, his muscles twitching like the flesh of a horse stung by many flies. When he finally rolled off, his face was gray and no one stopped him when he ran from the floor amid booming laughter.

"Get the money," the M.C. called. "That's good hard American cash!"

And we snatched and grabbed, snatched and grabbed. I was careful not to come too close to the rug now, and when I felt the hot whiskey breath descend upon me like a cloud of foul air I reached out and grabbed the leg of a chair. It was occupied and I held on desperately.

"Leggo, nigger! Leggo!"

The huge face wavered down to mine as he tried to push me free. But my body was slippery and he was too drunk. It was Mr. Colcord, who owned a chain of movie houses. Each time he grabbed me I slipped out of his hands. It became a real struggle. I feared the rug more than I did the drunk, so I held on, surprising myself for a moment by trying to topple *him* upon the rug. It was such an enormous idea that I found myself actually carrying it out. I tried not to be obvious, yet when I grabbed his leg, trying to tumble him out of the chair, he raised up roaring with laughter, and looking at me with soberness dead in the eye, kicked me viciously in the chest. The chair leg flew out of my hand and I felt myself going and rolled. It was as though I had rolled through a bed of hot coals. It seemed a whole century would pass before I would roll free, a century in which I was seared through the deepest levels of my body to the fearful breath within me and the breath seared and heated to the point of explosion. It'll all be over in a flash, I thought as I rolled clear. It'll all be over in a flash.

But not yet, the men on the other side were waiting, red faces swollen as though from apoplexy as they bent forward in their chairs. Seeing their fingers coming toward me I rolled away as a fumbled football rolls off the receiver's fingertips, back into the coals. That time I luckily sent the rug sliding out of place and heard the coins ringing against the floor and the boys scuffling to pick them up and the M. C. calling, "All right, boys, that's all. Go get dressed and get your money."

I was limp as a dish rag. My back felt as though it had been beaten with wires.

When we had dressed the M. C. came in and gave us each five dollars, except Tatlock, who got ten for being last in the ring. Then he told us to leave. I was not to get a chance to deliver my speech, I thought. I was going out into the dim alley in despair when I was stopped and told to go back. I returned to the ballroom, where the men were pushing back their chairs and gathering in groups to talk.

The M. C. knocked on a table for quiet. "Gentlemen," he said, "we almost forgot an important part of the program. A most serious part, gentlemen. This boy was brought here to deliver a speech which he made at his graduation yesterday . . ."

"Bravo!"

"I'm told that he is the smartest boy we've got out there in Greenwood. I'm told that he knows more big words than a pocket-sized dictionary."

Much applause and laughter.

"So now, gentlemen, I want you to give him your attention."

There was still laughter as I faced them, my mouth dry, my eye throbbing. I began slowly, but evidently my throat was tense, because they began shouting, "Louder! Louder!"

"We of the younger generation extol the wisdom of that great leader and educator," I shouted, "who first spoke these flaming words of wisdom: 'A ship lost at sea for many days suddenly sighted a friendly vessel. From the mast of the unfortunate vessel was seen a signal: "Water, water: we die of thirst!" The answer from the friedly vessel came back: "Cast down your bucket where you are." The captain of the distressed vessel, at last heeding the injunction, cast down his bucket, and it came up full of fresh sparkling water from the mouth of the Amazon River.' And like him I say, and in his words, 'To those of my race who depend upon bettering their condition in a foreign land, or who underestimate the importance of cultivating friendly relations with the Southern white man, who is his next-door neighbor, I would say: "Cast down your bucket where you are"—cast it down in making friends in every manly way of the people of all races by whom we are surrounded . . .' "

I spoke automatically and with such fervor that I did not realize that the men were still talking and laughing until my dry mouth, fil-ling up with blood from the cut, almost strangled me. I coughed, wanting to stop and go to one of the tall brass, sand-filled spittoons to relieve myself, but a few of the men, especially the superintendent, were listening and I was afraid. So I gulped it down, blood, saliva and all, and continued. (What powers of endurance I had during those days! What enthusiasm! What a belief in the rightness of things!) I spoke even louder in spite of the pain. But still they talked and still they laughed, as though deaf with cotton in dirty ears. So I spoke with greater emotional emphasis. I closed my ears and swallowed blood until I was nauseated. The speech seemed a hundred times as long as before, but I could not leave out a single word. All had to be said, each memorized nuance considered, rendered. Nor was that all. Whenever I uttered a word of three or more syllables a group of voices would yell for me to repeat it. I used the phrase "social responsibility" and they yelled:

"What's that word you say, boy?"

"Social responsibility," I said.

"What?"

"Social . . ."

"Louder."

". . . responsibility."

"More!"

"Respon—"

"Repeat!"

"—sibility."

The room filled with the uproar of laughter until, no doubt, distracted by having to gulp down my blood, I made a mistake and yelled a phrase I had often seen denounced in newspaper editorials, heard debated in private.

"Social . . ."

"What?" they yelled.

". . . equality—"

The laughter hung smokelike in the sudden stillness. I opened my eyes, puzzled. Sounds of displeasure filled the room. The M. C. rushed forward. They shouted hostile phrases at me. But I did not understand.

A small dry mustached man in the front row blared out, "Say that slowly, son!"

"What sir?"

"What you just said!"

"Social responsibility, sir." I said.

"You weren't being smart, were you, boy?" he said, not unkindly.

"No, sir!"

"You sure that about 'equality' was a mistake?"

"Oh, yes, sir," I said. "I was swallowing blood."

"Well, you had better speak more slowly so we can understand. We mean to do right by you, but you've got to know your place at all times. All right, now, go on with your speech."

I was afraid. I wanted to leave but I wanted also to speak and I was afraid they'd snatch me down.

"Thank you, sir," I said, beginning where I had left off, and having them ignore me as before.

Yet when I finished there was a thunderous applause. I was surprised to see the superintendent come forth with a package wrapped in white tissue paper, and gesturing for quiet, address the the men.

"Gentlemen, you see that I did not overpraise this boy. He makes a good speech and some day he'll lead his people in the proper paths. And I don't have to tell you that that is important in these days and times. This is a good, smart boy, and so to encourage him in the right direction, in the name of the Board of Education, I wish to present him a prize in the form of this . . ."

He paused, removing the tissue paper and revealing a gleaming calfskin case.

". . . in the form of this first-class article from Shad Whitmore's shop."

"Boy, he said, addressing me, "take this prize and keep it well. Consider it a badge of office. Prize it. Keep developing as you are and some day it will be filled with important papers that will help shape the destiny of your people."

I was so moved that I could hardly express my thanks. A rope of bloody saliva forming a shape like an undiscovered continent drooled upon the leather and I wiped it quickly away. I felt an importance that I had never dreamed.

"Open it and see what's inside," I was told.

My fingers a-tremble, I complied, smelling the fresh leather and finding an official-looking document inside. It was a scholarship to the state college for Negroes. My eyes filled with tears and I ran awkwardly off the floor.

I was overjoyed. I did not even mind when I discovered that the gold pieces I had scrambled for were brass pocket tokens advertising a certain make of automobile.

When I reached home everyone was excited. Next day the neighbors came to congratulate me. I even felt safe from grandfather whose deathbed curse usually spoiled my triumphs. I stood beneath his photograph with my brief case in hand and smiled triumphantly into his stolid black peasant's face. It was a face that fascinated me. The eyes seemed to follow everywhere I went.

That night I dreamed I was at a circus with him and that he refused to laugh at the clowns no matter what they did. Then later he told me to open my brief case and read what was inside and I did, finding an official envelope stamped with the state seal; and inside the envelope I found another and another, endlessly, and I thought I would fall of weariness. "Them's years," he said. "Now open that one." And I did and in it I found an engraved document containing a short message in letters of gold. "Read it," my grandfather said. "Out loud."

"To Whom It May Concern," I intoned. "Keep This Nigger-Boy Running."

I awoke with the old man's laughter ringing in my ears.

Questions for Discussion

1. THE NARRATOR explains in the first paragraph that as a young, inexperienced person he was looking for an identity, but did not know who he was until he came to realize that white people were not aware of blacks and that he was invisible to them. What problem does this point up in the relations between the races?

2. How DID the family react to the grandfather's dying words?

3. DID THE NARRATOR heed the words of his dying grandfather? Explain.

4. AT WHAT OCCASION was the narrator invited to repeat his graduation speech for the town's white citizens?

5. How WERE the men at the party acting?

6. WHAT WERE the boys in the battle royal supposed to do?

7. How WERE the boys tricked when it came to getting paid for the boxing exhibition?

8. WHY DID the white men get so upset when the narrator made a slip of the tongue and referred to "social equality" instead of "social responsibility?"

9. IN HIS SPEECH the narrator quoted a famous Negro leader as saying, "Cast down your bucket where you are . . ." What racial philosophy is exemplified by these words? What leader uttered these words? How is he regarded in the framework of today's racial conflict?

10. WHAT CAN you say about the white men, the most important men of the town, who made sport of small black boys? What did this reveal about the racial attitudes of the whites?

11. IN VIEW OF the contempt that the whites felt, how do you account for the superintendent's kindness in presenting the narrator with a brief case and a college scholarship?

12. WHAT IS your interpretation of the dream the narrator had in which his grandfather appeared?

13. COMPARE the invisible man in this story with the one in the story of the same title by H. G. Wells.

Building Vocabulary

Getting the meaning from the context. For each of the following sentences taken from the story, select from the choices given the word or phrase that means the same as the word in heavy type. Check your answer by looking up the word in a dictionary. Write the ones you get wrong in your special vocabulary list.

---

1. "I was **naive** (nah-eve')." (p. 87)

   A. intelligent B. simple C. changeable D. bold

2. "On my graduation day I delivered an **oration** (uh-ray'shun)." (p. 89)

   A. story B. thanksgiving C. speech D. eulogy

3. "We were led through a **rococo** (ruh-koh'koh) hall into an anteroom." (p. 89)

   A. fancifully ornamented B. reddish C. dimly lit D. very long

4. "I **pivoted** (piv'ut-id), strike out stiffly..." (p. 90)

   A. tripped B. shouted C. turned D. punched

5. "I lay **prone** (prohn), pretending that I was knocked out." (p. 90)

   A. faint B. calm C. flat D. panting

6. "It was complete **anarchy** (an'uhr-key). Everybody fought everybody else." (p. 90).

7. "... Their fists testing the smoke-filled air like the knobbed feelers of **hypersensitive** (high-puhr-sen'si-tiv) snails." (p. 90)

   A. drugged B. sluggish C. very receptive D. intelligent

8. "A blow to my head as I danced about... settled my **dilemma** (dih-lem'uh)." (p. 92)

   A. determination B. problem C. dizziness D. disaster

9. "... His elbows beating a **frenzied** (fren'zeed) tattoo upon the floor." (p. 93)

   A. wild B. painful C. rhythmic C. slow

10. "We of the younger generation **extol** (eks-tole') the wisdom of the great leader..." (p. 95)

   A. praise B. question C. encourage D. tolerate

A. disorder B. a king C. violence D. war

❦

The Theme

1. THE UNDERLYING idea, or theme of this story, is concerned with black-white relations and runs as a thread through the story. At the beginning the narrator relates how his grandfather was born a slave and after freedom worked hard and humbly. Why did he say their life was like a war? What was his dying advice?

2. WHAT DID the narrator's grandfather mean by saying he was a traitor? To whom was he a traitor, to his own people, or to the whites?

3. WHAT DID he mean by saying, "Live with your head in the lion's mouth?"

4. WHY DID the narrator feel guilty when he was praised for his good behavior?

5. IN THE LAST envelope in his dream the narrator found a message that he should be kept running. What does this mean in terms of the conflict between the races?

6. How WOULD you state the theme of the story in one or two sentences?

7. IN HIS GRADUATION speech the narrator showed that meekness was the basis of progress. How does this fit in with the theme of the story?

8. THE AUTHOR'S MEANING may be sprinkled throughout the story and the full impact of his message may not be revealed until the ending. Point out whether or not this is true here.

❦

Thinking and Writing

1. AT THE TIME he was graduated from high school the narrator believed that being humble was the essence of progress. If you agree with him, write a composition showing how colored people can improve their situation by showing humility to whites. If you disagree with him, show how militancy is a more effective way for colored folks to improve their lot.

2. MANY STUDENTS work at part-time jobs in order to earn extra spending money. For a fee the narrator participated in a battle

royal at a smoker. Describe the kind of work you have done in after-school or week-end activities.

3. THE GRANDFATHER said that he was a traitor after he gave up his gun in the Reconstruction days. Write an account of what might have happened if he and other blacks had kept their arms after Federal troops were withdrawn from the South.

About the Author

Ralph Ellison was born in Oklahoma City in 1914 and attended segregated schools where he developed a special interest in jazz and classical music. To further his ambition to become a composer of symphonic music, he went to Tuskegee Institute in Alabama, majoring in music and composing. Becoming interested in sculpture he left Tuskegee after three years and went to New York City in 1936 to develop his talent. Then he became attracted to literature and came under the influence of Richard Wright, the noted novelist.

In the 1940's Ellison had a number of short stories and articles published in which he expressed again and again his belief that white America had to recognize the blacks as human beings. In 1952 his *Invisible Man* was published and recognized as a work of major importance. It won the National Book Award for Fiction in 1953. He is also the author of *Shadow and Act*, a collection of essays.

In recent years Ralph Ellison has been devoting himself to teaching, as well as to writing. He has served as visiting instructor and lecturer in many universities, including Yale, Harvard, Rutgers, Fisk and Stony Brook, in addition to foreign universities in Germany, Spain, Italy, Mexico and Far Eastern countries.

Miss Cynthie

By Rudolph Fisher

A sprightly seventy-year old grandmother travels up from the South to visit her grandson who has made good in the big city. She has raised him strictly, in lieu of his mother, wanting him to become a preacher or a doctor, or at least an undertaker. The grandson meets her at the railroad station and has her baggage brought to a big, blue convertible with red wheels. She is whirled off to his luxurious apartment in Harlem. No, he has not achieved success in New York as an undertaker. She asks if he is a bootlegger. No, he is not; but he won't reveal what he is until she can see for herself the next night. Does he turn out to be a racketeer, a night-club operator, in the numbers racket? Let Mr. Fisher tell you in his own way.

For the first time in her life somebody had called her "madam." She had been standing, bewildered but unafraid, while innumerable Red Caps appropriated piece after piece of the baggage arrayed on the platform. Neither her brief seventy years' journey through life nor her long two days' travel northward had

102

dimmed the live brightness of her eyes, which, for all their bewilderment, had accurately selected her own treasures out of the row of luggage and guarded them vigilantly. "These yours, madam?"

The biggest Red Cap of all was smiling at her. He looked for all the world like Doc Crinshaw's oldest son back home. Her little brown face relaxed; she smiled back at him.

"They got to be. You all done took all the others."

He laughed aloud. Then— "Carry 'em in for you?"

She contemplated his bulk. "Reckon you can manage it— puny little feller like you?"

Thereupon they were friends. Still grinning broadly, he surrounded himself with her impedimenta, the enormous brown extension-case on one shoulder, the big straw suitcase in the opposite hand, the carpet-bag under one arm. She herself held fast to the umbrella. "Always like to have sump'm in my hand when I walk. Can't never tell when you'll run across a snake."

"There aren't any snakes in the city."

"There's snakes everywhere, chile."

They began the tedious hike up the interminable platform. She was small and quick. Her carriage was surprisingly erect, her gait astonishingly spry. She said:

"You liked to took my breath back yonder, boy, callin' me 'madam'. Back home everybody call me 'Miss Cynthie.' Even their chillun. Black folks, white folks too. 'Miss Cynthie.' Well, when you come up with that 'madam' o' yourn, I say to myself, 'Now, I wonder who that chile's a-grinnin' at?' 'Madam' stands for mist'ess o' the house, and I sho' ain' mist'ess of nothin' in this hyeh New York.' "

"Well, you see, we call everybody 'madam.' "

"Everybody?—Hm." The bright eyes twinkled. "Seem like that's worry me some—if I was a man."

He acknowledged his slip and observed, "I see this isn't your first trip to New York."

"First trip any place, son. First time I been over fifty mile from Waxhaw. Only travelin' I've done is in my head. Ain' seen many places, but I's seen a passel o' people. Reckon places is pretty much alike after people been in 'em awhile."

"Yes, ma'am. I guess that's right."

"You ain't no reg'lar bag-toter, is you?"

"Ma'am?"

"You talk too good."

"Well. I only do this in vacation-time. I'm still in school."

"You is. What you aimin' to be?"

"I'm studying medicine."

"You is?" She beamed. "Aimin' to be a doctor, huh? Thank the Lord for that. That's what I always wanted my David to be. My grandchile hyeh in New York. He's to meet me hyeh now."

"I bet you'll have a great time."

"Mussn't bet, chile. That's sinful. I tole him 'for' he left home, I say, 'Son, you the only one o' the chillun what's got a chance to amount to sump'm. Don't th'ow it away. Be a preacher or a doctor. Work yo' way up and don't stop short. If the Lord don't see fit for you to doctor the soul, then doctor the body. If you don't get to be a reg'lar doctor, be a tooth-doctor. If you jes' can't make that, be a foot-doctor. And if you don' get that fur, be a undertaker. That's the least you must be. That ain't so bad. Keep you acquainted with the house of the Lord. Always mind the house o' the Lord— whatever you do, do like a church-steeple: aim high and go straight.'"

"Did he get to be a doctor?"

"Don't b'lieve he did. Too late startin', I reckon. But he's done succeeded at sump'm. Mus' be at least a undertaker, 'cause he started sendin' the homefolks money, and he come home las' year dressed like Judge Pettiford's boy what went off to school in Virginia. Wouldn't tell none of us 'zackly what he was doin', but he said he wouldn't never be happy till I come and see for myself. So hyeh I is." Something softened her voice. "His mammy died befo' he knowed her. But he was always sech a good chile—" The something was apprehension. "Hope he *is* a undertaker."

They were mounting a flight of steep stairs leading to an exit-gate, about which clustered a few people still hoping to catch sight of arriving friends. Among these a tall young brown-skinned man in a light grey suit suddenly waved his panama and yelled, "Hey, Miss Cynthie!"

Miss Cynthie stopped, looked up, and waved back with a delighted umbrella. The Red Cap's eyes lifted too. His lower jaw sagged.

"Is that your grandson?"

"It sho' is," she said and distanced him for the rest of the climb. The grandson, with an abandonment that superbly ignored onlookers, folded the little woman in an exultant, smothering embrace. As soon as she could, she pushed him off with breathless mock impatience.

"Go 'way, you fool, you. Aimin' to squeeze my soul out of my body befo' I can get a look at this place?" She shook herself into the semblance of composure. "Well. You don't look hungry, anyhow."

"Ho-ho! Miss Cynthie in New York! Can y' imagine this? Come on. I'm parked on Eighth Avenue."

Another Red Cap came up. "Got a break, hey, boy?"

"Dave Tappen himself—can you beat that?"

"The old lady hasn't seen the station yet—starin' at him."

"That's not the half of it, bozo. That's Dave Tappen's Grandmother. And what do you s'pose she hopes?"

"What?"

"She hopes that Dave has turned out to be a successful undertaker!"

"Undertaker? Undertaker!"

They stared at each other a gaping moment, then doubled up with laughter.

"Look — through there — that's the Chrysler Building. Oh, Helle-lujah! I meant to bring you up Broadway—"

"David—"

"Ma'am?"

"This hyeh wagon yourn?"

"Nobody else's. Sweet buggy, ain't it?"

"David—you ain't turned out to be one of them moonshiners, is you?"

"Moonshiners—? Moon-Ho! No indeed, Miss Cynthie. I got a better racket 'n that."

"Better which?"

"Game. Business. Pick-up."

"Tell me, David. What is yo' racket?"

"Can't spill it yet, Miss Cynthie. Rather show you. Tomorrow night you'll know the worst. Can you make out till tomorrow night?"

"David, you know I always wanted you to be a doctor, even if 'twasn' nothin' but a foot-doctor. The very leas' I wanted you to be was a undertaker."

"Undertaker! Oh, Miss Cynthie! —with my sunny disposition?"

"Then you ain't even a undertaker?"

"Listen, Miss Cynthie. Just forget 'bout what I am for awhile. Just till tomorrow night. I want you to see for yourself. Tellin' you will spoil it. Now stop askin', you hear?—because I'm not answerin —I'm surprisin' you. And don't expect anybody you meet to tell you. It'll mess up the whole works. Understand? Now give the big city a break. There's the elevated train going up Columbus Avenue. Ain't that hot stuff?"

Miss Cynthie looked. "Humph!" she said. "Tain' half high as that trestle two miles from Waxhaw."

She thoroughly enjoyed the ride up Central Park West. The stagger lights, the extent of the park, the high, close, kingly buildings, remarkable because their stoves cooled them in summer as well as heated them in winter, all drew nods of mild interest. But what gave her special delight was not these: it was that David's car so effortlessly sped past the headlong drove of vehicles racing northward.

They stopped for a red light; when they started again their machine leaped forward with a triumphant eagerness that drew from her an unsuppressed "Hot you, David! That's it!"

He grinned appreciatively. "Why, you're a regular New Yorker already."

"New York nothin'! I done the same thing fifty years ago—befo' I knowed they was a New York."

"What!"

"'Deed so. Didn' I use to tell you 'bout my young mare, Betty? Chile, I'd hitch Betty up to yo' grandpa's buggy and pass anything on the road. Betty never knowed what another horse's dust smelt like. No 'ndeedy. Shuh, boy, this an't nothin' new to me. Why that broke-down Fo'd yo uncle Jake's got ain' nothin'—nothin' but a sorry mess. Done got so slow I jes' won' ride in it—I declare I'd rather walk. But this hyeh thing, now, this is right nice." She settled back in complete, complacent comfort, and they speed on, swift and silent.

Suddenly she sat erect with abrupt discovery.

"David—well-bless my soul!"

"What's the matter, Miss Cynthie?"

Then he saw what had caught her attention. They were travelling up Seventh Avenue now, and something was miraculously different. Not the road, that was as broad as ever, wide, white gleaming in the sun. Not the houses; they were lofty still, lordly, disdainful, supercilious. Not the cars; they continued to race impatiently onward, innumerable, precipitate, tumultuous. Something else, something at once obvious and subtle, insistent, pervasive, compelling.

"David—this mus' be Harlem!"

"Good Lord, Miss Cynthie—!"

"Don' use the name of the Lord in vain, David."

"But I mean—gee!—you're no fun at all. You get everything before a guy can tell you."

"You got plenty to tell me, David. But don' nobody need to tell me this. Look a yonder."

Not just a change of complexion. A completely dissimilar atmosphere. Sidewalks teeming with leisurely strollers, at once strangely dark and bright. Boys in white trousers, berets, and green shirts, with slickened black heads and proud swagger. Bareheaded girls in crisp organdie dresses, purple, canary, gay scarlet. And laughter, abandoned strong Negro laughter,

some falling full on the ear, some not heard at all, yet sensed—the warm life-breath of the tireless carnival to which Harlem's heart quickens in summer.

'This is it," admitted David. "Get a good eyeful. Here's One Hundred and Twenty-fifth Street —regular little Broadway. And here's the Alhambra, and up ahead we'll pass the Lafayette."

"What's them?"

"Theatres."

"Theatres? Theatres. Humph! Look, David—is that a colored folks church?" They were passing a fine gray-stone edifice.

"That. Oh. Sure it is. So's this one on this side."

"No! Well, ain' that fine? Splendid big church like that for colored folks."

Taking his cue from this, her first tribute to the city he said, "You ain't seen nothing yet. Wait a minute."

They swung left through a side-street and turned right on a boulevard. "What do you think o' that?" And he pointed to the quarter-million-dollar St. Mark's.

"That a colored church, too?"

"'Tain' no white one. And they built it themselves, you know. Nobody's hand-me-down gift."

She heaved a great happy sigh. "Oh, yes, it was a gift, David. It was a gift from on high." Then, "Look a, hyeh—which a one you belong to?"

"Me? Why, I don't belong to any—that is, none o' these. Mine's over in another section. Y'see, mine's Baptist. These are all Methodist. See?"

"M-m. Uh-huh. I see."

They circled a square and slipped into a quiet narrow street overlooking a park, stopping before the tallest of the apartment-houses in the single commanding row.

Alighting, Miss Cynthie gave this imposing structure one side-wise, upward glance, and said, "Y'all live like bees in a hive, don't y'?—I boun' the women does all the work, too." A moment later, "So this is a elevator? Feel like I'm glory-bound sho' nuff."

Along a tiled corridor and into David's apartment. Rooms leading into rooms. Luxurious couches, easy-chairs, a brown-walnut grand piano, gay-shaded floor lamps, panelled walls, deep rugs, treach-erous glass-wood floors—and a smiling golden-skinned girl in a gingham housedress, approaching with outstretched hands.

"This is Ruth, Miss Cynthie."

"Miss Cynthie!" said Ruth.

They clasped hands. "Been wantin' to see David's girl ever since he first wrote us 'bout her."

"Come—here's your room this way. Here's the bath. Get out of your things and get comfy. You must be worn out with the trip."

"Worn out? Worn out? Shuh. How you gon' get worn out in a train? Now if 'twas a horse, or Jake's no-count Fo'd—but a train —didn' but one thing bother me on that train."

"What?"

"When the man made them beds down, I jes' couldn' manage to undress same as at home. Why, s'posin' sump'm bus' the train open—where'd you be? Naked as a jay-bird in dew-berry time."

David took in her things and left her to get comfortable. He re-turned, and Ruth, despite his re-assuring embrace, whispered:

"Dave, you can't fool old folks —why don't you go ahead and tell her about yourself? Think of the shock she's going to get—at her age."

David shook his head. "She'll get over the shock if she's there looking on. If we just told her, she'd never understand. We've got to railroad her into it. Then she'll be happy."

"She's nice. But she's got the same ideas as all old folks—"

"Yea—but with her you can change 'em. Specially if every-thing is really all right. I know her. She's for church and all, but she believes in good times too, if they're right. Why, when I was a kid—" He broke off. "Listen!"

Miss Cynthie's voice came quite distinctly to them, singing a jaunty little rhyme:

Oh I danced with the gal with the hole in her stockin',
And her toe kep' a-kickin' and her heel kep' a-knockin'—

'Come up, Jesse, and get a drink o' gin,

'Cause you near to the heaven
as you'll ever get ag'in'.

"She taught me that when I
wasn't knee-high to a cricket,"
David said.

Miss Cynthia still sang softly
and merrily:

"Then I danced with the gal
with the dimple in her cheek,
And if she'd 'a' kep' a-smilin',
I'd 'a' danced for a week—"

"God forgive me," prayed Miss
Cynthie as she discovered David's
purpose the following night. She
let him and Ruth lead her, like an
early Christian martyr, into the
Lafayette Theatre. The blinding
glare of the lobby produced a
merciful self-anaesthesia, and she
entered the sudden dimness of the
interior as involuntarily as in a
dream. . . .

Attendants outdid each other
for Mr. Dave Tappen. She heard
him tell them, "Fix us up till we
go on," and found herself sitting
between Ruth and David in the
front row of a lower box. A mirac-
ulous device of the devil, a motion
picture that talked, was just ending. At her feet the orchestra was
assembling. The motion-picture
faded out amid a scattered round
of applause. Lights blazed and
the orchestra burst into an ungod-
ly rumpus.

She looked out over the seated
multitude, scanning row upon row
of illumined faces, black faces,
white faces, yellow, tan, brown,
bald heads, bobbed heads, kinky
and straight heads; and upon
every countenance, expectancy—
scowling expectancy in this case,
smiling in that, complacent here,
amused there, commentative else-
where, but everywhere suspense,
abeyance, anticipation.

Half a dozen people were ushered down the nearer aisle to reserved seats in the second row.
Some of them caught sight of David and Ruth and waved to them.
The chairs immediately behind
them in the box were being shifted. "Hello, Tap" Miss Cynthie
saw David turn, rise, and shake
hands with two men. One of them
was large, bald and pink, emanating good cheer; the other short,
thin, sallow with thick black hair
and a sour mien. Ruth also acknowledged their greeting. "This
is my grandmother," David said
proudly. "Miss Cynthie, meet my
managers, Lou and Lee Goldman." "Pleased to meet you,"
managed Miss Cynthie. "Great
lad, this boy of yours," said Lou
Goldman. "Great little partner
he's got, too," added Lee. They
also settled back expectantly.

"Here we go!"

The curtain rose to reveal a
cotton-field at dawn. Pickers in
blue denim overalls, bandanas,
and wide-brimmed straws, or in
gingham aprons and sun-bonnets,
were singing as they worked.
Their voices, from clearest so-
prano to richest bass, blended in
low concordances, first simply
humming a series of harmonies,

until, gradually, came words, like figures forming in mist. As the sound grew, the mist cleared, the words came round and full, and the sun rose bringing light as if in answer to the song. The chorus swelled, the radiance grew, the two, as if emanating from a single source, fused their crescendos, till at last they achieved a joint transcendence of tonal and visual brightness.

"Swell opener," said Lee Goldman.

"Ripe," agreed Lou.

David and Ruth arose. "Stay here and enjoy the show, Miss Cynthie. You'll see us again in a minute."

"Go to it, kids," said Lou Goldman.

"Yea—burn 'em up," said Lee.

Miss Cynthie hardly noted that she had been left, so absorbed was she in the spectacle. To her, the theatre had always been the antithesis of the church. As the one was the refuge of righteousness, so the other was the stronghold of transgression. But this first scene awakened memories, captured and held her attention by offering a blend of truth and novelty. Having thus baited her interest, the show now proceeded to play it like the trout through swift-flowing waters of wickedness. Resist as it might, her mind was caught and drawn into the impious subsequences.

The very music that had just rounded out so majestically now distorted itself into ragtime. The singers came forward and turned to dancers; boys, a crazy, swaying background, threw up their arms and kicked out their legs in a rhythmic jamboree; girls, an agile, brazen foreground, caught their skirts up to their hips and displayed their copper calves, knees, thighs in shameless, incredible steps. Miss Cynthie turned dismayed eyes upon the audience, to discover that mob of sinners devouring it all with fond satisfaction. Then the dancers separated and with final abandon, flung themselves off the stage in both directions.

Lee Goldman commented through the applause, "They work easy, them babies."

"Yea," said Lou. "Savin' the hot stuff for later."

Two black-faced cotton-pickers appropriated the scene, indulging in dialogue that their hearers found uproarious.

"Ah'm tired."

"Ah'm hongry."

"Dis job jes' wears me out."

"Starves me to death."

"Ah'm so tired—you know what Ah'd like to do?"

"What?"

"Ah'd like to go to sleep and dream I was sleepin'."

"What good dat do?"

"Den I could wake up and still be 'sleep."

"Well y'know what Ah'd like to do?"

"No. What?"

"Ah'd like to swaller me a hog and a hen."

"What good dat do?"

"Den Ah'd always be full o' ham and eggs."

"Ham? Shuh. Don't you know a hog has to be smoked 'fo' he's a ham?"

"Well, if I swaller him, he'll have a smoke all around him, won't he?"

Presently Miss Cynthie was smiling like everyone else, but her smile soon fled. For the comics departed, and the dancing girls returned, this time in scant travesties on their earlier voluminous costumes—tiny sun-bonnets perched jauntily on one side of their glistening bobs, bandanas reduced to scarlet neck-ribbons, waists mere brassieres, skirts mere gingham sashes.

And now Miss Cynthie's whole body stiffened with a new and surpassing shock; her bright eyes first widened with unbelief, then slowly grew dull with misery. In the midst of a sudden great volley of applause her grandson had broken through that bevy of agile wantons and begun to sing.

He too was dressed as a cotton-picker, but a Beau Brummell among cotton pickers; his hat bore a pleated green band, his bandana was silk, his overalls blue satin, his shoes black patent leather. His eyes flashed, his teeth gleamed, his body swayed, his arms waved, his words came fast and clear. As he sang, his companions danced a concerted tap, uniformly wild, ecstatic. When he stopped singing, he himself began to dance, and

without sacrificing crispness of execution, seemed to absorb into himself every measure of the energy which the girls, now merely standing off and swaying, had relinquished.

"Look at that boy go," said Lee Goldman.

"He ain't started yet," said Lou.

But surrounding comment, Dave's virtuosity, the eager enthusiasm of the audience were all alike lost on Miss Cynthie. She sat with stricken eyes watching this boy whom she'd raised from a babe, taught right from wrong, brought up in the church, and endowed with her prayers, this child whom she had dreamed of seeing a preacher, a regular doctor, a tooth-doctor, a foot-doctor, at the very least an undertaker— sat watching him disport himself for the benefit of a sinen—sick, flesh-hungry mob of lost souls, not one of whom knew or cared to know the loving kindness of God; sat watching a David she'd never foreseen, turned tool of the devil, disciple of lust, unholy prince among sinners.

For a long time she sat there watching with wretched eyes, saw portrayed on the stage David's arrival in Harlem, his escape from 'old friends' who tried to dupe him; saw him working as a trap-drummer in a night-club, where he fell in love with Ruth, a dancer; not the gentle Ruth Miss Cynthie knew, but a wild and shameless young savage who danced like seven devils—in only a girdle and breastplates; saw the two of them join in a song-and-dance act that eventually made them Broadway headliners, an act presented *in toto* as the pre-finale of this show. And not any of the melodies, not any of the sketches, not all the comic philosophy of the tired-and-hungry duo, gave her figure a moment's relaxation or brightened the dull defeat in her staring eyes. She sat apart, alone in the box, the symbol, the epitome of supreme failure. Let the rest of the theatre be riotous, clamoring for more and more of Dave Tappen, "Tap," the greatest tapster of all time, idol of uptown and downtown New York. For her, they were lauding simply an exhibition of sin which centered about her David.

"This'll run a year on Broadway," said Lee Goldman.

"Then we'll take it to Paris."

Encores and curtains with Ruth, and at last David came out on the stage alone. The clamor dwindled. And now he did something quite unfamiliar to even the most consistent of his followers. Softly, delicately, he began to tap a routine designed to fit a particular song. When he had established the rhythm, he began to sing the song:

"Oh I danced with the gal with the hole in her stockin',
And her toe kep' a-kickin' and her heel kep' a-knockin'—

Come up, Jesse, and get a drink o' gin,

'Cause you near to the heaven as you'll ever get ag'in'—"

As he danced and sang this song, frequently smiling across at Miss Cynthie, a visible change transformed her. She leaned forward incredulously, listened intently, then settled back in limp wonder. Her bewildered eyes turned on the crowd, on those serried rows of shriftless sinners. And she found in their faces now an overwhelmingly curious thing; a grin, a universal grin, a gleeful and sinless grin such as not the nakedest chorus in the performance had produced. In a few seconds, with her own song, David had dwarfed into unimportance, wiped off their faces, swept out of their minds every trace of what had seemed to be sin; had reduced it all to mere trivial detail and revealed these revelers as a crowd of children, enjoying the guileless antics of another child. And Miss Cynthie whispered:

"Bless my soul! They didn't mean nothin' . . . They jes didn't see no harm in it—"

"Then I danced with the gal with the dimple in her cheek,
And if she'd 'a' kep' a-smilin', I'd 'a' danced for a week—
'Come up, Jesse—' "

The crowd laughed, clapped their hands, whistled. Someone

threw David a bright yellow flower. "From Broadway!"

He caught the flower. A hush fell. He said:

"I'm really happy tonight, folks. Y'see this flower? Means success, don't it? Well, listen. The one who is really responsible for my success is here tonight with me. Now what do you think o' that?"

The hush deepened.

"Y'know folks, I'm sump'm like Adam—I never had no mother. But I've got a grandmother. Down home everybody calls her Miss Cynthie. And everybody loves her. Take that song I just did for you. Miss Cynthie taught me that when I wasn't knee-high to a cricket. But that wasn't all she taught me. Far back as I can remember, she used to always say one thing: Son, do like a church steeple—aim high and go straight. And for doin' it—" he grinned, contemplating the flower—"I get this."

He strode across to the edge of the stage that touched Miss Cynthie's box. He held up the flower.

"So y'see, folks, this isn't mine. It's really Miss Cynthie's." He leaned over to hand it to her. Miss Cynthie's last trace of doubt was swept away. She drew a deep breath of revelation; her bewilderment vanished, her redoubtable composure returned, her eyes lighted up; and no one but David, still holding the flower toward her, heard her sharply whispered reprimand:

"Keep it, you fool. Where's yo' manners—givin' 'way what somebody give you?"

David grinned:

"Take it, tyro. What you tryin' to do—crab my act?"

Thereupon, Miss Cynthie, smiling at him with bright, meaningful eyes, leaned over without rising from her chair, jerked a tiny twig off the stem of the flower, then sat decisively back, resolutely folding her arms, with only a leaf in her hand.

"This'll do me," she said.

The finale didn't matter. People filed out of the theatre. Miss Cynthie sat awaiting her children, her foot absently patting time to the orchestra's jazz recessional. Perhaps she was thinking, "God moves in a mysterious way," but her lips were unquestionably forming the words:

"—danced with the gal—hole in in her stockin'—
—toe kep' a-kickin'—heel kep' a knockin'."

Questions for Discussion

1. WHY WAS Miss Cynthie so surprised when the Red Cap addressed her as "Madam?"

2. WHAT WERE Miss Cynthie's ambitions for her grandson? Why were those ambitions never realized?

3. WE ARE KEPT GUESSING as to what Miss Cynthie's grandson really is. How does the author keep the reader in a state of suspense in this story?

4. WHAT IS the first clue in the story that David Tappen, Miss Cynthie's grandson, is some one special?

5. AT THIS POINT in the story, what did you think David was going to turn out to be?

6. WHAT INDICATIONS are there in the story that Miss Cynthie has spirit and a young outlook on life that you wouldn't expect to find in a seventy-year-old grandmother?

7. MISS CYNTHIA VIEWED the skyscrapers of New York, elevated trains, the broad streets with speeding traffic. Yet she didn't say a word. What was the first thing she exclaimed about? What does this tell us about her?

8. DAVE TAPPEN took his grandmother to the theater. How did Miss Cynthie feel about theater-going? What kind of people usually have this attitude toward all forms of entertainment?

9. WHY WAS Miss Cynthie so utterly distressed when she learned that her beloved grandson was not a doctor, not even an undertaker, but an entertainer?

10. AT THE END of his act Dave Tappen sang the folk tune which his grandmother had taught him. What effect did it have on Miss Cynthie and the whole audience? Why did it change the despairing way Miss Cynthie was viewing her grandson's performance?

11. HIS GRANDMOTHER'S ADVICE was "aim high and go straight." In becoming a Broadway entertainer, did Dave follow that advice? In what way?

12. DO YOU THINK Miss Cynthie would have been more pleased if her grandson had become an undertaker? Support your answer with references to the story.

13. MISS CYNTHIE is quite different from the usual picture we have of a grandmother. What kind of person is she? Do you like her? Tell why you do or don't.

♧

Building Vocabulary

Getting the Meaning from the Context. In each of the following sentences taken from the story, select from the choices given, the word or phrase that means the same as the word in heavy type. Check your answer by looking up the word in a dictionary. Write the ones you get wrong in your special vocabulary list.

———

1. ... "He surrounded himself with her **impedimenta** (im-ped-ih-men'tuh) ..." (p. 103)
A. implements   B. directions   C. annoying glances   D. baggage

2. ". . . The dancing girls returned . . . in scant **travesties** (trav'es-tees) of their earlier voluminous costumes." (p. 110)
A. imitations   B. vests   C. travelers   D. stockings

3. ". . . His companions danced a concerted tap, uniformly wild, **ecstatic** (ek-stat'ik)." (p. 110)
A. sorry   B. high   C. joyful   D. exaggerated

4. "Dave's **virtuosity** (vuhr-tyoo-os'ih-tee), the eager enthusiasm of the audience were all lost alike on Miss Cynthie." (p. 110)

A. skill   B. morality   C. witty answer   D. handsomeness

5. "She sat apart, ... the symbol, the **epitome** (ih-pit'uh-mee) of supreme failure." (p. 111)
A. name   B. summary   C. peak   D. depth

6. "She leaned forward **incredulously** (in-kred'yoo-lus-lee), listened intently ..." (p. 111)
A. unbelievingly   B. keenly   C. enjoyably   D. foolishly

7. "Her bewildered eyes turned on the crowd, on those **serried** (ser'reed) rows ..." (p. 111)
A. well-dressed   B. serious looking   C. pressed together   D. orderly

8. ". . . David had revealed these **revelers** (rev'il-uhz) as a crowd of children ..." (p. 111)
A. sinners   B. merry-makers   C. strong men   D. athletes

9. ". . . Enjoying the guileless **antics** (an'tiks) of another child." (p. 111)

A. actions   B. high leaps   C. fantasies   D. funny behavior

10. ". . . Her bewilderment vanished, her **redoubtable** (ree-dout'uh-bl) composure returned . . ." (p. 112)

A. worthy of respect   B. without alarm   C. genuine   D. too far

Setting

1. THE SETTING is the environment for the action of a story. Included would be the physical background with shifts from one scene to another, the time period during which the action takes place, and the way in which the characters live. In "Miss Cynthie" the author gives us four different backdrops for the events of the story. What are the four settings in New York City?

2. FROM THE EVIDENCE in the story, approximately when does it take place?

3. MENTION some of the features of New York that elicited only faint interest on the part of Miss Cynthie.

4. How DID Miss Cynthie know she was in Harlem, even though she had never been in Harlem in her life?

5. How IS the atmosphere of Harlem different from other parts of the city?

6. A THEATER is the scene for the latter part of the story. Miss Cynthie attends although it is against her moral principles, believing popular entertainment to be the work of the devil. Explain how the theatrical background is necessary to work out the conflict in Miss Cynthie's mind regarding her grandson's choice of career.

⊙❀⊙

Thinking and Writing

1. Miss Cynthie was a stranger in New York City, but its big-ness didn't faze her. We have all been to other places and made mental comparisons with our own abode. Write a comparison of a place you have visited with your own place of residence.

2. Miss Cynthie wanted her grandson to be a preacher or a doctor and if he couldn't manage that to become a dentist, or a foot-doctor, or at least an undertaker. He turned out to be none of those things. Write about your own ambition in life and tell whether it is the same goal as envisioned by your parents.

3. Dave did not turn out to be what Miss Cynthie envisioned for him. He wasn't even an undertaker. Did she become recon-ciled to his career behind the footlights? Write an account of what you think she said to Dave after the show.

⊙❀⊙

About the Author

Writing was an avocation for Rudolph Fisher, since by profes-sion he was a doctor. Although he was born in Washington, D. C., he was educated in Rhode Island and received degrees from Brown University in Providence. Fisher then entered Howard Medical School and later took specialized work at the College of Physicians and Surgeons of Columbia University. He began his practice of medicine in 1927.

Fisher's literary career paralleled his medical career. While still in medical school he found time to write short stories that were published in the *Atlantic Monthly* and *Story Magazine*. In addition, he authored two novels before his untimely death in 1934 at the age of thirty-seven.

Mista
Courifer

The coffin-maker of Freetown, in Sierra Leone, was happy following the pattern of life he had laid out for himself. While his trade might have been lugubrious, he was quite content with his English clothes and his English house transplanted to Africa.

However, his son was cut out of different cloth. Should a son follow in his father's footsteps? The son of Mista Courifer caused him a great deal of grief. The son sought another kind of life for himself. Who was to say whether the son's ideas were old-fashioned or daringly modern?

Mista Courifer

By Adelaide Casely-Hayford

Not a sound was heard in the coffin-maker's workshop, that is to say no human sound. Mista Courifer, a solid citizen of Sierra Leone, was not given to much speech. His apprentices, knowing this, never dared address him unless he spoke first. Then they only carried on their conversation in whispers. Not that Mista Courifer did not know how to use his tongue. It was incessantly wagging to and fro in his mouth at every blow of the hammer. But his shop in the heart of Freetown was a part of his house. And, as he had once confided to a friend, he was a silent member of his own household from necessity. His wife, given to much speaking, could outtalk him.

"It's no use for argue wid woman," he said cautiously. "Just like 'e no use for teach woman carpentering; she nebba sabi for hit de nail on de head. If 'e argue, she'll hit eberyting but de nail; and so wid de carpentering."

So, around his wife, with the

119

exception of his tongue's continual wagging like a pendulum, his mouth was kept more or less shut. But whatever self-control he exercised in this respect at home was completely sent to the wind in his official capacity as the local preacher at chapel, for Mista Courifer was one of the pillars of the church, being equally at home in conducting a prayer meeting, superintending the Sunday school or occupying the pulpit.

His voice was remarkable for its wonderful gradations of pitch. He would insist on starting most of his tunes himself; consequently they nearly always ended in a solo. If he happened to pitch in the bass, he descended into such a *de profundis* that his congregations were left to flounder in a higher key; if he started in the treble, he soared so high that the children stared at him open-mouthed and their elders were lost in wonder and amazement. As for his prayers, he roared and volleyed and thundered to such an extent that poor little mites were quickly reduced to a state of collapse and started to whisper from sheer fright.

But he was most at home in the pulpit. It is true, his labors were altogether confined to the outlying village districts of Regent, Gloucester and Leicester, an arrangement with which he was by no means satisfied. Still, a village congregation is better than none at all.

His favorite themes were Jonah and Noah and he was forever pointing out the great similarity between the two, generally finishing his discourse after this manner: "You see my beloved Brebren, den two man berry much alike. All two lived in a sinful and adulterous generation. One get inside am ark; de odder get inside a whale. Day bof seek a refuge fom de swelling waves.

"And so it is today my beloved Brebren. No matter if we get inside a whale or get inside an ark, as long as we get inside some place of safety—as long as we can find some refuge, some hiding place from de wiles ob de debil."

But his congregation was by no means always convinced.

Mr. Courifer always wore black. He was one of the Sierra Leone gentlemen who consider everything European to be not only the right thing, but the *only* thing for the African, and having read somewhere that English undertakers generally appeared in somber attire, he immediately followed suit.

He even went so far as to build a European house. During his short stay in England, he had noticed how the houses were built and furnished and had forthwith erected himself one after the approved pattern—a house with stuffy little passages, narrow little staircases and poky rooms, all crammed with saddlebags and carpeted with Axminsters. No wonder his wife had to talk. It was so hopelessly uncomfortable, stuffy and unsanitary.

So Mr. Courifer wore black. It never struck him for a single moment that red would have been more appropriate, far more becoming, far less expensive and far more national. No! It must be black. He would have liked blue black, but he wore rusty black for economy.

There was one subject upon which Mr. Courifer could talk even at home, so no one ever mentioned it: his son, Tomas. Mr. Courifer had great expectations for his son; indeed in the back of his mind he had hopes of seeing him reach the high-water mark of red-tape officialism, for Tomas was in the government service. Not very high up, it is true, but still he was in it. It was an honor that impressed his father deeply, but Tomas unfortunately did not seem to think quite so much of it. The youth in question, however, was altogether neutral in his opinions in his father's presence. Although somewhat feminine as to attire, he was distinctly masculine in his speech. His neutrality was not a matter of choice, since no one was allowed to choose anything in the Courifer family but the paterfamilias himself.

From start to finish, Tomas's career had been cut out, and in spite of the fact that nature had endowed him with a black skin and an African temperament, Tomas was to be an Englishman.

He was even to be an Englishman in appearance.

Consequently, once a year mysterious bundles arrived by parcel post. When opened, they revealed marvelous checks and plaids in vivid greens and blues after the fashion of a Liverpool counter-jumper, waistcoats decorative in the extreme with their bold designs and rows of brass buttons, socks vying with the rainbow in glory and pumps very patent in appearance and very fragile as to texture.

Now, Tomas was no longer a minor and he keenly resented having his clothes chosen for him like a boy going to school for the first time. Indeed on one occasion, had it not been for his sister's timely interference, he would have chucked the whole collection into the fire.

Dear little Keren-happuch, eight years his junior and not at all attractive, with a very diminutive body and a very large heart. Such a mistake! People's hearts ought always to be in proportion to their size, otherwise it upsets the dimensions of the whole structure and often ends in its total collapse.

Keren was that type of little individual whom nobody worshipped, consequently she understood the art of worshipping others to the full. Tomas was the object of her adoration. Upon him she lavished the whole store of her boundless wealth and whatever hurt Tomas became positive torture as far as Keren-happuch was concerned.

"Tomas!" she said clinging to him with the tenacity of a bear, as she saw the faggots piled up high, ready for the conflagration. "Do yah! No burn am oh! Ole man go flog you oh! Den clos berry fine! I like am myself too much. I wish"—she added wistfully—"me na boy; I wish I could use am."

This was quite a new feature which had never struck Tomas before. Keren-happuch had never received a bundle of English clothes in her life, hence her great appreciation of them.

At first Tomas only laughed —the superior daredevil, don't-care-a-damn-about-consequences laugh of the brave before the deed. But after hearing that wistful little sentence, he forgot his own annoyance and awoke to his responsibilities as an elder brother.

A few Sundays later, Tomas Courifer, Jr., marched up the aisle of the little Wesleyan chapel in all his Liverpool magnificence accompanied by a very elated Keren-happuch whose natural unattractiveness had been further accentuated by a vivid cerise costume —a heterogeneous mass of frill and furbelows. But the glory of her array by no means outshone the brightness of her smile. Indeed that smile seemed to illuminate the whole church and to dispel the usual melancholy preceding the recital of Jonah and his woes.

Unfortunately, Tomas had a very poor opinion of the government service and in a burst of confidence he had told Keren that he meant to chuck it at the very first opportunity. In vain his sister expostulated and pointed out the advantages connected with it— the honor, the pension—and the awful nemesis upon the head of anyone incurring the head-of-the-family's ire.

"Why you want leave am, Tomas?" she asked desperately.

"Because I never get a proper holiday. I have been in the office four and a half years and have never had a whole week off yet. And," he went on vehemently, "these white chaps come and go, and a fresh one upsets what the old one has done and a newcomer upsets what he does and they all only stay for a year and a half and go away for four months, drawing big fat pay all the time, not to speak of passages, whereas a poor African like me has to work year in and year out with never a chance of a decent break. But you needn't be afraid, Keren dear," he added consolingly. "I shan't resign. I shall just behave so badly that they'll chuck me and then my ole man can't say very much."

Accordingly when Tomas, puffing a cigarette, sauntered into the office at 9 a.m. instead of 8 a.m. for the fourth time that week, Mr. Buckmaster, who had hitherto maintained a discreet silence and kept his eyes shut, opened them wide and administered a sharp rebuke. Tomas's conscience was profoundly stirred. Mr. Buckmaster was one of the few white men for whom he had a deep respect, aye, in the depth of his heart, he really had a sneaking regard. It was for fear of offending him that he had remained so long at his post.

But he had only lately heard that his chief was due for leave so he decided there and then to say a long good-by to a service which had treated him so shabbily. He was a vociferous reader of half-penny newspapers and he knew that the humblest shop assistant in England was entitled to a fort-night's holiday every year. Therefore it was ridiculous to argue that because he was an African working in Africa there was no need for a holiday. All his applications for leave were quietly pigeonholed for a more convenient season.

"Courifer!" Mr. Buckmaster said sternly. "Walk into my private office please." And Courifer knew that this was the beginning of the end.

"I suppose you know that the office hours are from 8 a.m. till 4 p.m. daily," commenced Mr. Buckmaster, in a freezing tone.

"Yes, er—Sir!" stammered Courifer with his heart in his mouth and his mouth twisted up into a hard sailor's knot.

"And I suppose you also know that smoking is strictly forbidden in the office?"

"Yes, er-er—Sir!" stammered the youth.

"Now hitherto," the even tones went on, "I have always looked upon you as an exemplary clerk, strictly obliging, punctual, accurate and honest, but for the last two or three weeks I have had nothing but complaints about you. And from what I myself have seen, I am afraid they are not altogether unmerited."

Mr. Buckmaster rose as he spoke, took a bunch of keys out of his pocket and unlocking his roll-top desk, drew out a sheaf of papers. "This is your work, is it not?" he said to the youth.

"Yes, er—er—Sir!" he stuttered, looking shamefacedly at the dirty, ink-stained, blotched sheets of closely typewritten matter.

"Then what in Heaven's name is the matter with you to produce such work?"

Tomas remained silent for a moment or two. He summoned up courage to look boldly at the stern countenance of his chief. And as he looked, the sternness seemed to melt away and he could see genuine concern there.

"Please, er—Sir!" he stammered, "May—I—er—just tell you everything?"

Half an hour later, a very quiet, subdued, penitent Tomas Courifer walked out of the office by a side door. Mr. Buckmaster followed later, taking with him an increased respect for the powers of endurance exercised by the growing West African youth.

Six weeks later, Mista Courifer

was busily occupied wagging his tongue when he looked up from his work to see a European man standing in his doorway.

The undertaker found speech and a chair simultaneously. "Good afternoon, Sah!" he said, dusting the chair before offering it to his visitor. "I hope you don't want a coffin, Sah!" which was a deep-sea lie for nothing pleased him more than the opportunity of making a coffin for a European. He was always so sure of the money. Such handsome money—paid it is true with a few ejaculations, but paid on the nail and without any deductions whatsoever. Now with his own people things were different. They demurred, they haggled, they bartered, they gave him detailed accounts of all their other expenses and then, after keeping him waiting for weeks, they would end by sending him half the amount with a stern exhortation to be thankful for that.

Mr. Buckmaster took the proffered chair and answered pleasantly: "No thank you, I don't intend dying just yet. I happened to be passing so I thought I should just like a word with you about your son."

Mr. Courifer bristled all over with exultation and expectation. Perhaps they were going to make his son a kind of undersecretary of state. What an unexpected honor for the Courifer family. What a rise in their social status; what a rise out of their neighbors. How good God was!.

"Of course you know he is in my office?"

"Oh yes, Sah. He often speaks about you."

"Well, I am going home very soon and as I may not be returning to Sierra Leone, I just wanted to tell you how pleased I should be at any time to give him a decent testimonial."

Mr. Courifer's countenance fell. What a comedown!

"Yes, Sah," he answered somewhat dubiously.

"I can recommend him highly as being steady, persevering, reliable and trustworthy. And you can always apply to me if ever such a thing be necessary."

Was that all! What a disappointment! Still it was something worth having. Mr. Buckmaster was an Englishman and a testimonial from him would certainly be a very valuable possession. He rubbed his hands together as he said:

"Well I am berry much obliged to you, Sah, berry much obliged. And as time is short and we nebba know what a day may bring forth, would you mind writing one down now, Sah?"

"Certainly. If you will give me a sheet of paper, I shall do so at once."

Before Tomas returned home from his evening work, the testimonial was already framed and hanging up amidst the moth-eaten velvet of the drawing room.

On the following Monday morning, Courifer Jr. bounced into his father's workshop, upsetting the equilibrium of the carpenter's bench and also of the voiceless apprentice hard at work.

"Well, Sah?" ejaculated his father, surveying him in disgust. "You berry late. Why you no go office dis morning?"

"Because I've got a whole two months' holiday, Sir!" Just think of it—two whole months—with nothing to do but just enjoy myself!"

"Tomas," his father said solemnly, peering at him over his glasses, "you must larn for make coffins. You get fine chance now."

Sotto Voce: "I'll be damned if I will!" Aloud: "No thank you, Sir. I am going to learn how to make love, after which I am going to learn how to build myself a nice mud hut."

"And who dis gal you want married?" thundered his father, ignoring the latter part of the sentence altogether.

A broad smile illuminated Tomas's countenance. "She is a very nice girl, Sir, a very nice girl. Very quiet and gentle and sweet, and she doesn't talk too much."

"I see. Is dat all?"

"Oh, no. She can sew and clean and make a nice little home. And she has plenty sense; she will make a good mother."

"Yes, notting pass dat!"

"She has been to school for a long time. She reads nice books and she writes, oh, such a nice letter," said Tomas, patting his breast-pocket affectionately.

"I see, I suppose she sabi cook good fashion?"

"I don't know, I don't think so, and it doesn't matter very much.

"What!" roared the old man, "You mean tell me you want married woman who no sabi cook?"

"I want to marry her because I love her, Sir!"

"Dat's all right, but for we country, de heart and de stomach always go togedder. For we country, black man no want married woman who no sabi cook! Dat de berry first requisitional. You own mudder sabi cook."

That's the reason why she has been nothing but your miserable drudge all these years, thought the young man. His face was very grave as he rejoined: "The style in our country is not at all nice, Sir. I don't like to see a wife slaving away in the kitchen all times to make good chop for her husband who sits down alone and eats the best of everything himself, and she and the children get only the leavings. No thank you! And besides, Sir, you are always telling me that you want me to be an Englishman. That is why I always try to talk good English to you."

"Yes, dat's all right. Dat's berry good. But I want make you look like Englishman. I don't say you must copy all der different way!"

"Well, Sir, if I try till I die, I shall never look like an Englishman, and I don't know that I want to. But there are some English customs that I like very much indeed. I like the way white men treat their wives; I like their home life; I like to see mother and father and the little family all sitting down eating their meals together."

"I see," retorted his father sarcastically. "And who go cook den meal. You tink say wid your four pound a month, you go able hire a perfessional cook?"

"Oh, I don't say so, Sir. And I am sure if Accastasia does not know how to cook now, she will before we are married. But what I want you to understand is just this, that whether she is able to cook or not, I shall marry her just the same."

"Berry well," shouted his father, wrath delineated in every feature, "but instead of building one mud hut you better go one time build one madhouse."

"Sir, thank you. But I know what I am about and a mud hut will suit us perfectly for the present."

"A mud hut!" ejaculated his father in horror. "You done use fine England house wid staircase and balustrade and tick carpet and handsome furnitures. You want to go live in mud hut? You ungrateful boy, you shame me, oh!"

"Dear me, no, Sir. I won't shame you. It's going to be a nice clean spacious mud hut. And what is more, it is going to be a sweet little home, just big enough for two. I am going to distemper the

walls pale green, like at the principal's rooms at Kerén's school."

"How you sabi den woman's rooms?"

"Because you have sent me two or three times to pay her school fees, so I have looked at those walls and I like them too much."

"I see. And what else you go do?" asked his father ironically.

"I am going to order some nice wicker chairs from the Islands and a few good pieces of linoleum for the floors and then—"

"And den what?"

"I shall bring home my bride."

Mr. Courifer's dejection grew deeper with each moment. A mud hut! This son of his—the hope of his life! A government officer! A would-be Englishman! To live in a mud hut! His disgust knew no bounds. "You ungrateful wretch!" he bellowed, "You go disgrace me. You go lower your pore father. You go lower your position for de office."

"I am sorry, Sir," retorted the young man. "I don't wish to offend you. I'm grateful for all you have done for me. But I have had a raise in salary and I want a home of my own which, after all, is only natural, and"—he went on steadily, staring his father straight in the face—"I may as well tell you at once, you need not order any more Liverpool suits for me."

"Why not?" thundered his irate parent, removing his specs lest any harm should befall them.

"Well, I am sorry to grieve you,

Sir, but I have been trying to live up to your European standards all this time. Now I am going to chuck it once and for all. I am going back to the native costume of my mother's people, and the next time I appear in chapel it will be as a Wolof."

The very next Sunday the awful shock of seeing his son walk up the aisle of the church in pantaloons and the bright loose over-jacket of a Wolof from Gambia, escorting a pretty young bride the color of cholocate, also in native dress, so unnerved Mista Courifer that his mind suddenly became a complete blank. He could not even remember Jonah and the whale, nor could his tongue possess one word to let fly, not one. The service had to be turned into a prayer meeting.

Mista Courifer is the local preacher no longer. Now he only makes coffins.

Questions for Discussion

1. As ONE of the African stories in this book, "Mista Courifer" has a distinctive flavor and atmosphere that sets it apart from the other stories. What accounts for this difference?

2. MISTA COURIFER affected everything English. How did he carry out this liking for English things in Sierra Leone?

3. How DID young Tomas feel about his father's desire to make an Englishman out of him?

4. WHAT GRIEVANCES did Tomas have against the government service? Was he justified in his complaints against this form of colonialism?

5. TOMAS KNEW his father would never stand for his resigning from his government post. What course of action did he decide to take about his job?

6. MISTA COURIFER was aghast when he heard his son wanted to marry a native girl and then go to live in a mud hut. What were the fundamental reasons for the conflict between father and son?

7. WHY DID Mista Courifer regard it as important for a bride to know how to cook? Do you consider it essential?

8. THERE WERE many things Tomas didn't like about English customs. What aspects of the English way of life did he admire?

9. Is IT POSSIBLE to make an English gentleman out of an African? Was Tomas wiser than his father in thinking it was impossible to transform an African into an Englishman? What meaning does this have for the future of Africa?

10. How WAS Mista Courifer's life changed by the action of his son in going native?

11. THE AFRICAN SPEECH employed in the story is a kind of pidgin English or a patois. How do you account for the contrast in the speech of the father and son?

12. Do YOU SEE any relationship in this father-son conflict to a broader picture of social development in Africa? Was Tomas returning to an old-fashioned way of living or was he pointing the way to the future? What message does the author leave with the reader?

Building Vocabulary

Getting the meaning from the context. In each of the following sentences taken from the story, select from the choices given the word or phrase that means the same as the word in heavy type. Check your answer by looking up the word in a dictionary. Write the ones you get wrong in your special vocabulary list.

---

1. "(His tongue) was **incessantly** (in-ses'int-lee) wagging to and fro in his mouth . . ." (p. 119)

   A. slowly B. continually C. rapidly D. surely

2. "His voice was remarkable for its wonderful **gradations** (gray-day'shuns) of pitch." (p. 120)

   A. certificates B. long stops C. short songs D. successive steps

3. ". . . generally finishing his **discourse** (dis-kaws') after this manner . . ." (p. 120)

   A. speech B. contest C. great distance D. discount

4. ". . . Keren . . . with a very **diminutive** (dih-min'you-tive) body and a very large heart." (p. 121)

   A. too tall B. far-sighted C. very small D. always clean

5. ". . . she saw the faggots piled up high, ready for the **conflagration** (kon-flih-gray'shun)," (p. 122)

   A. fire B. signal flag C. smoke D. confrontation

6. ". . . a vivid cerise costume— a **heterogeneous** (het-uhr-oh-jee'nee-us) mass of frill and furbelows." (p. 122)

   A. alike B. real C. unlucky D. dissimilar

7. ". . . I have always looked upon you as an **exemplary** (egg-zem'pli-ree) clerk . . ." (p. 123)

   A. given warning B. doing wrong C. serving as a pattern D. looking for work

8. "They **demurred** (dee-muhrd'), they haggled, they bartered . . ." (p. 124)

   A. praised B. scratched C. exclaimed D. delayed

9. "I am going to **distemper** (dis-tem'puh) the walls pale green . . ." (p. 126)

   A. to get angry B. to paint C. to look up D. to offer

10. '"Why not?" thundered his **irate** (i'rate) parent. (p. 126)

    A. fiery B. handsome C. helpful D. angry

Plot Structure

A SHORT STORY presents a problem confronting the main character. The author plans a series of happenings leading to a high point in the action in an attempt to find a solution to the difficulty. All these steps take shape as the plot structure.

1. MISTA COURIFER's PROBLEM had been developing long before he became aware of it. What is the first incident that foreshadows the conflict involving Mista Courifer and his son? Why does the problem exist?

2. POINT OUT ANOTHER incident in the plot of the story that marks Tomas' rebellion against his father's authority.

3. TOMAS DECIDES to solve his personal problem by doing such poor work that he would be dismissed from his government position. This course of action does not turn out as he anticipates. Instead, he reveals to his astounded father that he has been given a two month's vacation. What does he plan to do with his holiday? What difficulty does this revelation lead to?

4. THE CONFRONTATION between father and son in the coffin shop represents the highest point in the action, the climax of the story. What takes place in this scene?

5. WHAT KIND of solution does the author work out to resolve the impasse resulting from the contradictory set of values of father and son?

6. IN THE FRAMEWORK of the plot structure, the anti-climax (the last event, which is less important than the preceding climax) takes place when Tomas and his bride walk up the aisle of Mista Courifer's church in native dress. What startling effect does this have on Mista Courifer?

7. Did you find the solution to this father-son struggle satisfying? Was there anything Mista Courifer could have done to avoid rejection by his son? Explain.

༄

Thinking and Writing

1. YOUNG TOMAS WANTED to marry a sweet and gentle girl, but his father raised formidable objections to her when he learned she couldn't cook. Write an account of the qualities you would look for in the one that you would want to marry.

2. MISTA COURIFER looked up to the English colonizer as the epitome of a superior way of life; his son wanted to revert to native ways. Write an essay defending the position that you prefer—the white man's ways or native customs—in the light of today's social, political and economic aspirations.

3. THE DIFFERENT outlook on life of Tomas and his father represents a generation gap. Write an essay showing your relationship with your parents, whether or not you think alike on the issues of the day, whether you find yourself in harmony with them or disagreeing on most things.

༄

About the Author

Adelaide Casely-Hayford was born in 1868 in Africa of mixed African and English blood. She was educated in European schools but returned to Sierra Leone to open a school, together with her sister, in 1897. After her marriage she traveled widely, visiting many parts of the world, and even lived for a while in the United States. She wrote her autobiography when she was advanced in years and died in 1959 at the age of 91.

By Richard Wright

From

Native Son

What kind of homes do most American Negros live in? What is it like to be a resident of a ghetto? What opportunities are there for a black person in a white society? Richard Wright answers these questions in a disturbing novel, entitled Native Son. *In the book, Bigger Thomas unintentionally kills Mary Dalton, his employer's daughter. He tries to put the blame on her boy friend, but his own guilt is discovered. Going into hiding in the Chicago slums, he kills a second time in order to cover up his trail. After a chase across roof tops Bigger is captured, tried and sentenced to death, although his lawyer tries to show that society had a large share in the blame for Bigger's criminal acts.*

The following story is taken from the first chapter of Native Son *and gives us a picture of the home background of twenty-year-old Bigger Thomas, the central character in this tragic tale.*

Brrrrrriiiiiiiiiiiiinng!

An alarm clock clanged in the dark and silent room. A bed spring creaked. A woman's voice sang out impatiently:

"Bigger, shut that thing off!"

A surly grunt sounded above the tinny ring of metal. Naked feet swished dryly across the planks in the wooden floor and the clang ceased abruptly.

"Turn on the light, Bigger."

"Awright," came a sleepy mumble.

Light flooded the room and revealed a black boy standing in a narrow space between two iron beds, rubbing his eyes with the back of his hands. From a bed to his right the woman spoke again:

"Buddy, get up from there! I got a big washing on my hands today and I want you-all out of here."

Another black boy rolled from bed and stood up. The woman also rose and stood in her nightgown.

"Turn your heads so I can dress," she said.

The two boys averted their eyes and gazed into a far corner of the room. The woman rushed out of her nightgown and put on a pair of step-ins. She turned to the bed from which she had risen and called:

"Vera! Get up from there!"

"What time is it, Ma?" asked a muffled, adolescent voice from beneath a quilt.

"Get up from there, I say!"

"O.K., Ma."

A brown-skinned girl in a cotton gown got up and stretched her arms above her head and yawned. Sleepily, she sat on a chair and fumbled with her stockings. The two boys kept their faces averted while their mother and sister put on enough clothes to keep them from feeling ashamed; and the mother and sister did the same while the boys dressed. Abruptly, they all paused, holding their clothes in their hands, their attention caught by a light tapping in the thinly plastered walls of the room. They forgot their conspiracy against shame and their eyes strayed apprehensively over the floor.

"There he is again, Bigger!" the woman screamed, and the tiny one-room apartment galvanized into violent action. A chair toppled as the woman, half-dressed, and in her stocking feet, scrambled breathlessly upon the bed. Her two sons, barefoot, stood tense and motionless, their eyes searching anxiously under the bed and chairs. The girl ran into a corner, half-stooped and gathered the hem of her slip into both of her hands and held it tightly over her knees.

"Oh! Oh!" she wailed.

"There he goes!"

The woman pointed a shaking finger. Her eyes were round with fascinated horror.

"Where?"

"I don't see 'im!"

"Bigger, he's behind the trunk!" the girl whimpered.

"Vera!" the woman screamed. "Get up here on the bed! Don't let that thing bite you!"

Frantically, Vera climbed upon the bed and the woman caught hold of her. With their arms entwined about each other, the black mother and the brown daughter gazed open-mouthed at the trunk in the corner.

Bigger looked round the room wildly, then darted to a curtain and swept it aside and grabbed two heavy iron skillets from a wall above a gas stove. He whirled and called softly to his brother, his eyes glued to the trunk.

"Buddy!"

"Yeah?"

"Here, take this skillet."

"O.K."

"Now, get over by the door!"

"O.K."

Buddy crouched by the door and held the iron skillet by its handle, his arm flexed and poised. Save for the quick, deep breathing of the four people, the room was quiet. Bigger crept on tiptoe toward the trunk with the skillet clutched stiffly in his hand, his eyes dancing and watching every inch of the wooden floor in front of him .He paused and, without moving an eye or muscle, called:

"Buddy!"

"Hunh?"

"Put that box in front of the hole so he can't get out!"

"O.K."

Buddy ran to a wooden box and shoved it quickly in front of a gaping hole in the molding and then backed again to the door, holding the skillet ready. Bigger eased to the trunk and peered behind it cautiously. He saw nothing. Carefully, he stuck out his bare foot and pushed the trunk a few inches.

"There he is!" the mother screamed again.

A huge black rat squealed and leaped at Bigger's trouser-leg and snagged it in his teeth, hanging on.

"Goddamn!" Bigger whispered fiercely, whirling and kicking out his leg with all the strength of his body. The force of his movement shook the rat loose and it sailed through the air and struck a wall. Instantly, it rolled over and leaped again. Bigger dodged and the rat landed against a table leg. With clenched teeth, Bigger held the skillet; he was afraid to hurl it, fearing that he might miss. The rat squeaked and turned and ran in a narrow circle, looking for a place to hide; it leaped again past Big-

ger and scurried on dry rasping feet to one side of the box and then to the other, searching for the hole. Then it turned and reared upon its hind legs.

"Hit 'im, Bigger!" Buddy shouted.

"Kill 'im!" the woman screamed.

The rat's belly pulsed with fear. Bigger advanced a step and the rat emitted a long thin song of defiance, its black beady eyes glittering, its tiny forefeet pawing the air restlessly. Bigger swung the skillet; it skidded over the floor, missing the rat, and clattered to a stop against a wall.

"Goddamn!"

The rat leaped. Bigger sprang to one side. The rat stopped under a chair and let out a furious screak. Bigger moved slowly backward toward the door.

"Gimme that skillet, Buddy," he asked quietly, not taking his eyes from the rat.

Buddy extended his hand. Bigger caught the skillet and lifted it high in the air. The rat scuttled across the floor and stopped again at the box and searched quickly for the hole; then it reared once more and bared long yellow fangs, piping shrilly, belly quivering.

Bigger aimed and let the skillet fly with a heavy grunt. There was a shattering of wood as the box caved in. The woman screamed and hid her face in her hands. Bigger tiptoed forward and peered.

"I got 'im," he muttered, his

clenched teeth bared in a smile. "By God, I got 'im."

He kicked the splintered box out of the way and the flat black body of the rat lay exposed, its two long yellow tusks showing distinctly. Bigger took a shoe and pounded the rat's head, crushing it, cursing hysterically.

. . . .

The woman on the bed sank to her knees and buried her face in the quilts and sobbed:

"Lord, Lord, have mercy. . . ."

"Aw, Mama," Vera whimpered, bending to her. "Don't cry. It's dead now."

The two brothers stood over the dead rat and spoke in tones of awed admiration.

. . . .

"He's over a foot long."

"How in hell do they get so big?"

"Eating garbage and anything else they can get."

"Look, Bigger, there's a three-inch rip in your pant-leg."

"Yeah; he was after me, all right."

"Please, Bigger, take 'im out," Vera begged.

"Aw, don't be so scary," Buddy said.

The woman on the bed continued to sob. Bigger took a piece of newspaper and gingerly lifted the rat by its tail and held it out at arm's length.

"Bigger, take 'im out," Vera begged again.

Bigger laughed and approached the bed with the dangling rat, swinging it to and fro like a pendulum, enjoying his sister's fear.

"Bigger!" Vera gasped convulsively; she screamed and swayed and closed her eyes and fell headlong across her mother and rolled limply from the bed to the floor.

"Bigger, for God's sake!" the mother sobbed, rising and bending over Vera. "Don't do that! Throw that rat out!"

He laid the rat down and started to dress.

"Bigger, help lift Vera to the bed," the mother said.

He paused and turned round.

"What's the matter?" he asked, feigning ignorance.

"Do what I asked you, will you, boy?"

He went to the bed and helped his mother lift Vera. Vera's eyes were closed. He turned away and finished dressing. He wrapped the rat in a newspaper and went out of the door and down the stairs and put it into a garbage can at the corner of the alley. When he returned to the room his mother was still bent over Vera, placing a wet towel upon her head. She straightened and faced him, her cheeks and eyes wet with tears and her lips tight with anger.

"Boy, sometimes I wonder what makes you act like you do."

"What I do now?" he demanded belligerently.

"Sometimes you act the biggest fool I ever saw."

"What you talking about?"

"You scared your sister with

that rat and she fainted! Ain't you got no sense at all?"

"Aw, I didn't know she was that scary."

"Buddy!" the mother called.

"Yessum."

"Take a newspaper and spread it over that spot."

"Yessum."

Buddy opened out a newspaper and covered the smear of blood on the floor where the rat had been crushed. Bigger went to the window and stood looking out abstractedly into the street. His mother glared at his back.

"Bigger, sometimes I wonder why I birthed you," she said bitterly.

Bigger looked at her and turned away.

"Maybe you oughtn't've. Maybe you ought to left me where I was."

"You shut your sassy mouth."

"Aw, for chrissakes!" Bigger said, lighting a cigarette.

"Buddy, pick up them skillets and put 'em in the sink," the mother said.

"Yessum."

Bigger walked across the floor and sat on the bed. His mother's eyes followed him.

"We wouldn't have to live in this garbage dump if you had any manhood in you," she said.

"Aw, don't start that again."

"How you feel, Vera?" the mother asked.

Vera raised her head and looked about the room as though expecting to see another rat.

"Oh, Mama!"

"You poor thing!"

"I couldn't help it. Bigger scared me."

"Did you hurt yourself?"

"I bumped my head."

"Here; take it easy. You'll be all right."

"How come Bigger acts that way?" Vera asked, crying again.

"He's just crazy," the mother said. "Just plain dumb black crazy."

"I'll be late for my sewing class at the Y.W.C.A.," Vera said.

"Here; stretch out on the bed. You'll feel better in a little while," the mother said.

She left Vera on the bed and turned a pair of cold eyes upon Bigger.

"Suppose you wake up some morning and find your sister dead? What would you think then?" she asked. "Suppose those rats cut our veins at night when we sleep? Naw! Nothing like that ever bothers you! All you care about is your own pleasure! Even when the relief offers you a job you won't take it till they threaten to cut off your food and starve you! Bigger, honest, you the most nocountest man I ever seen in all my life!"

"You done told me that a thousand times," he said, not looking round.

"Well, I'm telling you agin! And mark my word, some of these days you going to set down and cry. Some of these days you going to wish you had made something out of yourself, instead of just a tramp. But it'll be too late then."

"Stop prophesying about me," he said.

"I prophesy much as I please! And if you don't like it, you can get out. We can get along without you. We can live in one room just like we living now, even with you gone," she said.

"Aw, for chrissakes!" he said, his voice filled with nervous irritation.

"You'll regret how you living some day," she went on. "If you don't stop running with that gang of yours and do right you'll end up where you never thought you would. You think I don't know what you boys is doing, but I do. And the gallows is at the end of the road you traveling, boy. Just remember that." She turned and looked at Buddy. "Throw that box outside, Buddy."

"Yessum."

There was silence. Buddy took the box out. The mother went behind the curtain to the gas stove. Vera sat up in bed and swung her feet to the floor.

"Lay back down, Vera," the mother said.

"I feel all right now, Ma. I got to go to my sewing class."

"Well, if you feel like it, set the table," the mother said, going behind the curtain again. "Lord, I get so tired of this I don't know what to do." her voice floated plaintively from behind the cur-

tain. "All I ever do is try to make a home for you children and you don't care."

"Aw, Ma," Vera protested. "Don't say that."

"Vera sometimes I just want to lay down and quit."

"Ma, please don't say that."

"I can't last many more years, living like this."

"I'll be old enough to work soon, Ma."

"I reckon I'll be dead then. I reckon God'll call me home."

Vera went behind the curtain and Bigger heard her trying to comfort his mother. He shut their voices out of his mind. He hated his family because he knew that they were suffering and that he was powerless to help them. He knew that the moment he allowed himself to feel to its fullness how they lived, the shame and misery of their lives, he would be swept out of himself with fear and despair. So he held toward them an attitude of iron reserve; he lived with them, but behind a wall, a curtain. And toward himself he was even more exacting. He knew that the moment he allowed what his life meant to enter fully into his consciousness, he would either kill himself or someone else. So he denied himself and acted tough.

He got up and crushed his cigarette upon the window sill. Vera came into the room and placed knives and forks upon the table.

"Get ready to eat, you-all," the mother called.

He sat at the table. The odor of frying bacon and boiling coffee drifted to him from behind the curtain. His mother's voice floated to him in song.

Life is like a mountain railroad
With an engineer that's brave
We must make the run success-
ful
From the cradle to the
grave . . . .

The song irked him and he was glad when she stopped and came into the room with a pot of coffee and a plate of crinkled bacon. Vera brought the bread in and they sat down. His mother closed her eyes and lowered her head and mumbled,

"Lord, we thank Thee for the food You done placed before us for the nourishment of our bodies. Amen." She lifted her eyes and without changing her tone of voice, said, "You going to have to learn to get up earlier than this, Bigger, to hold a job."

He did not answer or look up.

"You want me to pour you some coffee?" Vera asked.

"Yeah."

"You going to take the job, ain't you, Bigger?" his mother asked.

He laid down his fork and stared at her.

I told you last night I was going to take it. How many times you want to ask me?"

"Well, don't bite her head off," Vera said. "She only asked you a question."

"Pass the bread and stop being smart."

"You know you have to see Mr. Dalton at five-thirty," his mother said.

"You done said that ten times."

"I don't want you to forget, son,"

"And you know how you can forget," Vera said.

"Aw, lay off Bigger," Buddy said. "He told you he was going to take the job."

"Don't tell 'em nothing," Bigger said.

"You shut your mouth, Buddy, or get up from this table," the mother said. "I'm not going to take any stinking sass from you. One fool in the family's enough."

"Lay off, Ma," Buddy said.

"Bigger's setting here like he ain't glad to get a job," she said.

"What you want me to do? Shout?" Bigger asked.

"Oh, Bigger!" his sister said.

"I wish you'd keep your big mouth out of this!" he told his sister.

"If you get that job," his mother said in a low, kind tone of voice, busy slicing a loaf of bread, "I can fix up a nice place for you children. You could be comfortable and not have to live like pigs."

"Bigger ain't decent enough to think of nothing like that," Vera said.

"God, I wish you-all would let me eat," Bigger said.

His mother talked on as though

she had not heard him and he stopped listening.

"Ma's talking to you, Bigger," Vera said.

"So what?"

"Don't be that way, Bigger!"

He laid down his fork and his strong black fingers gripped the edge of the table; there was silence save for the tinkling of his brother's fork against a plate. He kept staring at his sister till her eyes fell.

"I wish you'd let me eat," he said again.

As he ate he felt that they were thinking of the job he was to get that evening and it made him angry; he felt that they had tricked him into a cheap surrender.

"I need some carfare," he said.

"Here's all I got," his mother said, pushing a quarter to the side of his plate.

He put the quarter in his pocket and drained his cup of coffee in one long swallow. He got his coat and cap and went to the door.

"You know, Bigger," his mother said, "if you don't take that job the relief'll cut us off. We won't have any food."

"I told you I'd take it!" he shouted and slammed the door.

Questions for Discussion

1. WHAT IS the background for the story?

2. WHAT INCIDENTS reveal how crowded this family of four was in their one room?

3. How DID Bigger get along with the other members of his family?

4. WHAT WAS the nature of the conflict between Bigger and his mother?

5. BIGGER'S TOUGH ATTITUDE toward his family was a shield. Why did he find it necessary to put up a wall between himself and the others?

6. IN WHAT ways is Bigger like many other young American Negroes?

7. How DOES one who is caught up in a life of misery try to escape from the despair all around him?

8. WHAT DO you think the battle with the big black rat symbolizes in the life of this family?

9. WHY DID Bigger feel resentful about the job the Welfare Department found for him?

10. WHAT ARE the tensions in this story? What are the roots of these tensions?

11. WHAT WOULD you guess about the educational background of the family from the level of English usage in the story?

12. IF THE THOMAS FAMILY had been white, do you think their lives would have been less degrading? Why?

13. IF BIGGER had a father at home would the family situation have been different? In what way?

14. WHAT IS the author's purpose in writing this story?

Vocabulary

It is often possible to guess the meaning of an unfamiliar word by the way it is used in relation to the other ideas in the paragraph. We refer to this as learning a word from the context in which it appears, that is, the passage helps to explain the meaning of the word. Let us take the world *apprehensively* on page 134. In the paragraph Bigger's mother and sister heard a scratching in the wall "and their eyes strayed *apprehensively* over the floor." Then they see the rat running across the room. From the context we can assume that they were watching for something and at the same time fearful of seeing it. In fact, one of the meanings of *apprehensively* is *anticipating something with dread or anxiety*.

Let's see if we can hit upon the meaning of another word on the same page, *galvanized*. Bigger's mother spied the rat, screamed, "and the tiny one-room apartment *galvanized* into violent action." We can deduce from the way the word is used that everybody got excited and things started to happen, as if they had received an electric shock. The dictionary meaning of the word is *stimulated as if by electricity*. (*Galvanized* is derived from a man's name, Luigi Galvani, an Italian who was connected with the discovery of electric currents in the eighteenth century.)

In the same way, try to discover from the context the meanings of these words:

feigning (page 136)   abstractedly (page 137)   plaintively (page 138)

Now look up each word in the dictionary and see how close you came to the correct meaning. Add the words to your private vocabulary list.

The Characters

1. WHO ARE the persons in this story?

2. WHAT KIND of person is Bigger? What qualities does one need in order to engage in a battle with a big, aggressive rat? Try to use at least five adjectives in describing Bigger.

3. How DOES the character of Bigger play a large part in the story?

4. How DO the two boys, Bigger and Buddy, differ in character?

5. WHAT ATTITUDE does Bigger exhibit toward his sister, Vera? What are some of the phrases he uses in talking to her? How does his attitude compare with that of most older brothers toward younger sisters?

6. WHAT KIND of person is Vera, the girl of the family?

7. BIGGER FEELS that his mother is always nagging him. Mrs. Thomas feels that it is her duty to turn the boy away from the dangerous path he is following. With which one do you sympathize? Why?

8. DO THE PEOPLE in the story seem like real people? What makes them seem true to life, or unreal, according to your way of thinking?

9. WHICH PERSON in the family did you like the most? Why?

Thinking and Writing

1. BIGGER'S FAMILY lived in one room in a Chicago slum. Write a comparison of the apartment in which you live and Bigger's apartment.

2. WRITE ABOUT the members of your family, including such things as the mood at mealtimes when everyone is assembled, the kind of work performed by individuals in the group, how each one gets along with the others, leisure-time activities, and the characteristics of each person in the family.

3. BIGGER WAS FILLED with bitterness and despair because he could see no hope in his future. Put yourself in Bigger's place and write about what you would do to get yourself out of a seeming dead-end.

4. SEVERAL YEARS AGO Michael Harrington wrote a book called *The Other America* about the millions of poor Americans who have a sub-standard existence in this, the richest country in the world. What methods do you advocate to relieve the poverty-stricken of this nation, like the Bigger family, and have them share in the good things of life?

About the Author

Richard Wright (1908-1960) was born on a plantation in Mississippi, the son of a farm hand. By the time he was ten, he was left to shift for himself, his father having deserted the family and his mother having become paralyzed. Without parental control, young Richard became difficult to restrain. He lied, stole, got into fights and became a trial to the relatives with whom he was living. He was ever on the quest to earn a few dollars to alleviate the extreme poverty in which they lived.

He tells us in *Black Boy* that on every hand he encountered almost incredible brutality on the part of white Southerners who aimed to keep blacks "in their place." Looking for a better life and wishing to further his early ambition to become a writer, he went North. In Chicago, he became interested in the labor movement in the 1930's and later joined the Communist Party. He won writing fellowships in 1938 and 1939 and eventually became the outstanding Negro writer of the first half of the twentieth century, achieving wide success with his sociological novel *Native Son* (1940) and with his painfully revealing autobiography *Black Boy* (1945).

In order to escape racial injustice in America, Wright became an expatriate, moving to Paris in 1946 with his family. In 1953 he visited a number of African countries and published his observations of the Gold Coast in *Black Power* (1954).

Professor

Professor

By Langston Hughes

Higher education for blacks is undergoing close scrutiny as an area for the extension of minority rights. Intense pressures are being exerted to open the college gates to large numbers of students from the disadvantaged segments of our population. A re-shaping of college curricula is taking place with separate Schools of Black Studies being organized in many institutions of higher learning. It is too soon to see what pattern is emerging, but one thing is clear—changes are taking place in black education.

"Professor," by Langston Hughes, is concerned with the question of what kind of college education for blacks. Dr. Brown has achieved his Ph.D. the hard way, working nights as a porter and waiter for seven years. Now he is a sociologist and a respected scholar. He has been unable to get a position in a Northern college and is now on the faculty of a Southern college. A philanthropist has offered to supply his school with funds to raise its standards and he himself would benefit by getting a large salary to do the research he loved. There is a price to accepting this tempting offer. Is Prof. Brown willing to pay the price?

Promptly at seven a big car drew up in front of the Booker T. Washington Hotel, and a white chauffeur in uniform got out and went toward the door, intending to ask at the desk for a colored professor named T. Walton Brown. But the professor was already sitting in the lobby, a white scarf around his neck and his black overcoat ready to button over his dinner clothes.

As soon as the chauffeur entered, the professor approached. 'Mr. Chandler's car?" he asked hesitantly.

"Yes, sir," said the white chauffeur to the neat little Negro. "Are you Dr. Walton Brown?"

"I am," said the professor, smiling and bowing a little.

The chauffeur opened the street door for Dr. Brown, then ran to the car and held the door open there, too. Inside the big car and on the long black running board as well, the lights came on. The professor stepped in among the soft cushions, the deep rug, and the cut-glass vases holding flowers. With the greatest of deference the chauffeur quickly tucked a covering of fur about the professor's knees, closed the door, entered his own seat in front beyond the glass partition, and the big car purred away. Within the lobby of the cheap hotel a few ill-clad Negroes watched the whole procedure in amazement.

"A big shot!" somebody said.

At the corner as the car passed, two or three ash-colored children ran across the street in front of the wheel, their skinny legs and poor clothes plain in the glare of the headlights as the chauffeur slowed down to let them pass. Then the car turned and ran the whole length of a Negro street that was lined with pawn-shops, beer joints, pig's knuckle stands, cheap movies, hair-dressing parlors, and other ramshackle places of business patronized by the poor blacks of the district. Inside the big car the professor, Dr. Walton Brown, regretted that in all the large Midwestern cities where he had lectured on his present tour in behalf of his college, the main Negro streets presented the same sleazy and disagreeable appearance: pig's knuckle joints, pawn-shops, beer parlors.

The professor looked away from the unpleasant sight of this typical Negro street, poor and unkempt. He looked ahead through the glass at the dignified white neck of the uniformed chauffeur in front of him. The professor in his dinner clothes, his brown face even browner above the white silk scarf at his neck, felt warm and comfortable under the fur rug. But he felt, too, a little unsafe at being driven through the streets of this city on the edge of the South in an expensive car, by a white chauffeur.

"But, then," he thought, "this is the wealthy Mr. Ralph P. Chandler's car, and surely no harm can come to me here. The Chandlers are a power in the Middle West, and in the South as well. Theirs is one of the great fortunes of America. In philanthropy, nobody exceeds them in well-planned generosity on a large and highly publicized scale. They are a power in Negro education, too — as long as it remains *Negro* and does not get tangled up in integration. That is why I am visiting them tonight at their invitation."

Just now the Chandlers were interested in the little Negro college at which the professor taught. They wanted to make it one of the major Negro colleges of America. And in particular the Chandlers were interested in his Department of Sociology. They were thinking of endowing a chair of research there and employing a man of ability for it. A Ph.D. and a scholar. A man of some prestige, like the professor. For his *The Sociol-*

ogy of Prejudice (that restrained and conservative study of Dr. T. Walton Brown's) had recently come to the attention of the Chandler Committee. And a representative of their philanthropies, visiting the campus, had conversed with the professor at some length about his book and his views. This representative of the committee found Dr. Brown highly gratifying, because in almost every case the professor's views agreed with the white man's own.

"A fine, sane, dependable young Negro," was the description that came to the Chandler Committee from their traveling representative.

So now the power himself, Mr. Ralph P. Chandler, and Mrs. Chandler, learning that he was lecturing at one of the colored churches of the town, had invited him to dinner at their mansion in this city on the edge of the South. Their car had come to call for him at the colored Booker T. Washington Hotel — where the hot water was always cold, the dresser drawers stuck, and the professor shivered as he got into his dinner clothes.

But now he was in this big warm car and they were moving swiftly down a fine boulevard, the black slums far behind them. The professor was glad. He had been very much distressed at having the white chauffeur call for him at this cheap hotel. But, then, none of the white hotels in this American city would house Negroes, no matter how cultured they might be. Mar-

ian Anderson herself had been unable to find decent accommodations there, so the colored papers said, on the day of her concert.

Sighing, the professor looked out of the car at the wide lawns and fine homes that lined the well-lighted boulevard where white people lived. After a time the car turned into a fashionable suburban road and he saw no more houses, but only ivy-hung walls, neat shrubs and boxwoods that indicated not merely homes beyond but vast estates. Shortly, the car whirled into a paved driveway, past a small lodge, through a park full of fountains and trees, and up to a private house as large as a hotel. From a tall portico a great hanging lantern cast a soft glow on the black and chrome body of the big car. The white chauffeur jumped out and deferentially opened the door for the colored professor. An English butler welcomed him at the entrance and took his coat, hat, and scarf. Then he led the professor into a large drawing room where two men and a woman were standing chatting near the fireplace.

The professor hesitated, not knowing who was who, but Mr. and Mrs. Chandler came forward, introduced themselves, shook hands, and in turn presented their other guest of the evening, Dr. Bulwick of the local Municipal College — a college that Dr. Brown recalled did *not* admit Negroes.

"I am happy to know you," said

Dr. Bulwick. "I am also a sociologist."

"I have heard of you," said Dr. Brown graciously.

The butler came with sherry in a silver pitcher. They sat down, and the whites began to talk politely, to ask Dr. Brown about his lecture tour, if his audiences were good, if they were mostly Negro or mixed, and if there was much interest in his college, much money being given.

Then Dr. Bulwick began to ask about his book, *The Sociology of Prejudice*, where he got his material, under whom he had studied, and if he thought the Negro Problem would ever be solved.

Dr. Brown said genially, "We are making progress," which was what he always said, though he often felt he was lying.

"Yes," said Dr. Bulwick, "that is very true. Why, at our city college here we've been conducting some fine interracial experiments. I have had several colored ministers and high-school teachers visit my classes. We found them most intelligent people."

In spite of himself Dr. Brown had to say, "But you have no colored students at your college, have you?"

"No," said Dr. Bulwick, "and that is too bad! But that is one of our difficulties here. There is no college for Negroes — although nearly forty per cent of our population is colored. Some of us have thought it might be wise to establish a separate junior college for

our Negroes, but the politicians opposed it on the score of no funds. And we cannot take them as students on our campus. That, at present, is impossible. It's too bad."

"But do you not think, Dr. Brown," interposed Mrs. Chandler, who wore diamonds on her wrists and smiled every time she spoke, "do you not think *your* people are happier in schools of their own — that it is really better for both groups not to mix them?"

In spite of himself Dr. Brown replied, "That depends, Mrs. Chandler. I could not have gotten my degree in any schools of our own."

"True, true," said Mr. Chandler. "Advanced studies, of course, cannot be gotten. But when your colleges are developed — as we hope they will be, and our committee plans to aid in their development — when their departments are headed by men like yourself, for instance, then you can no longer say, 'That depends.'"

"You are right," Dr. Brown agreed diplomatically, coming to himself and thinking of his mission in that house, "You are right," Dr. Brown said, thinking, too, of that endowed chair of sociology and himself in the chair, the ten thousand dollars a year that he would probably be paid, the surveys he might make and the books he could publish. "You are right," said Dr. Brown diplomatically to Ralph P. Chandler. But in the back of his head was that ghetto street full of sleazy misery he had just driven through, and the segregated hotel where the hot water was always cold, and the colored churches where he lectured, and the Jim Crow schools where Negroes always had less equipment and far less money than white institutions; and that separate justice of the South where his people sat on trial but the whites were judge and jury forever; and all the segregated Jim Crow things that America gave Negroes and that were never equal to the things she gave the whites. But Dr. Brown said, "You are right, Mr. Chandler," for, after all, Mr. Chandler had the money!

So he began to talk earnestly to the Chandlers there in the warm drawing room about the need for bigger and better black colleges, for more and more surveys of *Negro* life, and a well-developed department of sociology at his own little institution.

"Dinner is served," said the butler.

They rose and went into a dining room where there were flowers on the table and candles, white linen and silver, and where Dr. Brown was seated at the right of the hostess and the talk was light over the soup, but serious and sociological again by the time the meat was served.

"The American Negro must not be taken in by communism," Dr. Bulwick was saying with great positiveness as the butler passed the peas.

"He won't," agreed Dr. Brown. "I assure you, our leadership stands squarely against it." He looked at the Chandlers and bowed. "All the best people stand against it."

"America has done too much for the Negro," said Mr. Chandler, "for him to seek to destroy it."

Dr. Brown bobbed and bowed. "In your *Sociology of Prejudice*," said Dr. Bulwick, "I highly approve of the closing note, your magnificent appeal to the old standards of Christian morality and the simple concepts of justice by which America functions."

"Yes," said Dr. Brown, nodding his dark head and thinking how on ten thousand dollars a year he might take his family to South America in the summer where for three months they wouldn't feel like Negroes. "Yes, Dr. Bulwick," he nodded, "I firmly believe as you do that if the best elements of both races came together in Christian fellowship, we would solve this problem of ours."

"How beautiful," said Mrs. Chandler.

"And practical, too," said her husband. "But now to come back to your college — university, I believe you call it — to bring that institution up to really first-class standards you would need ... ?"

"We would need ... " said Dr. Brown, speaking as a mouthpiece of the administration, and speaking, too, as mouthpiece for the Negro students of his section of the South, and speaking for himself as a once ragged youth who had attended the college when its rating was lower than that of a Northern high school so that he had to study two years in Boston before he could enter a white college, when he had worked nights as redcap in the station and then as a waiter for seven years until he got his Ph.D., and then couldn't get a job in the North but had to go back down South to the work where he was now — but which might develop into a glorious opportunity at ten thousand dollars a year to make surveys and put down figures that other scholars might study to get their Ph.D.'s, and that would bring him in enough to just once take his family on a vacation to South America where they wouldn't feel that they were Negroes. "We would need, Mr. Chandler . . . "

And the things Dr. Brown's little college needed were small enough in the eyes of the Chandlers. The sane and conservative way in which Dr. Brown presented his case delighted the philanthropic heart of the Chandlers. And Mr. Chandler and Dr. Bulwick both felt that instead of building a junior college for Negroes in their own town, they could rightfully advise local colored students to go down South to

that fine little campus where they had a professor of their own race like Dr. Brown.

Over the coffee, in the drawing room, they talked about the coming theatrical season. And Mrs. Chandler spoke of how she loved Negro singers, and smiled and smiled.

In due time the professor rose to go. The car was called and he shook hands with Dr. Bulwick and the Chandlers. The white people were delighted with Dr. Brown. He could see it in their faces, just as in the past he could always tell as a waiter when he had pleased a table full of whites by tender steaks and good service.

"Tell the president of your college he shall hear from us shortly," said the Chandlers. "We'll probably send a man down again soon to talk to him about his expansion program." And they bowed farewell.

As the car sped him back toward town, Dr. Brown sat under its soft fur rug among the deep cushions and thought how with ten thousand dollars a year earned by dancing properly to the tune of Jim Crow education, he could carry his whole family to South America for a summer where they wouldn't need to feel like Negroes.

Questions for Discussion

1. WHERE DOES the story take place?

2. How DOES the author acquaint us with the situation at the opening of the story?

3. PROF. BROWN was staying at the Booker T. Washington, a cheap hotel, where he was uncomfortable. What was he doing in this Midwestern city? In what section of the city was the hotel located? Why didn't he move to a better hotel?

4. WHAT WAS unusual about the deference of the chauffeur toward Dr. Walton Brown? Do you see any satire here on the author's part?

5. WHAT DISPLEASED the Professor as the limousine drove through the streets away from his hotel?

6. WHY WAS the wealthy Mr. Chandler interested in the professor and in the small Negro college where he taught?

7. WHY DID Dr. Brown say that Negroes were making progress, if he really felt that was not true?

8. How DO you feel about Mrs. Chandler's statement that Negroes are better off in schools of their own? Are Black Separatists playing into the hands of the Chandlers of the country by demanding their own schools?

9. MR. CHANDLER was a philanthropist who made large donations to Negro colleges. Was he really interested in higher education for blacks, or do you think he had some ulterior motive in making these endowments?

10. Do YOU think Dr. Brown is a hypocrite? How can you defend his submissiveness to the racist philosophy of the Chandlers?

11. How DOES the author show the depth of Dr. Brown's resentment against racial discrimination in the United States?

12. THE CONFLICT in this story is not so much between two people as it is between two parts of Dr. Brown. What is the conflict that is going on in his mind during his visit with the Chandlers?

13. How WOULD you characterize Dr. Brown? Would you dismiss him as an "Uncle Tom" or view him with sympathy in the light of his ultimate educational goals?

14. This story was written a few years ago. If Dr. Brown were visiting that city today, is it likely he would be forced to stay at a segregated hotel? Why not?

Building Vocabulary

Getting the meaning from the context. For each of the following sentences taken from the story, select from the choices given the word or phrase that means the same as the bold face word. Check your answer by looking up the word in the dictionary. Write the ones you get wrong in your special vocabulary list.

---

1. "...The main Negro streets presented the same **sleazy** (slay'zee) and disagreeable appearance ..." (p. 148)
A. smelly B. dark C. flimsy D. dirty

2. "...The unpleasant sight of this typical Negro street, poor and **unkempt** (uhn-kempt')." (p. 148)
A. noisy B. untidy C. tree-less D. old-looking

3. "In **philanthropy** (fih-lan'-throh-pee), nobody exceeds them in well-planned generosity ..." (p. 148)
A. gardening   B. stamp-collecting   C. social planning D. love for mankind

4. "...The Chandlers were interested in his Department of **Sociology** (soh-see-ol'oh-jee)." (p. 148)
A. social science   B. language C. psychology   D. synthetic chemistry

5. "They were thinking of **endowing** (en-dow'ing) a chair of research there ..." (p. 148)
A. giving joy   B. repairing C. furnishing with money D. elaborating

6. "...The committee found Dr. Brown highly **gratifying** (grat'-ih-figh-ing) ..." (p. 149)
A. sorrowful B. critical C. satisfying D. unsatisfactory

7. "The white chauffeur jumped out and **deferentially** (def-uhr-en'shul-lee) opened the door for the colored professor." (p. 149)
A. quickly B. gruffly C. fearfully D. respectfully

8. "...The simple **concepts** (kon'-septs) of justice by which America functions." (p. 151)
A. ideas B. forms C. courts D. rules

⚮

The Theme

BY THE theme of a story is meant the message the author wishes to convey to the reader. It is the point of the story or the inside meaning. Very often the theme says something about life in general or something about the way people behave. In this story the theme is involved with Dr. Brown's thinking and his actions. Through Dr. Brown the author draws a general conclusion that applies to many black people who act like the professor. The following questions help to point the way to the *theme* of the story.

1. ON HIS way to the Chandlers, Dr. Brown reminds himself, "They are a power in Negro education—as long as it remains *Negro* and does not get tangled up in integration. That is why I am visiting them tonight at their invitation."

WHAT DOES this thought indicate about Dr. Brown's position regarding education for Negroes?

2. DR. BROWN's scholarly sociological study of prejudice is characterized as "restrained and conservative." A representative of the Chandler Committee, after visiting the professor on his campus reported that he was "a fine, sane dependable young Negro." In the light of these comments how would you characterize the public image of Dr. Brown?

3. ALTHOUGH HE didn't put it into words, how did Dr. Brown really feel about solving the "Negro Problem?"

4. WHAT IS the implication of Dr. Brown's question directed to Dr. Bulwick of the local Municipal College, "But you have no colored students at your college, have you?"

5. DR. BROWN agreed with Mr. Chandler that advanced degrees could be obtained at Negro colleges when they were improved; at the same time he couldn't help thinking of the discrimination and degradation suffered by Negroes because of segregation.

Why did Dr. Brown straddle the fence in his conversation with the Chandlers instead of taking a forthright position?

6. DR. BROWN outlined to the Chandlers the things his college needed to put it in the first rank. He knew he could get the money for expansion by supporting Jim Crow in higher education. Why did he try to please the white people if he felt inwardly that segregated education was undesirable for blacks?

7. IN THE light of the thinking you have done in answering the above questions, how would you state the theme of the story?

⟨✗⟩

Thinking and Writing

1. PROF. BROWN had to stop at a cheap, segregated hotel in a black slum where he couldn't get hot water and the bureau drawers stuck. Today, he would be accepted at any first-class hotel in that city. Write about the progress that has been made in the area of civil rights in the last decade.

2. SUPPOSE Prof. Brown were an outspoken person and did not wish to keep his real thoughts to himself and did not care about getting an endowment from Mr. Chandler. Write what Prof. Brown might have said about the "Negro Problem" if he felt free to speak his mind.

3. AMERICAN Negros who can afford it go to Europe or Latin America because they can live there without being always reminded they are black. Prof. Brown's greatest desire was to take his whole family to South America for a summer where they wouldn't have to feel like Negroes. Write a composition about the treatment of colored people in places outside the United States.

4. MR. CHANDLER says "America has done too much for the Negro for him to seek to destroy it." If you agree with this statement write a composition pointing out the advantages for a Negro to live in the United States. If you disagree, show what this country has failed to do for the Negro.

⟨✗⟩

About the Author

ℒangston Hughes (1902-1967) was born in Missouri and became the victim of a broken home at a very early age. His father separated from the family and went off to Mexico to live. His mother re-married and Langston was brought up by his grandmother until she died. From her he gained his identity as a spokesman of rights for Negroes, for she was the widow of one of the five blacks who accompanied John Brown on the raid that was to strike an armed blow for Negros slaves.

Hughes went to high school in Cleveland and after graduation made a trip to Mexico to visit his father. While crossing the Mississippi River he got the inspiration for the remarkable poem, "The Negro Speaks of Rivers," written when he was a teen-ager. He attended Columbia University for one year, then became a seaman on a freighter, followed by various jobs in France and Italy. On returning to the United States he attended Lincoln University in Pennsylvania and received an A.B. degree in 1929.

His first published volume was a book of poetry, *The Weary Blues*, in 1926. His last volume was *The Best Short Stories By Negro Writers*, which he edited and published in 1967 just before his death. In between these works was a lifetime of almost 50 years of writing and editing. Altogether, Hughes authored or edited 64 books and pamphlets. His own writings spanned almost all forms of literature: novels, short stories, poems, essays, plays, and autobiography. In all these different formats Hughes wrote about one paramount subject — what it meant to be a black in America — the incomprehensible gap between the races exemplified by the prototype of Simple, in the Simple stories, who was asked what the cranks were for that he worked to produce. The answer was "White folks don't tell colored folks what cranks crank."

Living with an aunt and uncle in a third-floor Harlem apartment, Hughes did most of his writing through the night after the sounds of the noisy life around him had quieted, finishing his day's quota by 7 A. M.

Rat
Joiner
Routs
the
Klan

BY TED POSTON

*This is one of several short stories written by Poston about incidents
that occurred during his childhood days in Hopkinsville, Kentucky, the
heart of the tobacco-growing region, where the field hands were blacks.
Living in a so-called "border state", the author grew up in a segregated
society where the whites still gloried in the pre-Civil War traditions
and the Negroes were always reminded of "their place." One such re-
minder was the Rex Theater in Hopkinsville where the audience was
segregated. Negroes were compelled to sit in the balcony which was
termed "the peanut gallery", undoubtedly because of the goober con-
sumption in that section.*

*How could a group of boys legally prevent the showing of a motion
picture that their elders objected to? The boys in Hopkinsville came up
with a diverting answer, thereby making a contribution to the cause of
civil rights without recourse to the courts.*

THERE had never been a Ku Klux Klan in Hopkinsville, Kentucky. So it was sort of surprising how our leading colored citizens got all worked up when they heard that *The Birth of a Nation* was coming to the Rex Theatre down on Ninth Street.

It was we young ones who brought them the news — although it didn't mean anything to us. And it was we young ones who got them out of it when the situation finally reached a stalemate.

The whole thing started one Saturday morning when Bronco Billy Anderson was being featured at the Rex in *The Revenge of the Ranger*. And, of course, not a one of us could afford to miss that.

Naturally, the Booker T. Washington Colored Grammar School was not open on Saturdays, but that meant only one extra hour's sleep. For all of us had to be at the Rex at 9 A.M. to be sure that we could get front row seats in the peanut gallery which was reserved for all of our colored citizens.

It was absolutely essential that we be there when the doors first opened or else the bigger boys would get there first and take the choice seats.

We always thought the big boys were unfair, but there was nothing we could do about it. No self-respecting young colored citizen would dream of squealing to the white folks about it. And further-more, if we did, we knew the big boys would bop us for doing it.

But this was our problem: The Rex Theater charged only five cents admission for all of our col-ored citizens under ten years of age. But since Miss Lucy, the white ticket lady who took our nickels, was nearsighted, and saw us only through a peep-hole as we stood in line in the alley, there was a rumor around the colored community that none of us grew any older after we were nine years old until we suddenly reached twenty-one or more. For all you had to do was bend your knees, look up innocently, and slip your nickel through the slot, and she'd pass you right up the gallery stairs.

There was a story — which I never believed — that Jelly Roll

Benson never paid more than a nickel to get into the Rex until he was about thirty-five years old.

"That's why he walks with a stoop in his shoulders and a bend in his knees to this day," Rat Joiner always insisted. "He got that way from fooling Miss Lucy. He'd still be doin' it now, but he forgot to shave one morning. And she sus-pected for the first time that he was over ten."

But all this happened before that historic Saturday when we all rushed to see Bronco Billy Ander-son in *The Revenge of the Ranger*. All of us were crazy about Bronco Billy, but there was also another reason for going to see him. For in every picture, Bronco Billy's main side-kick was a cowboy named Buffalo Pete. And, believe it or not, Buffalo Pete was as highly visible and 100 per cent colored as any citizen up on Billy Goat Hill.

He was the only colored cowboy or colored anything we ever saw in the movies in those days, and we wouldn't think of missing him. Our enthusiasm was not even dim-med by the cynicism of Rat Joiner, who observed one day: "They don't never let him kill none of them white mens, no matter how evil they is. Oh yeah, they let him knock off a Indian every now and then. But only Bronco Billy kills them white bad mens."

There was an unconfirmed ru-mor around town that another

movie actor, named Noble Johnson, had Negro blood. But we
didn't pay that no mind. We figured that the high-yallers in our
colored community had dreamed
up that story for prestige purposes.
And anyway, Noble Johnson played in those silly love stories they
showed at the Rex on weekday
nights. And who would pay five
cents to see one of them?

But *The Revenge of the Ranger*
that Saturday was a real knock-
down picture and we saw it eight
times before they put us out at 5
P.M. in order to let the grownups
in for the evening, at fifteen cents
a head.

We got downstairs and out of
the alley at just about the same
time that the little white boys were
being put out also, and we noticed
that they were all carrying handbills in their fists. Nobody had
passed out any handbills upstairs,
but we had no difficulty getting
some when we found out that
Tack Haired Baker had been paid
twenty-five cents to stand by the
front door in the lobby and pass
them out.

We were a little disappointed
when we read them, because it
didn't mean anything to us then.
Bronco Billy and Buffalo Pete
weren't even mentioned anywhere
on the handbills. They read:

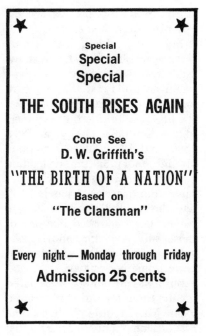

Most of us threw the handbills
away before we got home, and I
don't remember how I happened
to hold on to mine.

But I still had it in my hand
when I climbed up our front steps
and tried to make my way through
the usual Saturday crowd of elders
and sporting men who were holding their weekly session with Papa.
Papa was Professor E. Poston,
dean of men at Kentucky State
Industrial College for Negroes in
Frankfort and the official arbiter
of all bets and disputes which

piled up during his two-weekly absences from home.

My sister Lillian, who is only three years older than I, was showing off by sitting next to Papa while he explained that a Negro jockey named Isaac Murphy was the first man to ride three winners in the Kentucky Derby, in 1884, 1890, and 1891. So as I stepped around Smoky Smith, our leading colored gambling man, who had raised the question, I handed Lillian the handbill. This *Birth of a Nation* thing sounded like one of those silly love-story movies she was always going to, so I thought I was doing her a favor.

But I was absolutely unprepared for the commotion that was raised when Mr. Freddie Williams, the first deacon of our Virginia Baptist Church, happened to glance at the handbill and let out a screech.

"Don't that say *The Birth of a Nation?*" he yelled as he snatched it out of Lillian's hands. "And coming to the Rex Theatre here?"

He thrust the crumpled handbill in Papa's face and said: "Professor Poston, you've got to do something about this right away."

I still had no idea what had caused the commotion, but Mr. J. B. Petty, our local insurance man-historian, very soon put me right.

It seemed that this novel, *The Clansman,* and the moving picture *The Birth of a Nation* were something about a bunch of peckerwoods who dressed up in sheets and went around whipping the heads of unsuspecting colored citizens and yelling about white supremacy. And there was one place in both things about some Negro — "played by a white man," Mr. J. B. Petty explained—who chased some poor white woman off the top of a rock quarry, with her yelling, "Death before dishonor."

Mr. Freddie Williams was putting it right up to Papa.

"You know what it will mean to show this sort of thing to these hillbillies and peckerwoods around here, Professor Poston," he kept saying. "And I'm sure that the quality white folks will agree with you if you put it up to them right. I'm surprised that Mr. Max Kaplan even thought of letting this happen."

Now even I knew that Mr. Max Kaplan, who owned the Rex was not exactly quality white folks in the eyes of Hopkinsville, Kentucky, even if he was a very popular white citizen in the colored community.

And neither was Judge Hezekiah Witherspoon, our veteran Republican leader, quality either. But he ran Hopkinsville, Kentucky, and it was to him that the group decided that Papa should make his first appeal.

Papa went right down to see him that Saturday night, but the meeting wasn't altogether successful. As I heard Papa explaining it to Mama when he finally got home, Judge Witherspoon started talking about private enterprise and what were the Negroes excited about anyhow? But Papa had one more weapon up his sleeve, he explained to Mama.

"So I finally said to him," Papa recalled, " 'I don't know if you read the book, Judge Witherspoon, but the whole thing is about the terrible things the scalawags[1] and carpetbaggers[2] did to the people of the South during Reconstruction. And although I didn't want to mention the subject, Judge, you must remember that all of those scalawags and carpetbaggers were Republicans, so I wonder if you want people reminded of that?' "

Papa chuckled as he recalled Judge Witherspoon's reaction.

" 'Eph, you damn Democrat,' he yelled at me," Papa said. " 'You keep your politics out of this.' But I could see that he was shaken, and I just let him rave for a few minutes.

"But finally he said: 'I'm not gonna get mixed up in this thing. But you go and see Max Kaplan and tell him how the colored people feel about this thing. And tell him I'll back him up if he feels he's got to do something about it.' "

Papa was very set up about the meeting. "I'm going out to see Mr. Max Kaplan tomorrow morning. After all, Sunday is not his Sabbath and he won't be averse to talking a little business."

I still didn't quite understand what the shouting was all about. But I had no doubt that Mr. Max Kaplan would side with our colored citizens if Papa asked him to. For Mr. Max Kaplan was quite an unusual citizen even in Hopkinsville, Kentucky. He had come there years before I was born and had got into hot water the minute he built the Rex Theatre, because he had planned only ground-floor seats for white and colored citizens alike.

Of course, the white folks, including the quality ones, had beaten him down on that, and he had been forced to spend extra money to fix the peanut gallery up for us.

Reaching Pete Washington, a classmate of mine in the Booker T. Washington Colored Grammar School, once said he was glad Mr. Max Kaplan lost that fight. Reaching Pete didn't have a nickel one Saturday when *The Clutching Hand* serial was playing the Rex, so he kept on up the alley and slipped through the fire-escape door on the ground floor where the white folks sat.

It was dark, of course, and no-

[1] scalawags: native white Southerners who worked with the carpetbaggers and Negroes during the Reconstruction period to organize and dominate the state governments.

[2] carpetbaggers: Northerners who went south after the Civil War to become supporters of the Negroes and office holders in the newly organized state governments. They brought all their property with them in carpetbags, the luggage of the period.

body noticed that Reaching Pete had slipped in. But everybody knew it a few minutes later. For when Pete looked up, he was right under the screen and the pictures were twenty feet tall. And just at that moment, the Clutching Hand, a very mean crook who had a claw in place of his right hand, was reaching out for his next victim, and Pete thought he was reaching for him.

Pete closed his eyes and screamed so loud that they had to turn on the lights in the whole theatre to find out what was going on. The cops wanted to lock Reaching Pete up, but Mr. Max Kaplan wouldn't let them. He even let Reaching Pete go upstairs free of charge.

But that wasn't the only thing that endeared Mr. Max Kaplan to our colored community. There was the matter of Tapper Johnson, our motion-picture projectionist. When the white folks balked Mr. Max Kaplan and made him build a whole peanut gallery (after starting a whispering campaign that he was trying to bring his New York City ideas to Hopkinsville), he made up his mind to get even. So he decided to make his most highly paid employee one of our colored citizens. That was when he hired Tapper and trained him to be the only moving-picture-machine operator in all of Hopkinsville. And he paid Tapper thirty-five dollars each and every week.

And Tapper paid Mr. Max

Kaplan back real nice too. He became the best moving-picture operator for his size and age in all of Kentucky, and there were rumors that he could have gotten five dollars more a week in Clarksville, Tennessee, if Mr. Kaplan had ever given him a vacation or a day off to go see about it.

But Tapper didn't want a day off. He had only two loves in his life—his motion-picture machine and little Cecelia Penrod with whom he had been in love long before he quit the fourth grade in the Booker T. Washington Colored Grammar School.

His love affair with the Rex Theatre moving-picture machine went along smoothly. But not his love affair with little Cecelia. For Cecelia was one of the nieces of Mrs. Nixola Green, our high-yaller social leader. And she felt that Tapper was too dark to become a member of her family.

In fact, my sister Lillian was always saying that Mrs. Nixola was trying to marry Cecelia off to Pat Slaker (who naturally was yaller), but that Pat and Cecelia weren't paying each other any mind. Cecelia was in love with Tapper, Lillian said, although there wasn't much she could do about it. She never got to go to the Rex Theatre alone. Mrs. Nixola always insisted on accompanying her.

Papa probably had all this in mind that Sunday morning when he hopefully set out for Mr. Max Kaplan's home. But Papa was in for a disappointment. Mr. Kaplan wasn't in town. He'd left three weeks ago for California and he wasn't expected home until Wednesday.

Now *The Birth of a Nation* was due to start running Tuesday night. Time was running out as the elders of Freeman Methodist Chapel and the Virginia Street Baptist Church met that afternoon to receive Papa's report.

"Professor Poston," Mr. Freddie Williams finally said after the discussion had gone on for hours. "I know how you feel about poor white trash. But with Mr. Max Kaplan out of town, there's nothing we can do but appeal to S. J. Bolton."

It took some talking on the part of the elders, but Papa was finally persuaded to lay the matter before Mr. S. J. Bolton, Mr. Kaplan's manager of the Rex, and the results were disastrous, as he reported it to Mama later.

"This clay-eating cracker," Papa said later, in as near an approach to profanity as he ever permitted himself, "had the nerve to call me Eph. He said to me: 'Eph, what are you Nigras upset about? Why, my grandfather was one of the founders of the Klan. No Nigra who knows his place has anything to worry about in this glorious story of the re-rise of the South.'

"And then he added," Papa said, " 'Why Eph, you must know what my initials, S.J., stand for. Stonewall Jackson Bolton, of course.' "

Papa's indignation at the outcome of his conference was far exceeded by the reaction of the elders who met on our lawn that Sunday afternoon to hear his report.

But none of us young ones felt personally involved until Mr. Freddie Williams summed up the feelings of our elders.

"All right," he said, "if that is the way the white folks feel about it, let them. But I move that if *The Birth of a Nation* opens at the Rex Tuesday evening, then "The Death of the Rex" should set in that very night. Because if we don't patronize that peanut gallery Mr. Max Kaplan has for us, then they ain't gonna make enough money each week to pay even Tapper's salary. And that means not only us staying away, but our kids as well—Bronco Billy and Buffalo Pete notwithstanding."

Now this created a very desperate situation indeed, as I explained to my classmates at the Booker T. Washington Colored Grammar School the next morning.

But what could we do about it? We were all pretty downcast until Rat Joiner said: "I think I got an idea." And then he explained.

And as soon as school was out that day, we all went to work to raise the fifteen cents Rat said was necessary for the success of his plan. Coco-Cola bottles, scrap wire, everything went into the pot until we had the fifteen cents.

There was no picket line at the Rex the next night, but some of our most responsible colored citizens were loitering around the alley from the minute the evening tickets went on sale. And most of them were very upset when Rat Joiner, the pride of Billy Goat Hill, showed up as the only colored customer that night who plunked down fifteen cents and requested a peanut-gallery ticket from Miss Lucy.

In fact, there was talk about mentioning the fact to Reverend Timberlake, and having him read Roosevelt Alonzo Taylor Joiner out of the congregation of the Dirt's Avenue Methodist Church.

But that was before they found out the nature of Rat's mission.

For Rat entered the Rex just thirty minutes before the main feature was to go on, just when Tapper was preparing to rewind the film for Hopkinsville's first showing of *The Birth of a Nation.* Rat knocked on the door of the projection room, then came right to the matter at hand.

"Tapper," he said, "Mrs. Nixola Green has finally persuaded Cecelia to run off and marry Pat Slaker. They're up at Mrs. Nixola's house on First Street and they're going to head for Clarksville any minute. I know it ain't none of my business, but you always been fair to us and—"

Tapper waited to hear no more. He dashed out of the projection room and headed first for Mrs.

Nixola's house on First Street.

Of course, Cecelia wasn't there; the whole family was over in Earlington, Kentucky, attending a family reunion.

But Tapper didn't know this. He rushed down to Irving's Livery Stable and rented the fastest horse and rig for an emergency dash to Clarksville, Tennessee, where he hoped to head off the nuptials.

Well, the downstairs section of the Rex Theatre was crowded (with only Rat in the peanut gallery) before Mr. S. J. Bolton learned that Hopkinville's only movie projectionist was no longer in the Rex Theatre. He tried to stall the showing for a half hour, but when Tapper didn't show up then, Mr. S. J. Bolton tried to run the machine himself.

Rat, who had decided to stay inside since he had paid an unheard-of fifteen cents to be there anyway, explained to us later what happened.

"Tapper had started rewinding the film backward to get to the front," he said, "but Mr. S. J. Bolton didn't know that. So he picked up the first film roll he saw and started running it on that picture thing.

"Well, it turned out that it was the middle of the picture and backwards besides. So, instead of that colored gentleman (played by some white man) chasing that white lady off the top of the quarry, it started with the white lady at the bottom of the quarry.

And she was leaping to the top of the quarry so that the colored gentleman (who was really a white man) could grab her.

"The white folks didn't see much of the picture, because Mr. S. J. Bolton yanked that part off so fast that he tore up the whole thing. I waited another half hour and nothing else came on, so all of us went home."

So Hopkinsville, Kentucky, never got to see *The Birth of a Nation*. Mr. Max Kaplan came back the next day and substituted another film for *The Birth of a Nation*. There were always two schools of thought in the colored community after that—and even Papa couldn't settle the dispute.

One school held that Mr. Max Kaplan would never have let *The Birth of a Nation* be booked for the Rex if he had known anything about it and if he hadn't been in Los Angeles. And the other school contended that Mr. S. J. Bolton had so messed up the original print in trying to run it without Tapper that it couldn't have been shown anyway.

In any case, Mr. Max Kaplan took steps to see that a certain situation never obtained again. He had little Cecelia Penrod smuggled out of her house while Mrs. Nixola wasn't watching. And he took her and Tapper down to Judge Hezekiah Witherspoon who married both of them on the spot. Mrs. Nixola Green collapsed at the news and went over to Clarksville, Tennessee, to recuperate at the home of some of her high-yaller relatives.

When she came back she boasted that she had passed for white and had seen *The Birth of a Nation* at the Princess Theatre there.

"And it was a very good picture," she said, "I don't know what all the fuss over here was about."

Questions for Discussion

1. "THE BIRTH of a Nation" is a controversial motion picture that was made in 1915 by the noted movie director, D. W. Griffith and has been shown repeatedly through the years. Now it is exhibited only at anniversaries and in film festivals. What is the movie about?

2. WHY WERE the colored citizens of Hopkinsville so disturbed when they learned that the film was coming to the Rex Theater in town?

3. THE Ku Klux Klan has been outlawed. What effect has this had on acts of terror and lynchings in the South?

4. HOW DID the boys trick the unsuspecting cashier of the Rex Theater?

5. WHAT IS your opinion of the favorite movies of the boys of Hopkinsville? Have movie tastes changed in the last couple of decades? Explain. How do television programs reflect the taste of the viewing audience?

6. HOW WERE the "high-yallers" regarded in the colored community of Hopkinsville? Since the Black Power movement what changes have taken place in equating social status with skin color?

7. WHY DID the political leader of the town, Judge Witherspoon, refuse to do anything about stopping the showing of the film?

8. WHAT KIND of person was Mr. Max Kaplan, the owner of the Rex? Refer to incidents in the story to support your characterization.

9. THE COLORED community voted not to patronize the Rex Theater during the showing of "The Birth of a Nation." Could they have taken more direct action? What kind of action?

10. DESCRIBE the plan that Rat Joiner devised to stop the showing of the objectionable film.

11. MRS. NIXOLA GREEN saw "The Birth of a Nation" in Clarksville and when she came back to town was quoted as saying, "It was a very good picture. I don't know what all the fuss over here was about." What do you make of that remark?

12. WHAT IS the implied message or theme of this story in connection with taking action to resolve a racial crisis?

13. WHO WOULD you say is the most admirable character in this story? How would you describe him?

14. WHAT IS the setting of the story? Include in your answer a reference to the town's background, keeping in mind two facts:

a. In border states colored communities were not totally ignored as in other parts of the South. That is why Prof. Poston went to the political leader of the town for help.

b. There were different social classes in Hopkinsville, both in the white and black communities, as indicated by such terms as 'quality folks," "hill billies."

How important is the setting to the plot and characters? Could this story have been set in Mississippi or Alabama?

Mood

IN SOME stories the most significant element is mood, rather than plot, characterization, or conflict. This is the case with Edgar Allan Poe's stories, like "The Pit and the Pendulum" where the mood is stark horror. By mood is meant an emotion or feeling, such as fear, joy, anger, hate, grief, etc. There is a feeling of light-heartedness and fun pervading "Rat Joiner Routs the Klan" from the title to the very end. The mood of a story may depend upon the characters, the plot, the setting, the author's choice of words or style, or any combination of these factors.

1. IN THIS story the author uses several means to achieve a humorous mood. Point out some of the things that make this a funny story, even though at bottom it deals with a serious subject — black and white relationships.

2. WHICH DO you find the funniest incident in the story?

3. HOW APPROPRIATE is the use of slang in this story, like the word *bop* on page 160? Other slang words are *side-kick* (page 160), *pot* (page 165), *plunked* (page 166). How do these words aid the mood of the story?

4. SLANG TENDS to become dated, like "23-skidoo." Are the words in question 3 still current slang or have they become obsolete?

5. WHEN THE author uses the word "high-yaller" what effect does he intend to produce? Does this intent fit into the mood of the story?

6. THE AUTHOR uses unusual first names like Jelly Roll, Tack Haired and Tapper for humorous effect. Compare these odd names with the characters in any of Damon Runyon's Broadway stories, especially *Guys and Dolls,* or any other story you have read where the characters have absurd names.

7. HOW WOULD you compare the mood of this story with any of Langston Hughes' Simple stories?

Word Study

*A*bout 70% of the words in the English language come from Latin and Greek. Do you know the meaning of the Greek-derived word that is italicized in the following sentence? "Our enthusiasm was not even dimmed by the *cynicism* (sin'ih-sizm) of Rat Joiner . . ." (p. 160).

By showing *cynicism* Rat Joiner was expressing an attitude of sneering doubt about the sincerity of the motives of whites. How did the word come to take on this meaning of skepticism? The history of this word goes back to a school of philosophy in Athens, Greece in the third century B. C. These philosophers believed that moral living was the greatest good and cut themselves off from the rest of society which they considered selfish and evil. Whenever anyone approached them, these philosophers were rude, snarling and insulting. Hence, people called them dogs, which in Greek is *Cynics*. A cynic, then, is a person who is sarcastic and questions the goodness of people's actions. *Cynicism* would be the beliefs held by a cynic, that is, doubtfulness about the sincerity of people.

While *cynicism* is of Greek origin, the word *arbiter* (ah'bih-tuh) is of Latin derivation. Here is the sentence in which this word is found. "Papa was Professor E. Poston . . . the official *arbiter* of all bets and disputes . . ." (p. 161). The word is composed of the Latin prefix *ad,* meaning *to* and the Latin root *bitere,* meaning *go.* Originally, then, *arbiter* meant one who goes to a place to be a judge. Now the word means simply a person selected to judge a dispute, an umpire.

Look up the origin and the meaning of the italicized words in the sentences below. Two of these words come from Latin, the third comes from Middle English, a forerunner of modern English, spoken in England during the period 1100 to 1500.

"We figured that the high-yallers in our colored community had dreamed up that story for *prestige* (pres-teezh') purposes." (p. 161).

"... He hoped to head off the *nuptials* (nup'shuls)." (p. 166).

"And it was we young ones who got them out of it when the situation finally reached a *stale-mate*." (p. 159).

Thinking and Writing

1. THE NEGRO community wanted to prevent the showing of "The Birth of a Nation" because they believed it was a prejudiced portrayal of the Reconstruction Era following the Civil War, glorifying the Ku Klux Klan and making villains out of Negroes. Do you think it is right to censor movies for any reason? Explain your reasons if you are in favor of censorship or give reasons if you are against censorship.

2. THE BOYS of Hopkinsville favored westerns when they went to the movies; the girls preferred films involving romance. Write an essay describing the kinds of motion pictures you prefer, stating why they make an appeal to you.

3. CECELIA was in love with Tapper Johnson, the movie projectionist, but her aunt, Mrs. Nixola Green, wanted her to marry someone else. To what extent should a girl's family influence her choice of a fiance? Should young people be allowed to follow the dictates of their hearts when it comes to choosing mates? Should there be other considerations besides mutual attraction? Write an essay concerning the role one's family should play in courtship.

About the Author

𝒯ed Poston has been a newspaperman for many years. He has had a long association with the *New York Post* as a star reporter and writer of feature articles, having joined the paper in 1937.

He was born in Hopkinsville, Kentucky where he received his education. However, he attended college in a neighboring state, graduating with an A.B. degree from Tennessee Agricultural and Industrial State University in Nashville, Tennessee.

In addition to his work on the *New York Post*, Mr. Poston has written many short stories and articles for publication in such magazines as *Ebony*, *The Negro Digest*, *Saturday Review*, and *The Nation*.

During the World War II period, he served in a number of government agencies, including the post of Deputy Director of the Office of War Information.

In 1967, Mr. Poston was presented with an award by the New York Urban League for "sustained excellence in interpreting, analyzing and reporting the news and using the immense power of the press in advocating equality for all in the best American tradition."

A
Summer
Tragedy

By Arna Bontemps

A Summer Tragedy

Old Jeff Patton was a tenant farmer who worked 30 acres of land for a share of the crop. He has reached a crisis in his life. Farming is the only kind of living that Jeff knows. On the point of becoming physically incapacitated he feels he cannot make another crop. After forty-five years of sharecropping on the same farm he has reached the end of hope. What is left for Jeff and his blind and feeble wife?

Old Jeff Patton, the black share farmer, fumbled with his bow tie. His fingers trembled and the high stiff collar pinched his throat. A fellow loses his hand for such vanities after thirty or forty years of simple life. Once a year, or maybe twice if there's a wedding among his kinfolks, he may spruce up; but generally fancy clothes do nothing but adorn the wall of the big room and feed the moths. That had been Jeff Patton's experience. He had not worn his stiff-bosomed shirt more than a dozen times in all his married life. His swallow-tailed coat[1] lay on the bed beside him, freshly brushed and pressed, but it was as full of holes as the overalls in which he worked on weekdays. The moths had used it badly. Jeff twisted his mouth into a hideous toothless grimace as he contended with the obstinate bow. He stamped his good foot and decided to give up the struggle.

"Jennie," he called.

"What's that, Jeff?" His wife's shrunken voice came out of the adjoining room like an echo. It was hardly bigger than a whisper.

"I reckon you'll have to he'p me wid this heah bow tie, baby," he said meekly. "Dog if I can hitch it up."

Her answer was not strong enough to reach him, but presently the old woman came to the

---

door, feeling her way with a stick. She had a wasted, dead-leaf appearance. Her body, as scrawny and gnarled as a string bean, seemed less than nothing in the ocean of frayed and faded petticoats that surrounded her. These hung an inch or two above the tops of her heavy unlaced shoes and showed little grotesque piles where the stockings had fallen down from her negligible legs.

"You oughta could do a heap mo' wid a thing like that'n me—beingst as you got yo' good sight."

"Looks like I oughta could," he admitted. "But ma fingers is gone democrat on me. I get all mixed up in the looking glass an' can't tell wicha way to twist the devilish thing."

Jennie sat on the side of the bed and old Jeff Patton got down on one knee while she tied the bow knot. It was a slow and painful ordeal for each of them in this position. Jeff's bones cracked, his knee ached, and it was only after a half dozen attempts that Jennie worked a semblance of a bow into the tie.

"I got to dress maself now," the old woman whispered. "These is ma old shoes an' stockings, and I ain't so much as unwrapped ma dress."

"Well, don't worry 'bout me no mo', baby," Jeff said. "That 'bout finishes me. All I gotta do now is slip on that old coat 'n ves' an' I'll be fixed to leave."

Jennie disappeared again through the dim passage into the shed room. Being blind was no handicap to her in that black hole. Jeff heard the cane placed against the wall beside the door and knew that his wife was on easy ground. He put on his coat, took a battered top hat from the bedpost, and hobbled to the front door. He was ready to travel. As soon as Jennie could get on her Sunday shoes and her old black silk dress, they would start.

Outside the tiny log house, the day was warm and mellow with sunshine. A host of wasps were humming with busy excitement in the trunk of a dead sycamore. Gray squirrels were searching through the grass for hickory nuts and blue jays were in the trees, hopping from branch to branch. Pine woods stretched away to the left like a black sea. Among them were scattered scores of log houses like Jeff's, houses of black share farmers. Cows and pigs wandered freely among the trees. There was no danger of loss. Each farmer knew his own stock and knew his neighbor's as well as he knew his neighbor's children.

Down the slope to the right were the cultivated acres on which the colored folks worked. They extended to the river, more than two miles away, and they were today green with the unmade cotton crop. A tiny thread of a road, which passed directly in front of Jeff's place, ran through these green fields like a pencil mark.

Jeff, standing outside the door, with his absurd hat in his left hand, surveyed the wide scene tenderly. He had been forty-five years on these acres. He loved them with the unexplained affection that others have for the countries to which they belong.

The sun was hot on his head, his collar still pinched his throat, and the Sunday clothes were intolerably hot. Jeff transferred the hat to his right hand and began fanning with it. Suddenly the whisper that was Jennie's voice came out of the shed room.

"You can bring the car round front whilst you's waitin'", it said feebly. There was a tired pause; then it added, "I'll soon be fixed to go."

"A'right, baby," Jeff answered. "I'll get it in a minute."

But he didn't move. A thought struck him that made his mouth fall open. The mention of the car brought to his mind, with new intensity, the trip he and Jennie were about to take. Fear came into his eyes; excitement took his breath. Lord, Jesus!

"Jeff . . . O Jeff," the old woman's whisper called.

He awakened with a jolt. "Hunh, baby?"

"What you doin'?"

"Nuthin. Jes studyin'. I jes been turnin' things round'n round in ma mind."

"You could be gettin' the car," she said.

"Oh yes, right away, baby."

He started round to the shed, limping heavily on his bad leg. There were three frizzly chickens in the yard. All his other chickens had been killed or stolen recently. But the frizzly chickens had been saved somehow. That was fortunate indeed, for these curious creatures had a way of devouring "Poison" from the yard and in that way protecting against conjure and black luck and spells. But even the frizzly chickens seemed now to be in a stupor. Jeff thought they had some ailment; he expected all three of them to die shortly.

The shed in which the old T-model Ford stood was only a grass roof held up by four corner poles. It had been built by tremulous hands at a time when the little rattletrap car had been regarded as a peculiar treasure. And, miraculously, despite wind and downpour, it still stood.

Jeff adjusted the crank and put his weight upon it. The engine came to life with a sputter and bang that rattled the old car from radiator to taillight. Jeff hopped into the seat and put his foot on the accelerator. The sputtering and banging increased. The rattling became more violent. That was good. It was good banging, good sputtering and rattling, and it meant that the aged car was still in running condition. She could be depended on for this trip.

Again Jeff's thought halted as if paralyzed. The suggestion of the trip fell into the machinery of his mind like a wrench. He felt dazed and weak. He swung the car out into the yard, made a half turn and drove around to the front door. When he took his hands off the wheel, he noticed that he was trembling violently. He cut off the motor and climbed to the ground to wait for Jennie.

A few minutes later she was at the window, her voice rattling against the pane like a broken shutter.

"I'm ready, Jeff."

He did not answer, but limped into the house and took her by the arm. He led her slowly through the big room, down the step and across the yard.

"You reckon I'd oughta lock the do'?" he asked softly.

They stopped and Jennie weighed the question. Finally she shook her head,

"Ne' mind the do'," she said. "I don't see no cause to lock up things."

"You right," Jeff agreed. "No cause to lock up."

Jeff opened the door and helped his wife into the car. A quick shudder passed over him. Jesus! Again he trembled.

"How come you shaking so?" Jennie whispered.

"I don't know," he said.

"You mus' be scairt, Jeff."

"No, baby I ain't scairt."

He slammed the door after her and went around to crank up again. The motor started easily. Jeff wished that it had not been so responsive. He would have liked a few more minutes in which to turn things around in his head. As it was, with Jennie chiding him about being afraid, he had to keep going. He swung the car into the little pencil-mark road and started off toward the river, driving very slowly, very cautiously.

Chugging across the green countryside, the small battered Ford seemed tiny indeed. Jeff felt a familiar excitement, a thrill, as they came down the first slope to the immense levels on which the cotton was growing. He could not help reflecting that the crops were good. He knew what that meant, too; he had made forty-five of them with his own hands. It was true that he had worn out nearly a dozen mules, but that was the fault of old man Stevenson, the owner of the land. Major Stevenson had the odd notion that one mule was all a share farmer needed to work a thirty-acre plot. It was an expensive notion, the way it killed mules from overwork, but the old man held to it. Jeff thought it killed a good many share farmers as well as mules, but he had no sympathy for them. He had always been strong, and he had been taught to have no patience with weakness in men. Women or children might be tolerated if they were puny, but a weak man was a curse. Of course, his own children—

Jeff's thought halted there. He

and Jennie never mentioned their dead children any more. And naturally he did not wish to dwell upon them in his mind. Before he knew it, some remark would slip out of his mouth and that would make Jennie feel blue. Perhaps she would cry. A woman like Jennie could not easily throw off the grief that comes from losing five grown children within two years. Even Jeff was still staggered by the blow. His memory had not been much good recently. He frequently talked to himself. And, although he had kept it a secret, he knew that his courage had left him. He was terrified by the least unfamiliar sound at night. He was reluctant to venture far from home in the daytime. And that habit of trembling when he felt fearful was now far beyond his control. Sometimes he became afraid and trembled without knowing what had frightened him. The feeling would just come over him like a chill.

The car rattled slowly over the dusty road. Jennie sat erect and silent, with a little absurd hat pinned to her hair. Her useless eyes seemed very large, very white in their deep sockets. Suddenly Jeff heard her voice, and he inclined his head to catch the words.

"Is we passed Delia Moore's house yet?" she asked.

"Not yet," he said.

"You must be drivin' mighty slow, Jeff."

"We might just as well take our time, baby."

There was a pause. A little puff of steam was coming out of the radiator of the car. Heat wavered above the hood. Delia Moore's house was nearly a mile away. After a moment Jennie spoke again.

"You ain't really scairt, is you, Jeff?"

"Nah, baby, I ain't scairt."

"You know how we agreed—we gotta keep on goin'."

Jewels of perspiration appeared on Jeff's forehead. His eyes rounded, blinked, became fixed on the road.

"I don't know," he said with a shiver. "I reckon it's the only thing to do."

"Hm."

A flock of guinea fowls,[1] pecking in the road, were scattered by the passing car. Some of them took to their wings; others hid under bushes. A blue jay, swaying on a leafy twig, was annoying a roadside squirrel. Jeff held an even speed till he came near Delia's place. Then he slowed down noticeably.

Delia's house was really no house at all, but an abandoned store building converted into a dwelling. It sat near a cross-roads, beneath a single black cedar tree. There Delia, a cattish old creature of Jennie's age, lived alone. She had been there more years than

---

[1] guinea fowls: domestic birds, originally from Guinea

anybody could remember, and long ago had won the disfavor of such women as Jennie. For in her young days Delia had been gayer, yellower and saucier than seemed proper in those parts. Her ways with menfolks had been dark and suspicious. And the fact that she had had as many husbands as children did not help her reputation.

"Yonder's old Delia," Jeff said as they passed.

"What she doin'?"

"Jes sittin' in the do'," he said.

"She see us?"

"Hm," Jeff said. "Musta did."

That relieved Jennie. It strengthened her to know that her old enemy had seen her pass in her best clothes. That would give the old she-devil something to chew her gums and fret about, Jennie thought. Wouldn't she have a fit if she didn't find out? Old evil Delia! This would be just the thing for her. It would pay her back for being so evil. It would also pay her, Jennie thought, for the way she used to grin at Jeff— long ago when her teeth were good.

The road became smooth and red, and Jeff could tell by the smell of the air that they were nearing the river. He could see the rise where the road turned and ran along parallel to the stream. The car chugged on monotonously. After a long silent spell, Jennie leaned against Jeff and spoke.

"How many bale o' cotton you think we got standin'?" she said.

Jeff wrinkled his forehead as he calculated.

"'Bout twenty-five, I reckon."

"How many you make las' year?"

"Twenty-eight," he said. "How come you ask that?"

"I's jes thinkin'," Jennie said quietly.

"It don't make a speck o' difference though," Jeff reflected. "If we get much or if we get little, we still gonna be in debt to old man Stevenson when he gets through counting up agin us. It's took us a long time to learn that."

Jennie was not listening to these words. She had fallen into a trance-like meditation. Her lips twitched. She chewed her gums and rubbed her gnarled hands nervously. Suddenly she leaned forward, buried her face in the nervous hands and burst into tears. She cried aloud in a dry cracked voice that suggested the rattle of fodder on dead stalks. She cried aloud like a child, for she had never learned to suppress a genuine sob. Her slight old frame shook heavily and seemed hardly able to sustain such violent grief.

"What's the matter, baby?" Jeff asked awkwardly. "Why you cryin' like all that?"

"I's jes thinkin'," she said.

"So you the one what's scairt now, hunh!"

"I ain't scairt, Jeff. I's jes thinkin'

'bout leavin' eve'thing like this—eve'thing we been used to. It's right sad-like."

Jeff did not answer, and presently Jennie buried her face again and cried.

The sun was almost overhead. It beat down furiously on the dusty wagon-path road, on the parched roadside grass and the tiny battered car. Jeff's hands, gripping the wheel, became wet with perspiration; his forehead sparkled. Jeff's lips parted. His mouth shaped a hideous grimace. His face suggested the face of a man being burned. But the torture passed and his expression softened again.

"You mustn't cry, baby," he said to his wife. "We gotta be strong. We can't break down."

Jennie waited a few seconds, then said, "You reckon we oughta do it, Jeff? You reckon we oughta go 'head an' do it, really?"

Jeff's voice choked; his eyes blurred. He was terrified to hear Jennie say the thing that had been in his mind all morning. She had egged him on when he had wanted more than anything in the world to wait, to reconsider, to think things over a little longer. Now she was getting cold feet. Actually there was no need of thinking the question through again. It would only end in making the same painful decision once more. Jeff knew that. There was no need of fooling around longer.

"We jes as well to do like we planned," he said. "They ain't

nothin' else for us now—it's the bes' thing."

Jeff thought of the handicaps, the near impossibility, of making another crop with his leg bothering him more and more each week. Then there was always the chance that he would have another stroke, like the one that had made him lame. Another one might kill him. The least it could do would be to leave him helpless. Jeff gasped—Lord, Jesus! He could not bear to think of being helpless, like a baby, on Jennie's hands. Frail, blind Jennie.

The little pounding motor of the car worked harder and harder. The puff of steam from the cracked radiator became larger. Jeff realized that they were climbing a little rise. A moment later the road turned abruptly and he looked down upon the face of the river.

"Jeff."

"Hunh?"

"Is that the water I hear?"

"Hm. Tha's it."

"Well, which way you goin' now?"

"Down this-a way," he said. "The road runs 'long 'side o' the water a lil piece."

She waited a while calmly. Then she said, "Drive faster."

"A'right, baby," Jeff said.

The water roared in the bed of the river. It was fifty or sixty feet below the level of the road. Between the road and the water there was a long smooth slope, sharply inclined. The slope was dry, the clay hardened by prolonged summer heat. The water below, roaring in a narrow channel, was noisy and wild.

"Jeff."

"Hunh?"

"How far you goin'?"

"Jes a lil piece down the road."

"You ain't scairt, is you, Jeff?"

"Nah, baby," he said trembling. "I ain't scairt."

"Remember how we planned it, Jeff. We gotta do it like we said. Brave-like."

"Hm."

Jeff's brain darkened. Things suddenly seemed unreal, like figures in a dream. Thoughts swam in his mind foolishly, hysterically, like little blind fish in a pool within a dense cave. They rushed, crossed one another, jostled, collided, retreated and rushed again. Jeff soon became dizzy. He shuddered violently and turned to his wife.

"Jennie, I can't do it. I can't." His voice broke pitifully.

She did not appear to be listening. All the grief had gone from her face. She sat erect, her unseeing eyes wide open, strained and frightful. Her glossy black skin had become dull. She seemed as thin, as sharp and bony, as a starved bird. Now, having suffered and endured the sadness of tearing herself away from beloved things, she showed no anguish. She was absorbed with her own thoughts, and she didn't even hear Jeff's voice shouting in her ear.

Jeff said nothing more. For an instant there was light in his cavernous brain. The great chamber was, for less than a second, peopled by characters he knew and loved. They were simple, healthy creatures, and they behaved in a manner that he could understand. They had quality. But since he had already taken leave of them long ago, the remembrance did not break his heart again. Young Jeff Patton was among them, the Jeff Patton of fifty years ago who went down to New Orleans with a crowd of country boys to the Mardi Gras doings. The gay young crowd, boys with candy-striped shirts and rouged-brown girls in noisy silks, was like a picture in his head. Yet it did not make him sad. On that very trip Slim Burns had killed Joe Beasley—the crowd had been broken up. Since then Jeff Patton's world had been the Greenbriar Plantation. If there had been other Mardi Gras carnivals, he had not heard of them. Since then there had been no time; the years had fallen on him like waves. Now he was old, worn out. Another paralytic stroke (like the one he had already suffered) would put him on his back for keeps. In that condition, with a frail blind woman to look after him, he would be worse off than if he were dead.

Suddenly Jeff's hands became steady. He actually felt brave. He slowed down the motor of the car and carefully pulled off the road. Below, the water of the stream boomed, a soft thunder in the deep channel. Jeff ran the car onto the clay slope, pointed it directly toward the stream and put his foot heavily on the accelerator. The little car leaped furiously down the steep incline toward the water. The movement was nearly as swift and direct as a fall. The two old black folks, sitting quietly side by side, showed no excitement. In another instant the car hit the water and dropped immediately out of sight.

A little later it lodged in the mud of a shallow place. One wheel of the crushed and upturned little Ford became visible above the rushing water.

Questions for Discussion

1. OLD JEFF was getting ready for a trip. How does the author show that this was a very significant trip for Jeff and his wife and one that he faced with fearfulness?

2. A SHARE CROPPER does not have many occasions to wear a dress suit. How many times had Jeff worn his? Where was it kept when not in use? What condition was it in? Why was he having so much difficulty in making up the bow tie? How appropriate was the dress suit for the occasion he intended it for?

3. THE OLD T-model Ford that Jeff owned was a prototype of today's fastbacks. From your knowledge of classic cars can you describe Jeff's car. Why did he have to crank it?

4. AS JEFF started out he drove very slowly and cautiously. In view of the tragic destination of the car, why do you think the driver took such great care?

5. JEFF WORKED his farm for forty-five years. What did he have to show for his hard labor? Whose fault was it? Is there a better system for farming the land?

6. THE OLD couple decided not to lock the door when they left their cabin. As they were driving Jennie said they had to keep on going. At this point in the story where did you think they were going? Did the author succeed in keeping you in a state of suspense? At what point did you first suspect the nature of the tragedy in the title of the story?

7. WHAT WERE the factors that led the old couple to the decision to end their lives? What was the most impelling reason as far as Jeff was concerned?

8. DESCRIBE the conflicts you find in this story, both internal (within a person's mind) and external.

9. WHAT ROLE does the setting play in this story? Could the tragedy have been played out against a different physical background?

10. COULD THE story have had a happier endng? What ending would you suggest?

11. SUICIDE IS very often the action of a sick mind. Sometimes suicide is prompted by cowardice. Do either of these reasons apply to "A Summer Tragedy?" Are there any circumstances under which suicide may be justified, e.g. to save one's honor or to avert physical torture?

⚜

Building Vocabulary

Antonyms. In previous vocabulary exercises you have been asked to supply synonyms for unusual words, that is, words that have the same meaning. Now you are being asked to supply *antonyms*, that is, words that have the opposite meaning. Here is an example: *sad* is the antonym of *happy.* Most dictionaries include synonyms and antonyms after the word definition with the headings SYN (synonym) and ANT (antonym).

In Column A below is listed a group of words to be found in the story of the pages indicated. In Column B is a list of antonyms. Match each word in Column A with the correct antonym from Column B.

COLUMN A	COLUMN B
1. grimace (gri-mais') (p. 175)	a. easy test
2. negligible (neg'lih-jih-b'l) (p. 176)	b. smooth
3. ordeal (awr-dee'uhl) (p. 176)	c. important
4. meditation (med-ih-tay'-shun) (p. 180)	d. fine food
5. gnarled (nahrld) (p. 180)	e. unreal
6. fodder (fod'uh) (p. 180)	f. happy smile
7. genuine (jen'yoo-in) (p. 180)	g. solid
8. cavernous (kav'uh-ness) (p. 182)	h. lack of thought

⚜

Characterization

1. HOW SOON do you learn something about the central characters of the story, Jeff and Jennie Patton?

2. WHAT METHOD does the author use to reveal character traits of Jeff and Jennie?

3. WHAT QUALITIES in Jeff do you admire? Are there any traits that are discreditable? Would you consider him a failure in life? Explain your answer.

4. JEFF'S LOVE and tenderness for his wife sound a warm note throughout the story. What was Jennie's feeling for her husband?

5. JEFF ACTED like a man in mortal fear, trembling and shuddering at various points. The author states that his courage had left him. Yet he denied to Jennie that he was scared. Would you characterize him as a coward? Explain.

6. JEFF HAD no patience with weakness in others, taking pride in his own strength. How would you regard that trait, as a fault in his character or as evidence of his toughness? Explain.

7. WHEN THEY passed Delia Moore's house, Jennie wanted to be sure that Delia saw her going by in her best clothes. What very feminine characteristics are revealed in Jennie through her thoughts about old Delia?

Thinking and Writing

1. THE SHARE farmer and his wife felt that life was closing in on them and that it was better to commit suicide than face a bleak future. Can you propose any alternative for these two gentle people? In two or three paragraphs write a plan for life, that is, what they might have done instead of their last desperate act.

2. THEIR DEAD children were a continuing source of grief to the Pattons. The author mentions that they lost all five of their children in a period of two years. Drawing upon your imagination, write a composition showing how the children might have met their deaths.

3. WRITE ABOUT the young Jeff Patton before he married and became a share farmer, when he was a robust young man who enjoyed good times and who traveled with a crowd of country boys and girls to the Mardi Gras in New Orleans.

About the Author

Mr. Bontemps was born in Louisiana in 1902. He received an A.B. degree from Pacific Union College, California, in 1923. Coming to Harlem in the nineteen twenties he became associated with the bright and talented young writers of the "Harlem Renaissance" and began to write and publish poetry which received a number of awards. He became a high school teacher and principal in private schools until 1941. After attaining a degree in library science, in 1943 he became Librarian at Fisk University in Nashville, Tennessee. After twenty-two years at Fisk he left in 1966 to become a professor at the University of Illinois in Chicago. Since 1969 he has been a lecturer and curator at Yale University.

He has written novels, volumes of poetry, biographies, history and has also edited a number of collections, some in collaboration with Langston Hughes. Among his publications are: *Story of the Negro* (1948); *Lonesome Boy* (1955); *Frederick Douglass* (1959); *100 Years of Negro Freedom* (1961); *American Negro Poetry* (1963); and *Hold Fast to Dreams* (1969).

We're The Only Colored People Here

By Gwendolyn Brooks

We all need something to take us out of our humdrum lives. Some of us go to sporting events, like baseball games, or visit the theatre. Some of us participate personally in sports, like golfing or swimming. Others derive vicarious pleasure by reading stories about adventurous or interesting people. But most commonly, people are taken out of their lives by viewing motion pictures.

Here is a short story about a couple engaging in that everyday event of going to the movies and finding a spell laid over them. This selection is from a novel by a prize-winning poet, Gwendolyn Brooks.

WHEN they went out to the car there were just the very finest bits of white powder coming down, with an almost comical little ethereal hauteur, to add themselves to the really important, piled-up masses of their kind.

And it wasn't cold.

Maud Martha laughed happily to herself. It was pleasant out, and tonight she and Paul were very close to each other.

He held the door open for her— instead of going on round to the driving side, getting in, and leaving her to get in at her side as best she might. When he took this way of calling her "lady" and informing her of his love she felt precious, protected, delicious. She gave him an excited look of gratitude. He smiled indulgently.

"Want it to be the Owl again?"

"Oh, no, no, Paul. Let's not go there tonight. I feel too good inside for that. Let's go downtown?"

She had to suggest that with a question mark at the end, always. He usually had three protests. Too hard to park. Too much money. Too many white folks. And tonight she could almost certainly expect a no, she feared, because he had come out in his blue work shirt. There was a spot of apricot juice on the collar, too! His shoes were not shined.

. . . But he nodded!

"We've never been to the World Playhouse," she said cautiously.

"They have a good picture. I'd feel rich in there."

"You really wanta?"

"Please?"

"Sure."

It wasn't like other movie houses. People from the Studebaker Theatre which, as Maud Martha whispered to Paul, was "all-locked-arms" with the World Playhouse, were strolling up and down the lobby, laughing softly, smoking with gentle grace.

"There must be a play going on in there and this is probably an intermission," Maud Martha whispered again.

"I don't know why you feel you got to whisper," whispered Paul. "Nobody else is whispering in here." He looked around, resentfully, wanting to see a few, just a few colored faces. There were only their own.

Maud Martha laughed a nervous defiant little laugh; and spoke loudly. "There certainly isn't any reason to whisper. Silly, huh."

The strolling women were cleverly gowned. Some of them had flowers or flashers in their hair. They looked—cooked. Well cared-for. And as though they had never seen a roach or rat in their lives. Or gone without heat for a week. And the men had even edges. They were men, Maud Martha thought, who wouldn't stoop to fret over less than a thousand dollars."

"We're the only colored people here," said Paul.

She hated him a little. "Oh . . . Who . . . cares."

"Well, what I want to know is, where do you pay the . . . fares."

"There's the box office. Go on up."

He went on up. It was closed.

"Well," sighed Maud Martha, "I guess the picture has started already. But we can't have missed much. Go on up to that girl at the candy counter and ask her where we should pay our money."

He didn't want to do that. The girl was lovely and blonde and cold-eyed, and her arms were akimbo, and the set of her head was eloquent. No one else was at the counter.

"Well. We'll wait a minute. And see—"

Maud Martha hated him again. Coward. She ought to flounce over to the girl herself—show him up . . .

The people in the lobby tried to avoid looking curiously at two shy Negroes wanting desperately not to seem shy. The white women looked at the Negro woman in her outfit with which no special fault could be found, but which made them think, somehow, of close rooms, and wee, close lives. They looked at her hair. They were always slightly surprised, but agreeably so, when they did. They supposed it was the hair that had got her that yellowish, good-looking Negro man without a tie.

An usher opened a door of the World Playhouse part and ran quickly down the few steps that led from it to the lobby. Paul opened his mouth.

"Say, fella. Where do we get tickets for the movie?"

The usher glanced at Paul's feet before answering. Then he said cooly, but not unpleasantly, "I'll take the money."

They were able to go in.

And the picture! Maud Martha was so glad that they had not gone to the Owl! Here was technicolor, and the love story was sweet. And there was classical music that silvered its way into you and made your back cold. And the theater itself! It was no palace, no such Great Shakes as the Tivoli out south, for instance (where many colored people went every night). But you felt good sitting there, yes, good, and as if when you left it you would be going home to a sweet-smelling apartment with flowers on little gleaming tables; and wonderful silver on night-blue velvet, in chests; and crackly sheets; and lace spreads on such beds as you saw at Marshall Field's. Instead of back to your kit'n't apt., with the garbage of your floor's families in a big can just outside your door, and the gray sound of little gray feet scratching away from it as you drag up those flights of narrow complaining stairs.

Paul pressed her hand. Paul said, "We oughta do this more often."

And again. "We'll have to do this more often. And go to plays, too. I mean at that Blackstone, and Studebaker."

She pressed back, smiling beautifully to herself in the darkness. Though she knew that once the spell was over it would be a year, two years, more, before he would return to the World Playhouse. And he might never go to a real play. But she was learning to love moments. To love moments for themselves.

When the picture was over, and the lights revealed them for what they were, the Negroes stood up among the furs and good cloth and faint perfume, looked about them eagerly. They hoped they would meet no cruel eyes. They hoped no one would look intruded upon. They had enjoyed the picture so, they were so happy, they wanted to laugh, to say warmly to the other outgoers, "Good, huh? Wasn't it swell?"

This, of course, they could not do. But if only no one would look intruded upon . . .

Questions for Discussion

1. THE STORY begins with a poetic description of falling snow. This should not be surprising because Gwendolyn Brooks is a noted poet. What image does she picture in the first paragraph?

2. GWENDOLYN BROOKS has an extraordinary facility with words. Point out some unusual figures of speech she uses, like the reference to the background music in the films.

3. THERE IS A WARM, romantic feeling of two people in love pervading the story. Give two examples of how the author shows the affection between these two.

4. WHAT IS the setting for this story? A clue is given by the reference to Marshal Field's, a department store that is nationally known. In what city is this famous store located?

5. THE WORLD PLAYHOUSE was an unusual movie house, being affiliated with an adjacent theatre and sharing the same lobby. Do you know any "art" movie houses that show artistic or experimental films that appeal to a limited audience with sophisticated tastes?

6. MAUD MARTHA AND PAUL were ill-at-ease in the lobby of the theatre and found themselves whispering. What were the reasons for their feeling so uncomfortable?

7. EVEN though they enjoyed the movie immensely why did Maud Martha have the feeling that it would be a long time before they ever went back to the World Playhouse?

8. WHAT IS THE SITUATION around which this story centers?

9. WHAT IS THE BASIC IDEA of the story?

10. How APPROPRIATE is the title of the story?

11. THIS IS a very short story. Would you say it is a story of characterization or plot? Give reasons for your answer.

Word Study

*A*ll the words in our language have a history in the course of which many have undergone changes before developing their present-day meanings. In many cases, the origin of a word may be traced back to earlier forms in two or three languages. Let us take the word *ethereal* (eh-theer'ee-uhl), found on page 189 of the story. This word pertaining to *ether* (the upper regions of space) means spiritlike or airy. *Ether* comes from the Latin word *aether* which in turn is derived from an earlier Greek word *aither*. This historical explanation, or etymology, is found in brackets following the dictionary pronunciation of the word. The language of origin is indicated by an abbreviation, like O F., Old French. The meanings of abbreviations are explained at the beginning of the dictionary.

Using a dictionary, look up the history of each of the following words which occur in the story on the page noted. In each case note the language or languages from which the word is derived, that is, the origin. Also write the meaning of each word.

---

1. hauteur (haw-tyoor') page 189.
2. akimbo (uh-kim'boh) page 190.
3. flounce (flouns) page 190.
4. classical (klass'ih-kl) page 190.

The Characters

1. AS A specialized type of literature, the short story has three essential components, namely, a plot, a background, and characters. In this story the two central characters are Maud Martha and her husband, Paul, two middle-class black people. Give a word picture of them from the suggestions dropped by the author.

2. MAUD MARTHA made envious mental comparisons between her lot and the well-cared-for people in the lobby. Does this indicate a flaw in her character? Explain.

3. WHICH ONE is the more dominant personality? Point to something in the story to support your answer.

4. ON TWO OCCASIONS Maud Martha hated her husband: when he pointed out that there were no other colored people there and when he hesitated to ask the hard-eyed blonde where to get the movie tickets. What significance do you attribute to this? How does it illuminate their characteristics?

5. WHAT LONGINGS were brought out in Maud Martha as she watched the film? What chance did she have of satisfying such desires?

6. WHEN THE lights went up at the end of the movie, they were revealed as the only black people in the audience. They hoped that the white people wouldn't mind their being there. They didn't want to intrude on anyone. What character traits are revealed by this feeling?

7. WHICH ONE do you like better as a personality — Maud Martha or Paul? Why?

Thinking and Writing

1. THE AUTHOR gives us snatches of the way in which our romantic couple live — close rooms; wee, close lives; garbage in a big can and little gray feet scratching. Build upon these phrases and write two or three paragraphs describing the apartment that they live in as you imagine it.

2. THE MOVIE they saw at the World Playhouse was a love story. Make up the plot of such a movie that would send Maud Martha out with a happy, glowing feeling at the end.

3. THE PEOPLE in the lobby of the Studebaker Theatre regarded the black couple with well-hidden curiosity. Imagine that you were in that intermission crowd and saw these two out-of-place people who seemed so shy, she an unprepossessing young black woman and he a handsome, light-complexioned Negro. Write what your thoughts would be about the couple, possibly whether they seemed ill-mated, how they were dressed, speculations about what kind of work they did and how they lived.

ᐸ𝓧ᐳ

About the Author

Although born in Kansas in 1917, Gwendolyn Brooks has lived practically all her life in Chicago. She began writing poems while in school and later submitted her work for publication in the Chicago *Defender,* a Negro newspaper. Her formal education was completed at Wilson Junior College in Chicago, from which she was graduated in 1936. Miss Brooks won first prizes for her poetry at the Midwestern Writers' Conference for the years 1943, 1944 and 1945. In 1945 she also had her first book of poetry published, *A Street in Bronzeville.* Her second volume, *Annie Allen* won the Pulitzer Poetry Prize in 1950.

In 1953 appeared her sole novel, *Maud Martha,* about the life and disappointments of a black girl. Three more volumes of poetry followed: *The Bean Eaters, Bronzeville Poems for Boys and Girls,* and *Selected Poems.* in 1968 she published her seventh book *In the Mecca* which includes a long poem about a Chicago housing project. Much of her poetry deals with inner city life and derives from a first-hand knowledge of Chicago's ghetto.

Miss Brooks has been conducting a writing workshop for emerging writers in Chicago and has been donating cash prizes for fiction and poetry. She was named Illinois Poet Laureate in 1968, a title previously held by Carl Sandburg.

Selected Bibliography

Chapman, Abraham, ed. *Black Voices*. Mentor, 1968

Clarke, John H., ed. *American Negro Short Stories*. Hill & Wang, 1966

Dunbar, Paul L. *The Heart of Happy Hollow*. Negro Universities Press, 1969

Emanuel, James and Gross, T. L. *Dark Symphony*. Free Press, 1968

Hill, Herbert, ed. *Soon One Morning*. Knopf, 1963

Hughes, Langston, ed. *An African Treasury*. Pyramid, 1960

Hughes, Langston, ed. *The Best Short Stories by Negro Writers*. Little, Brown, 1967

Hughes, Langston. *Something in Common and other Stories*. Hill & Wang, 1963

Hurston, Zora N. *Mules and Men*. Lippincott, 1935

Jones LeRoi. *Tales*. Grove, 1967

Jones, LeRoi and Neal, Larry, ed. *Black Fire*. Morrow, 1968

Kelly, William M. *Dancers on the Shore*. Doubleday, 1964

Marshall, Paule. *Soul Clap Hands and Sing*. Atheneum, 1961

Rive, Richard, ed. *Modern African Prose*. Heineman, 1967

Toomer, Jean. *Cane*. Harper & Row, 1969

Wright, Richard. *Eight Men*. Avon, 1961

The Black Almanac

From Involuntary Servitude (1619-1860) to a Return to the Mainstream?(1973-1976)

by Alton Hornsby, Jr.

All of the important biographical details, institutions,
significant events, laws, court decisions,
programs and manifestos—affecting The Black American.

INVOLUNTARY SERVITUDE 1619-1860 WAR AND FREEDOM 1861-1876
THE NADIR 1877-1900 THE AGE OF BOOKER T. WASHINGTON 1901-1917
BETWEEN WAR AND DEPRESSION 1918-1932 A NEW DEAL—A NEW LIFE? 1933-1940
WAR AGAIN 1941-1945 THE ATTACK AGAINST SEGREGATION 1945-1954
THE ERA OF CIVIL RIGHTS 1954-1964 AN AGE OF DISILLUSIONMENT 1964-1973
A RETURN TO THE MAINSTREAM 1973-1976? FEATURES AN EXTENSIVE BIBLIOGRAPHY

Barron's Educational Series, Inc. $5.95